monsoonbooks

A CROWD OF TWISTED THINGS

Dawn Farnham is the author of The Straits Quartet, a bestselling series of historical romance set in 19th-century Singapore, as well as numerous short stories, plays and children's books. A former longterm resident of Singapore, Dawn now calls Perth, Australia, home. Learn more about Dawn at *www.dawnfarnham.com*.

Books by Dawn Farnham

THE STRAITS QUARTET
The Red Thread (Vol.1)
The Shallow Seas (Vol.2)
The Hills of Singapore (Vol.3)
The English Concubine (Vol.4)

Anthologies featuring short stories
by Dawn Farnham

Crime Scene Singapore
Crime Scene Asia (Vol.1)
Love and Lust in Singapore
The Best of Southeast Asian Erotica

A CROWD OF TWISTED THINGS

Dawn Farnham

monsoon

monsoonbooks

Published in 2013
by Monsoon Books Pte Ltd
71 Ayer Rajah Crescent #01-01, Mediapolis Phase Ø, Singapore 139951
www.monsoonbooks.com.sg

First edition.

ISBN (paperback): 978-981-4423-08-3
ISBN (ebook): 978-981-4423-09-0

Cover design by Cover Kitchen.

Frontcover photograph of crowds near Singapore's Supreme Court
breaking the police cordon during the Maria Hertogh riot
(11 December 1950, Singapore)©collection of Kenneth Chia,
courtesy of National Archives of Singapore.

National Library Board, Singapore Cataloguing-in-Publication Data
Farnham, Dawn, 1949-
A crowd of twisted things / Dawn Farnham. – First edition. – Singapore :
Monsoon Books Pte Ltd, 2013.
pages cm
ISBN : 978-981-4423-08-3 (paperback)

1. Mothers and daughters – Fiction. 2. Singapore – History – 1945-1963
– Fiction. 3. Riots – Singapore – History – Fiction. I. Title.

PR6106
823.92 -- dc23   OCN851119729

Printed in the United States
16 15 14 13   1 2 3 4 5

For my husband Roger Crabb
Journalist and Chief Correspondent

The Gloucestershire Echo, England
Agence France-Presse: Paris
Reuters: Paris, Beijing, Hong Kong, Seoul, Tokyo,
London and Singapore.

Newsmen are like the noble elephants. They travel in herds and think alike. They don't trust the jackals and hyenas who try to trick them in their never-ending pursuit of the green grass of truth. They have big ears and never forget.

The memory throws up high and dry

A crowd of twisted things;

A twisted branch upon the beach

Eaten smooth, and polished

As if the world gave up

The secret of its skeleton,

Stiff and white.

'Rhapsody on a Windy Night'

T.S. Eliot

The small beat in Annie's temple quivered like a captive moth. The gold carriage clock on the bedside table ticked. The banded chik chak looked down, splay-footed, from the wall and tut-tutted three times, its long tail curled into a question mark, its gibbous eyes immobile.

Perhaps it was this, the croaky call of the inquiring gecko, which found an echo in the still quick centre of her brain. Perhaps it was the sting of the mosquito or the sudden song of a night bird or the movement of the sudden breeze against her skin, but her body jerked into consciousness and the delicate skin of her hand splashed blood as it knifed into the corner of the bedside table. Her throat yawned in a silent scream, her body kicked. Not now, it said to the innermost workings of her cells, not yet. She drank in a great draught of warm air, roaring like a violent wind over her gullet. Her skin erupted in sweat, her heart hammered. The air rushed out of her lungs and she sucked again.

The tick of the clock sounded in the silence, beating the seconds away. Little by little, the turmoil and spasms of nerves and blood receded. The bellows calmed, the heart knock faded. Her eyes opened.

She was on her bed, in her room. The long low light was in that moment of tropical daylight when the sky fills with the last blush of the sun, the heavy heat leaves the day, the big hawks make shadow circles in the fading sky and flocks of swifts whirl into the fading treetops with a thunderous chirping. She took a shuddering breath and put a palm to her slippery brow.

The hush of the house lent the jungle an orchestral clarity. Against a choir of tinny crickets came the conversations of the frogs wallowing in the muddy drains and the throaty rasping booms of the bullfrogs. Above this she caught the trill of the nightjar, the twilight bird, the insistent whirr of its spinning-wheel notes giving prelude to the night. Its image lay behind her lashes, its long-tailed shadowy form moth-like against the dusky sky.

The Malays call it the graveyard bird, for its love of the undisturbed realms of the dead. This thought roused her from torpor. Sitting up was a struggle but being upright settled the whirling in her brain, and she put her legs to the floor with decision as the fingers of darkness snuffed out the day. Her hand ached and she looked down at the dripping blood. She opened the bedside drawer and took up a white handkerchief and wrapped it around the seeping wound. The cloth flushed red like a rose opening its petals. She hardly noticed the scattering of white pills on the bottom of the drawer.

The house was silent. That was puzzling. At this hour the boy filled her bath, and the distant sounds of clatter and chatter trickled in from the kitchen in the garden. Ronald usually had drinks around six. Her brow furrowed and she pressed her fingers to the aching, insistent pulse in her temples. No. Wait. That was before. Before the Japs had begun the shelling. She looked up, as if a silver missile might come crashing through the ceiling. Perhaps the silence meant it was over.

Ronald, when he spoke to her at all, told her impatiently that there was nothing to worry about. Dwarfs, he blustered, myopic dwarfs. Perhaps he was right. The dwarfs had given up.

She put out a hand to her bedside table to steady herself and got to her feet. An insect whined, and she slapped at her arm. The pain in her hand jangled. Why were the paraffin lamps not lit?

'Ah Lin,' she called, but her voice rasped weakly and echoed faintly along the corridors of the old house without answer.

She groped on the table and found the candlestick and matches. A bomb had fractured the Tanglin substation and electricity was but a distant memory. The memsahibs had all come like a flock of waddling geese, to look at the lumps of concrete and tangled metal, and at the splintered, tipping trees, their roots standing out of the ground like long gnarled fingers. The old Malay guard had been killed and his family had wailed piteously as they'd gathered up his flung remains. Annie had seen dead bodies before, in Ipoh, but none as splintered as this; she'd felt a shameful, gory curiosity.

Annie understood nothing of the whys and wherefores of this war. In Ipoh, the half-hidden cloistered life of the convent meant the outside world could, if you chose to do so, be ignored. Here, in Singapore, it was as if Tanglin was surrounded by the same high walls. The town was bombed to rubble but these leafy suburbs were virtually unscathed. Until that moment, it was possible, with a will, for the women to ignore this incomprehensible conflict. Now, there was blood on the village green and the geese were honking.

Yet few of the families left. It wasn't the right thing to do, the white thing to do. It sent the wrong message to the natives. That's how it was stated: the wrong message to the natives.

Annie, who knew she was at least half a native of somewhere not white, had few acquaintances and no friends amongst the chattering British mems and cared little for what they did. Some of the women and children, she'd heard, had rushed off down to the port when the news had come that the Japs had crossed the Straits, but Ronald had set his face against departure, offered himself to some volunteer military outfit, and so here they were. Annie had no idea where they would, in any case, have departed to. Ronald, as far as she knew, had no family at all.

The match fizzed and she put it unsteadily to the wick and waited until it caught. A feeble halo of light glowed, just enough to see her own feet, bare and pale, shuffling through the black soot. The candle flickered in the breeze that had sprung up as the heat had melted away from the day, and she put her aching hand around the flame in protection, inhaling, as she walked, the smell of the acrid smoke from the burning oil at Tanjong Pagar Harbour.

The strains of the notes of a piano floated to her ear. Ronald was playing 'Begin the Beguine'. He had suddenly returned yesterday afternoon, filthy, and had retired, without a word, to his room.

She cared nothing for Ronald. They had become married simply because he, at fifty-six years old, had seen her at a Christmas concert given by the convent, met the Mother Superior and asked for her hand. That a girl like Annie, without parents or background, should receive a proposal of marriage from a white man of considerable fortune was deemed miraculous. She had needed no persuasion. Ronald and his money were her escape route, and she had jumped at it.

She stopped at the door of her daughter's room. Where was the ayah? She held the candle up to the cot. It was empty. Suzy must be with Ronald. Suzy was the only thing in the whole world that Annie loved.

Her feet padded along the sooty boards, towards the glow of light from the living room. Ronald was hunched over the piano, his thinning hair revealing his shiny scalp, his hands moving gracefully along the keys.

The piano had not been tuned for months, even before the bombing had begun, and in the humidity some of the keys had warped; the notes now clunked and veered around like drunken peg-legged sailors. He'd reached 'to live it again is past all endeavour, except when that tune clutches my heart'. His lips moved slightly, singing under his breath. He seemed far away, as if he were a young man again, dreaming of a girl.

He'd been forced to practise many hours a day. He was fond of telling her that, repeating himself so often she wondered if his mind was wandering. Discipline, discipline, he'd pontificate, is what keeps the British Empire together. Discipline was a favourite topic for Ronald. Others were the feckless and unordered nature of women, the supremacy of the male species of the British variety and the cowardice and infamy of the French. Ronald, she had discovered, though from Australia, an entirely different country, was, by temperament and loyalty, English. The fine distinction between these varying nations of the Anglosphere eluded her completely.

She often wondered why Ronald had chosen her as his bride,

given his general dislike of anything not entirely English, but, of course, had never asked him.

'Where is everybody?' she said.

Ronald's head shot up. He stared at her, his face blank with confusion. Then his eyes dulled, as if nothing on earth was worth thinking about. He pulled his fingers abruptly from the keys and rose ponderously. He was a man of corpulent habits and he walked heavily to the cabinet and poured gin into a cut crystal glass. Fresh food had become a little short in the past week but there were shelves of tinned food, including Ronald's favourite Oxford English marmalade, and, of course, the house was floating in gin.

Annie spoke to his back.

'Ronald, what's going on?'

Ronald's shoulders heaved and he turned, not meeting her eyes.

'It's over. That fool Percival's surrendered.'

Ronald dropped heavily into a chair.

Annie put the candlestick on the card table.

Surrender? The word stabbed into her brain. Surrender? But that was impossible. It meant unspeakable horror. She, like everyone in Singapore, had heard the lurid stories about the rapes in China, the beheadings, the bayoneted babies.

'But you said ...' she began.

His head whipped up and he shot a look of pure hatred at her.

Panic wriggled in her stomach. Her eyes darted round the room and she took two quick steps to the sofa, expecting to see the baby there.

'Where's Suzy?'

Ronald raised the glass to his fleshy lips.

'I've no idea why I married you,' he said. 'But it doesn't matter anymore.'

1

'I have a mother's love for my child whom I brought into this world, and I desire that she be restored to me.'

Affidavit sworn by Adeline Hertogh

(Bergen op Zoom, Netherlands, 14 August 1950)

The twin-engine Airspeed Consul began its slow descent, metal glinting, propellers droning, passing low over the spit of palm-fringed beach at Tanjong Rhu. Its shadow undulated across the waters of the Kallang River. The engine noise grew to a roar and the airliner dropped gently to the ground.

The door of the plane opened. The passengers emerged one by one, teetered a moment, blinking, then stumbled down the steps, shell-shocked by the heat, and made quickly for the terminal building.

Annie stepped into the shade and under the whirling ceiling fans with the same gratitude as all the others. When called she went up to the official, a Chinese man with crooked teeth, and handed over her passport.

She looked around. On the other side of a low barrier were a small group of men, women and children awaiting the passengers. Several waved but not to her as far as she could see.

She had been told to expect a reporter from *The Melbourne Mercury*, a young man called Charlie Ransome.

She went through the barrier, darting looks to her right and left. The passengers' luggage had been unloaded and left together to one side. Gradually the pile diminished. She waited until her red suitcase sat, alone and forlorn, in the middle of the floor then joined it.

The last passenger departed, the immigration officials packed up, the ceiling fans ceased stirring the humid air, and the building fell into silence. A guard approached her.

'Sorry, Miss, you'll have to wait outside. I have to lock up.'

'Oh, yes.'

Annie picked up her suitcase and went outside. At that moment a car raced into the parking area and came to a halt.

A young man jumped out and rushed over to her.

'Mrs Collins?'

'Mr Ransome?'

'Yes. I'm so sorry to be late. Got stuck and …'

'It's all right. You're here now.'

'Yes. My word. But very sorry.'

Charlie's gaze lingered on her a little longer than was polite.

Annie contemplated Charlie Ransome. He was young and good-looking, fresh-faced and probably naïve. But he seemed good-natured. She was quite certain he had been expecting to see some ancient crone, fat and English, someone who'd fit the part of the wife of an old crony of Sir Alfred Maybridge.

'Not what you expected,' she said. 'Someone older, fatter, English?'

Charlie flushed a little. 'My word, no. I ...'

She put out a white-gloved hand and he took it. She withdrew it with only the most momentary pressure.

She pressed a handkerchief to her neck.

'I'd forgotten how hot it is here. Shall we go?'

Charlie nodded, obviously relieved.

'This way. My driver's waiting.'

He picked up her suitcase.

A Sikh driver opened the door of the Ford for Annie, with a small incline of his turbaned head.

'Thank you,' she said.

'Memsahib,' he said.

'So, Mrs Collins, your husband was a friend of Sir Alfred?' Charlie said as they settled into the car.

'Yes.'

The driver loaded the red suitcase into the boot, regained his seat and set off.

'Old school pals, was it?'

'No.'

Charlie fell silent.

Annie dabbed her forehead and put her face to the window, but the hot breeze offered no relief.

She watched as the car left the airport and bumped onto the main road, turning to cross the bridges into the town. She had never been to this part of Singapore. The airport had been there before the war, of course, but she had never ventured into these parts with their islands of palm trees and meandering river vistas.

As they approached the town, she began to recognise, if not the buildings, at least the architecture: the pretty shophouses with their arched and shuttered windows and their delicate tile-work, which even neglect could not totally conceal. Hawker stalls draped with grimy cloths and sheets of rusting corrugated iron filled every lane. Row upon row of long bamboo poles projected from every orifice of the shophouses, festooned with drooping shirts and pants and sarongs that hung like festival flags. The smell of hot spice and sour durian wafted in. The rickshaws were now trishaws, with a ceaseless tinkling of bells. Bony, half-naked Chinese men carried towering wares on their bouncing poles and the children did the same, the baskets twice their size. People jostled in the crowded streets, while the Malay policeman, clothed in his impeccable solar topee and his long white gloves, stood on his dais and directed traffic.

A vendor had spilled the wares from his small-wheeled cart, and dusters, towels and cheap household goods lay scattered on the ground. The car came to a halt as a verbal melee began and chattering hordes rushed forward, some to help, some to steal. A policeman blew his whistle insistently. She caught sight of the white spiral staircases curling up behind the buildings, in the warren of lanes on either side. The dismal days spent wandering the maze-like corridors of the convent in Ipoh slid into her mind.

Her first memory was fear of the dark, of the nursery at the convent and its hot darkness. She must have been three or four. The next memories were of a slap, because she had wet the bed, and of the high taunting laughter of children, because she didn't know her name.

A voice intruded on these thoughts.

'... a long time, then. Since you were here.'

She glanced at him.

'Look, would you mind if we didn't talk just now. I'm a bit tired.'

Charlie slumped again into silence.

When she saw the Raffles Hotel appear in the distance, she leaned forward. The car pulled round the straggling group of trishaws and their sprawled, somnolent drivers waiting for customers. Charlie held the door open, and Annie got out. The big ugly verandah that projected from its front façade was still there. It looked much as it had when she'd left it five years ago, a little grubbier perhaps, but she knew that, once inside, the grandeur of her recollections would be revealed. She felt nervous flutters begin in the pit of her stomach. Her journey into the past, for better or worse, would begin here.

'Come on. Get you settled.'

'Mr Ransome, I'll manage from here, if you don't mind. Can we meet the day after tomorrow at eleven or so? I'll explain everything.'

Charlie's face attempted not to show the relief he felt, but only partially succeeded.

'My word. Absolutely. Perhaps you'll come to my place for lunch?'

Charlie indicated the driver. 'Mahmoud will get you.'

Mahmoud inclined his head to her. 'Thursday at eleven, Memsahib.'

'Yes, please.'

She turned to Charlie. The poor man must think her a grumpy cow.

'Thank you,' she said and smiled.

Charlie smiled too. It was a nice smile.

Australians, in her experience, were straightforward and friendly. Though she knew it was involuntary, she was grateful for his kindness and attention. She judged him trustworthy enough for the task that lay ahead. Whether he, or even she herself, was up to it she did not know.

2

'The Malay foster-mother of 13-year-old Maria strongly denied today that she wanted money or any other form of compensation for Maria. Information originating from Holland in which Maria's father is claimed to have said that Aminah asked for 1000 Straits dollars in exchange for Maria was labelled as "slander" by Aminah. She wants to keep Maria for whom she has shown motherly love and care.'

de Telegraaf, Holland, 18 May 1950

Annie nursed an ice-cold Tiger and watched the tiny swifts swoop down to the tables in search of crumbs. One alighted fearlessly on the edge of her table, caught in a mote of dust and late sunlight and chirped a cheeky greeting.

She sat waiting for Desmond in a small Chinese kopitiam on North Bridge Road. She'd forgotten the way the creatures of the outside world penetrated the inner in Malaya. Birds in the bars, monkeys on the terraces, chik chaks clucking and running up and down the walls.

Around her some of the city took its small moment of leisure.

A group of schoolboys shared Coca-Colas and furtive secrets. Three Malay workers drank teh tarik, the sweet frothy 'pulled' tea she recalled from her childhood. The sisters occasionally had taken them into the town and all the girls, with their innocent and cloistered eyes, had found it a place of wonders. They'd stared at the way the orange-shirted showman could flamboyantly drag a long stream of tea from one cup to another without spilling a drop.

A group of nonyas in their fine voile kebaya and flower-printed sarongs, sipped coffee and examined their purchases, chattering, ignoring their small, whining children as the two or three maids attempted to spoon chendol into the children's mouths, chasing their ever-moving heads with the spoon, the shaved ice melting into the red bean and palm sugar, the little pea-green floury pellets flying off as the children batted their hands. Annie wanted to slap them and recognised acquired Australian attitudes in her feeling about these spoiled kids and their sad, ignored, little maids. She was glad when they left.

Two English squaddies drank beer, lounging in the chairs, smoking. One caught her eye and she turned away.

Major Desmond Carson was attached to the Australian Commission in Singapore. Annie knew he had something to do with the Emergency in Malaya. Desmond's father and Ronald had been friends. Annie had found him through Sir Alfred and corresponded with him on and off for the last year but they had never met. Sir Alfred Maybridge had written to Ronald's aunt, Mabel, when the war had ended and the fate of companions slowly became known.

Alfred and Ronald, as very young men, had fought together on the beaches and hills of Gallipoli. Survivors of those terrible campaigns carried a bond that was timeless. Only death could break it. Sir Alfred had travelled to Perth to visit her and promised to help her in any way he could. He had spoken in sorrowful tones of a Ronald she had never met, a man of vigour, courage and loyalty. She had not told him the entire truth. It didn't matter now and she didn't care to tarnish the memory of his brother-in-arms.

She put her chin in her hand and surveyed the passing scene. She tried for a moment to recapture the mood of those prewar days but it was impossible. She had changed too much. Yet the city itself, despite its obvious squalor, seemed unchanged. The red roofs of the convent and the institution still stood solidly on Bras Basah Road; the bells on the trishaws still rang stridently demanding a fare; even the squaddies seemed to walk in the same way, arrogantly pushing their way through the crowds.

Why was nothing changed, she thought. Why were the British still here? They had come back as if nothing had happened, as if they hadn't abjectly surrendered their role of invincible protector and thrown the people here into years of black misery. She hadn't known it then but she did now.

'Hello. Annie, is it?'

She looked up into the tanned, smiling face of a tall man, thirty something, with a shock of wavy brown hair. Nice-looking, she thought, in that rugged Australian way.

'Desmond?'

She put out her hand and Desmond took it, glancing at the

two white scars on her wrist. She made no attempt to hide them.

'Sit down. It's lovely to meet you.'

He ordered a beer.

'Does it feel strange to be back?'

Annie smiled. She knew him from their letters, which were friendly and understanding. He had been the only person to show any sort of interest in her search which did not discourage her.

'Yes. Strange to find it all so familiar. I suppose I thought the war would have left more of a mark.'

'The Japs made Singapore their headquarters. They needed it intact. The marks are deeper. The scars are on the people.'

'Yes. I was just wondering why they don't kick the British out.'

Desmond laughed.

'After the Occupation I think most people were ecstatic to get the British back, get back to normal. Normality is under-rated.'

Annie nodded and finished her beer. Desmond, attentive, caught the waiter's eye and ordered another.

She smiled at him as she put down the beer glass.

'Beer drinking. Habit I got into in Perth. Aunt Mabel loved her beer and didn't give a damn what anyone thought.'

'Sounds like my Aunt Jean. Perhaps Australian aunts are all the same.'

She smiled.

'You talked about normality. I'd like to get back to normality. I'd like to find my daughter.'

Desmond frowned.

'It's like looking for a needle in a haystack. I suppose the Brits are doing their best but it isn't very good. Food shortages, housing shortages, over-population. The Japs left a bloody great mess of course and you have to remember it's not yet five years since the war ended.'

He spread his hands as if trying to encompass the difficulty of the situation.

'Finding the Hertogh girl was a fluke and only happened because she was so white and the district officer noticed her.'

'Yes, yes, I know. You've told me. Suzy is darker than me, with black hair and eyes something like mine. I'm so light it was a surprise. That's why Ronald ...'

Annie still found it hard to admit the truth of Ronald's shame and felt her hatred for him flare up. Occasionally it died down especially after she had learned more about him from his aunt, but it was always there like a low, banked fire, waiting.

'... was ashamed. I've no idea what he thought would happen, why he even married me. In the end neither did he.'

Desmond put his hand to hers.

'Annie, I don't want to give you false hope.'

Annie removed her hand. She looked up into his eyes.

'Any kind of hope is fine for now. All I ask is that if Mr Ransome and I do find something that you bring your influence to bear on the British authorities.'

'What little I have.'

'But you have some,' Annie said and Desmond smiled.

'Well, I know the Commissioner and he knows the Governor very well. They play cards together. So if you get something concrete, I can promise to take it to them and do what we can.'

'Thank you.'

'I have made some enquiries about this Ransome. What do you know about him?'

'Not much. He's a journalist with *The Melbourne Mercury*. He's rather young but seems very nice.'

'He arrived a month or so ago. He's as green as a blade of grass and knows nothing at all about this place. He's here to close down *The Mercury* offices. They're pulling out.'

Annie smiled.

'I know all that. That's why I had to come right now and that's why we need you.'

Desmond shrugged.

'You see. I need him because his boss is Sir Alfred Maybridge, owner of *The Mercury*. Sir Alfred and Ronald fought together in the Great War. He's thrown his powers behind me. Charlie Ransome has no choice. He has to help me whether he likes it or not.'

'I see.'

'There's a bit of a story in it too. Long-lost child of Gallipoli hero found again after eight years, that sort of thing. I'm hoping that will tempt him to greater exertions.'

'Annie,' Desmond said and reached his fingers across the table again.

She ignored them.

'I know. No false hopes. But this is the only chance I'll get. All the fates have conspired to bring this moment together. Until I'm absolutely certain, one way or the other, I can't leave here.'

'Well, then, good luck.'

'Thanks, but good luck is nine parts determination.'

'You're the one who talked of fates.'

'Maybe that's the one part.'

She smiled. Silence fell between them. They drank slowly and watched the street.

'Would you care to have dinner with me, Annie?'

Annie turned her gaze to him.

'I understood you were married.'

Desmond shrugged.

'I am, officially. But she lives in Australia and isn't much interested in me anymore.'

'Oh. Sorry.'

'Don't be. I'm not. Wartime romance which flickered briefly then died out. Common enough story. Fortunately no children.'

Annie contemplated him. She could see Desmond found her attractive and she liked him. More importantly she needed him.

'Dinner would be nice.'

Desmond smiled his pleasure.

'Dinner,' she said firmly.

3

'Aminah is my mother. I don't want to go.' Nadra

'She is my daughter, you know, and she is my love.'

Aminah binte Ma'arof

(22 April 1950)

She took up the Raffles hotel tea cup. The liberation, she thought wryly, had left the crockery intact. The Japanese fight to the death had not happened. The atom bomb had seen to that.

The angel-faced boy in the small white jacket and the green sarong put the teapot on the table, bowed and smiled. She smiled back.

She'd heard, when she had been first brought here to this building, that, at the end, Japanese officers had put guns to their heads, stuck swords into their guts or blown themselves up in these rooms and gardens. She hadn't thought about it at all in 1945. After living in the malarial huts of the prisoner-of-war camp, it had been, to homeless, half-starved women such as themselves, almost preposterous to find themselves in such exquisite accommodations. Like a banquet after starvation, many women found it almost mortally overwhelming. They slept together, huddled in the corner of these palatial rooms for weeks. Annie had revelled in the cleanliness and space and privacy but she had also understood those other hollow-eyed women for whom freedom had become unnerving. She had, then, never given a thought to the hated Japanese, but now she did.

Perhaps one despairing officer, his eyes fixed on the East, the emperor's name on his lips, had slit his belly, right here where she was sitting. Her eyes drifted to the tiles. Something like that ought to leave a trace, but no sigh of those events echoed in the stones and trees around her. The garden was innocently tranquil, the great fans of traveller's palms shading the paths, the heliotrope and hibiscus falling in clusters against the walls, timeless and heedless.

She looked at her watch, finished her tea and made her way through the wide shady corridors to the front of the hotel. The old Ford stood like a poor, faded cousin of the new, shiny automobiles that flanked it on either side. She liked it for its age and wear, but doubtless she was the only one who did. The rage was for the new, for putting the war behind and looking to the future.

Mahmoud stood idly chatting to one of the Sikh doormen. When he saw her he pulled to attention and opened the car door. She had hardly noticed him the first time they'd met but now she took him in. He was a magnificent-looking man. Somewhere in his late thirties. Tall and well made, his face strong, his beard resplendent, his head noble under a turban of brilliant saffron orange. She knew nothing of Sikhs or their beliefs but she thought that they certainly were good looking.

'Thank you. What is your name?'

'Mahmoud, Memsahib,' he said, closing the door.

He pulled into the traffic of Beach Road, an alarming mixture of buses, cars and bicycles, trishaws and carts, swerving to avoid an oncoming truck overflowing with Malay workers and a British army staff car which honked imperiously.

'Mahmoud, I'm Eurasian. I know nothing at all about my parents but what I do know is that I am not entirely white, nor possibly even English, and that therefore I believe it is impossible for me to be a pukka memsahib.'

This seemed to give Mahmoud pause.

'My name is Annie. Can you call me that?'

'No, Memsahib. That is not proper.'

Annie laughed.

'What would you suggest then? Memsahib is not proper either.'

Mahmoud fell silent. Annie began to feel guilty.

'I'm sorry. I didn't mean to offend.'

'Oh no, Memsahib. No offence. I am thinking about what is proper.'

A trishaw darted in front of the car as its driver saw a fare, and Mahmoud braked suddenly but made no admonishing honk of the horn. She liked him for that.

The traffic was lighter on Orchard Road and the shops passed quickly by. She saw Amber Mansions, Malayan Motors, the Pavilion Cinema and Cold Storage. The building that had once been Collins & Warne Motor Company was now part of Borneo Motors but apart from this and a large new building here and there, little had changed. Warne had survived the war but Ronald had not. The company had done well in the immediate postwar years, supplying and servicing vehicles for the British Military Administration.

Warne had been in Changi with the Major in charge of BMA requisitions. It was what the Chinese called 'chi ku,' eating bitter. These men had eaten bitterness together and, like Sir Alfred and Ronald at Gallipoli, it had forged hoops of steely friendship.

Warne had gone into rubber manufacture under the civilian administration and sold the company and its lucrative connections for a handsome profit in 1949 and returned to England. Warne had never tried to disconnect Ronald's name from the company, which spoke a great deal for the loyalty and friendship of the two men. Considering how little she had liked him the clear signs of deep affection that Ronald inspired in others surprised her. But then she had never known him. She had met him not young but old, not full of promise and vigour, but overtaken by time. Now he and his partner had made her a wealthy woman.

The car engaged green, leafy Holland Road, leaving the shops and businesses behind. These were the tranquil suburbs where mansions surrounded by manicured lawns hid behind jungle trees. Mahmoud turned the car on to Peirce Road. The Indian guard drew to attention at the gates of a large property, as the car climbed the gentle slope of a driveway shaded by palms and tembusu trees and came to a halt under the porte-cochere.

A striking Chinese woman of some forty odd years of age opened the front door. She was elegant and groomed, dressed in a black chipao, every hair of her head in place. A gold cross lay against the black cloth. It gave her the grim air of a figure from the Inquisition.

Annie stepped inside onto the black-and-white tiled floor.

'Good day, madam,' the woman said. 'You have come to see Mr Ransome.'

Annie detected disapproval in the barely accented tones, as if Mr Ransome were a stray dog that had somehow found its way into the house, defecated on the dining room floor and refused to leave.

Straight-backed, she led Annie through the house to the extensive and lush grounds of the back garden. Under the arms of a rain tree sat a white wicker table and four chairs. Two Malay gardeners were crouched, weeding, moving slowly, like tortoises, across the lawn.

'I'm afraid Mr Ransome had company last night and may be some time.'

So few words but they told a big story. Annie thanked the woman graciously and watched her glide elegantly back to the house. Mr Ransome's company was a person or persons of which this impeccable Christian woman thoroughly disapproved. Probably even more than she disapproved of Mr Ransome himself. He had risen late from his activities and slumbered beyond the decent hour. Perhaps he was even asleep now.

Annie took off her gloves and took up *The Straits Times* that lay on the table.

Two minutes had barely elapsed when Charlie came rushing across the lawn.

'Sorry, sorry. Delayed. Something ...'

'It's perfectly all right. I am very comfortable here.'

Charlie's hair was damp. Clearly he had rushed out of his bath, having completely forgotten all about her.

Madame Wing crossed the lawn with a tray. Charlie leaped to his feet. Madame Wing placed the tray on the table, ignoring him. It contained a jug of iced lime juice, two glasses and a plate of sandwiches.

Charlie smiled at her wanly but she took no notice and disappeared into the house.

Charlie sat.

'Servants,' he said. 'Not used to them. Make me nervous.'

He poured a glass of the juice and drank it all down in one go. He picked up the sandwiches and proceeded to eat three at once.

'How did you get here?'

'Mahmoud picked me up.'

'Oh. Right.'

Annie took a sandwich and inspected its interior.

'Mr Ransome. What did Sir Alfred tell you?'

'Charlie, please. Nothing. Look after you.'

'Well, then I probably need to explain.'

Charlie nodded and took another sandwich.

'I need you to help me find my daughter, Charlie. And please, call me Annie.'

Charlie frowned. Annie poured two glasses of lime juice. She ran her finger down the rivulets of condensation that sprang from the glass.

'I am not at all sure how I can help. I've only just got here myself.'

'Perhaps you will allow me to tell you my story. It is quite simple.'

'My word. Yes, indeed.'

Charlie took a pack of cigarettes from his jacket and offered her one. Annie took it and when the formalities of lighting were finished, she sat back.

'I married my husband, Ronald Collins, when I was seventeen. We had a child, Suzanne, in November 1941. On the day that Singapore fell Ronald gave our daughter away and tried to murder me.'

Charlie flicked the ash from his cigarette. Annie could see she had got his full attention.

'I thought, at first, that he had killed her but, for some reason, he had found it very easy to murder me, but rather more difficult to kill his own child. So he gave her to the Malay nursemaid with some money and sent her away.'

Annie paused and sipped her lime juice.

'I knew nothing about this woman, not even her name. We called her simply "Ayah". Perhaps she was a good woman but we knew nothing about them, the servants. Nothing about their lives.'

Annie looked at Charlie, her eyes hard.

'You know, no babies died in Changi. Someone told me that.'

Charlie moved in his chair.

'I'm sorry if this makes you uncomfortable. The war was uncomfortable.'

'It doesn't make me uncomfortable. My father was in the war. North Africa.'

Annie stared at Charlie, her brow furrowing slightly.

'He survived?'

'Yes.'

'Well, Ronald didn't survive. I did. That's it.'

'I'm sorry.'

'Yes, well,' Annie said. 'That's all over. It's not why I'm here. It's background, as you journalists say.'

She stubbed out her cigarette.

Charlie sat back.

'After the war I went to Ronald's old aunt in Perth. She died last year. She was a very, very good woman. The refugee services discovered her for me. Despite the fact that I wasn't white, they let me in because I was Ronald's widow. Fortunately the marriage was verified through the civil authorities in Ipoh and at the church. I had no papers at all. I was lucky. She took me in even though I was this funny looking stranger. She'd lost her son in the Somme and now her nephew. I'd lost a husband and a daughter. We understood each other. Sometimes that kind of loss is more important than the colour of your skin. I started to write letters. The Red Cross, refugee organisations, government offices, all that. Years of letters but nothing came of it.'

She took up the newspaper folded to the article about Maria Hertogh and put it in front of Charlie.

'Then I heard about Maria, the little girl, lost, like Suzy, given up like Suzy so she would live, and then found again.'

'And so you came here to find her,' Charlie said.

'Yes, to find Suzy. I have to be here to do it, and I need your help.'

'I see.'

'I have money, plenty of it.'

'Right, well that's helpful to a certain extent.'

'My old address is here in Tanglin, just around the corner. My housekeeper's first name is all I know about her. The only other names I remember are the driver and the gardener.'

'Would you like some tea? I'd like some tea.'

Charlie looked around. Annie raise her hand to a little Malay boy crouched on the edge of the garden. He leapt to his feet and raced towards them. He bowed then stood to attention like a good soldier.

Annie smiled.

'Apa nama?'

The boy looked down shyly and murmured, 'Joseph, Puan.'

A Christian name. Annie was surprised.

'Joseph? Bisa berbahasa Inggeris?'

'Yes,' he said proudly.

'Very good,' Annie said and smiled at the little boy. 'Some tea, please, Joseph.'

He bowed very seriously and raced off.

'You speak the lingo?'

'Badly. Not as well as I should, considering the years I've lived in Malaya. But then the first seventeen were spent in an English convent, learning vowel sounds. The lingo was not encouraged.'

Madame Wing emerged again from the house and sailed over the grass, carrying another tray. Annie saw Charlie's legs twitch, and he instinctively moved to rise. Annie put out her hand.

'Sit down, Charlie. It's not expected.'

When Madame Wing had set down the tray she stood, straight-backed, waiting.

'Anything else, Sir?' she said.

Charlie gave a quick shake of his head. 'Thank you very much,' he said. 'Thank you.'

Annie smiled.

'Madame Wing, may I ask you about Joseph?'

The housekeeper inclined her head.

'He's a Malay boy but his name is Joseph. Do you know why?'

'I do not. However, if you wish, I could find out.'

'Thank you. I would be obliged.'

Madame Wing left them.

'He couldn't have been more than a toddler during the war. What things has his little mind seen?'

Charlie was looking at Madame Wing's receding back with a look of profound melancholy.

'Are you all right, Charlie?'

Charlie looked at her and shrugged.

'Yes. My word. More tea?'

*   *   *

The house on Swettenham Road seemed to have been swallowed by the jungle. The gate and the number were visible but beyond lay an impenetrable wall of greenery.

'It's here,' Annie said, pushing the gate, which did not budge. 'It's the last house so it was always surrounded by the jungle.

Monkeys used to come onto the lawn and throw rambutan skins at us. Monkeys are bad-tempered, you know, like hungover Australian reporters.'

Charlie made a face at her and set off following the tumbledown wall that surrounded the house. Mahmoud had insisted on accompanying them.

'There,' Charlie said. There was a gap in the jungle and a trampled path. He took Annie's hand to help her over the deep ditch that lay along the wall and they went inside. The house looked much like Charlie's but was in a vastly more dilapidated state. The walls were cracked and flaking, washing hung on bamboo poles from every window and draped over bushes as if the garden had suddenly burst into a bloom of faded and dusty flowers. Flimsy huts with an ingenious variety of plastic, leaf, metal and wooden roofs dotted almost every inch of the grounds. The air hung with the faint smell of effluent.

A dog began to bark ferociously. Suddenly the place was filled with faces, every window and verandah crowded with men, women and children. They looked hollow, hungry and sullen. Everyone stared at them silently. The dog continued to bark, now joined by another.

'What on earth?' said Charlie. 'Who are all these people?'

'Squatters. It's turned into a kampong. Kampong Swettenham,' said Annie.

Voices erupted, everyone talking at once and the barking dogs appeared around a corner and began to jump up and down.

Mahmoud stepped forward and silence fell. His presence clearly represented authority. A lot of Singapore's policemen were

Sikhs. Someone grabbed the dogs, which whined then also fell silent.

'Sahib,' Mahmoud said, 'they think you've come to evict them.'

'Oh,' Charlie said and put up his hands in reassurance. 'For heaven's sake, Mahmoud, tell them we're not the police and we've just got some questions.'

Mahmoud made this announcement in Malay and the electric nervousness that had filled the air dissipated. A parchment-faced withered man dressed in a faded sarong and a white cap stepped forward. He made a series of decisive noises, and a pair of battered chairs were borne head high down to the path.

'You have questions?' he said in English. 'Please sit, Puan.'

'Thank you,' Annie said. 'This is Charlie and Mahmoud, my friends. Your English is excellent, Haji.'

'I worked on the docks before the war,' he said and smiled a toothless grin.

'I lived in this house before the war,' Annie said. 'I think these are my dining chairs.'

A circle of dirty, raggedy children had gathered around them silently watching and rubbing their noses. Annie opened her handbag. She took out a large bag of liquorice allsorts and handed it to the old man.

'Will the children have some sweets?' she said and the old man nodded and signalled to an older boy to come forward. He murmured in his ear and the boy took the bag and shouted to the children and they all evaporated into the garden.

Annie took a paper from her bag and handed it to the old

man.

'When I lived here I had a housekeeper. Her name was Ah Lin and she had a distinctive gold tooth. Also there was a gardener named Ah Chun and we had an Indian driver I called Ragi, but possibly that wasn't his real name. I've written them down and put their approximate ages alongside.'

The old man looked at the paper.

'I want to find them, if I can. As you can see there is a reward for information. They are not in any trouble. It is a personal matter. I want to thank them.'

The old man nodded.

'You should not offer a reward. It will bring much information but none of it will be true. Let me first ask.'

He folded the paper.

'You suffered. In the war. They took you?'

Annie looked into his eyes and saw grief hooked there.

'Yes. And you?'

'No. My sons. One was in the Malay Regiment. He died fighting at Pasir Panjang. My young son was also later shot.'

Annie shook her head. It was unbearable.

'I'm sorry. My husband died too, building a railway in Siam.'

The old man put his hand to hers and she grasped it tightly, though a feeling of guilt crept into her at the false impression of grief for Ronald her words might have relayed, which, in some way, seemed to cheapen his. She released his hand.

The old Haji smiled at her.

'Death is our wedding with eternity. Come, come, whoever you are, wanderer, worshipper, lover of leaving. Ours is not a caravan of despair. We must believe.'

Annie rose and bowed slightly.

'I will ask,' he said. 'Some time is necessary. People come and go through here who do not always live here.'

'Thank you, Haji.'

'Assalamu Alaikum,' the old man said.

'Wa Alaikum Salam,' Annie said.

She stood looking around at the house and garden, seeing it as it had been once, not happy, she supposed, but sometimes content, occasionally very unhappy, but, after a life of nothing, it had been quiet and her domain, the place where the feel of Suzy's little body was strongest. She turned and left the garden.

Mahmoud opened the car door and they got inside.

'Thanks,' Annie said.

'Hope something comes of it.'

Annie nodded and looked out of the window as they moved down the winding road under the spreading black arms and lacy green canopy of the rain trees.

'What did you call that old man? Haji, was it?' Charlie said.

Annie had no desire to answer him. He knew nothing. Nothing of this place, of its hurt, of its people.

'Why? Why do you want to know?' She almost spat out the words. She saw Mahmoud glance at her in the rearview mirror.

'Well,' he said. It sounded so pathetic she felt sorry for her harshness.

'He was wearing what we used to call the Haji cap. It means he has been to Mecca. But he is a Sufi. The old men always talk in poetry. They seem to know absolute quantities of beautiful poetry about love and religion.'

She looked through the open window, the warm wind moving her hair about her face.

'Pointless dreams of beauty in an ugly world,' she murmured and Charlie barely caught the words.

'I'll come back in a week,' Annie said abruptly. 'Can you give me a lift into town?'

'Of course. Raffles, Mahmoud, and then the office.'

Mahmoud inclined his head. 'Yes, Sahib,' he said and Charlie raised his eyebrows.

'Please don't call me Sahib. Makes me sound like some ridiculous tiger-hunting, pommy fool.'

Annie ignored them, watching as the familiar roads of her past existence flew before her eyes.

4

'Mother, don't leave me,' cries 13-year-old Maria Huberdina
Hertogh after an hour had been spent persuading her to get into
the car at the Singapore Supreme Court, following a decision by
the Chief Justice that she be delivered into the care of the
Netherlands Consul-General.

The Straits Times, 20 May 1950

The crush at the Great World was hot enough to melt bones.
The entertainment park spread over several crowded acres,
with miles of cheek-by-jowl lines of ramshackle buildings, tents
and booths, restaurants and bars, filled with pushing, shoving,
hawking, spitting, screaming, laughing patrons of every colour
and creed.

Desmond had Annie's hand in his. He wanted her to see the
Ronggeng, the swaying dance of Java. Small, fine-boned women
with dark oiled hair and colourful sarongs moved their bare feet
and turned their hands this way and that. The earth was dry and
dust flew with each movement. The orchestra sat cross-legged on a
raised dais behind their gongs, drums and xylophones. The sound

was slow, hypnotic. The music from a Chinese opera caught at the edges of it in a cacophony of discord.

The air was filled with aromas of frying food, incense, fish stew and durian.

Annie felt sweat pouring off her.

'Desmond,' she said. 'I need to get away to somewhere quiet.'

'Yes, sorry Annie. This place can be a bit overwhelming.'

Desmond led her quickly to a small calm shore. It was the space in front of a cinema. The billboard announced *King Solomon's Mines* starring Deborah Kerr and Stewart Granger.

Annie eyed Miss Kerr, who looked back at her, eyes wide with concerned amazement, perhaps at finding herself in this African predicament. The doors opened and the cinema began to empty.

Charlie Ransome came out with a willowy, beautiful Chinese woman on his arm. With a look of surprise he recognised Annie.

'Hello, Annie.'

The Chinese woman pulled away and waved to him. In an instant she had disappeared down a side alley. Charlie gazed after her, and Annie saw a look of concern cross his face.

It disappeared as Annie walked up to him.

'Charlie, this is Desmond Carson from the Australian Commission. Desmond, this is Charlie from *The Mercury*.'

The two men shook hands.

'Nice to meet you. Annie's told me how you're helping to find her daughter. The Australian government, naturally, wishes to be of service in any way possible. But we're pretty small fry here.'

Annie was looking up at Desmond, smiling.

'I've told Desmond that it's still early days. But I am hopeful.'

'Yes, we have to be hopeful,' Desmond said, and Charlie frowned. Annie knew what he was thinking. Her quest was hopeless. Nothing had come of her visit to the Haji so far. But what was a week or so when she had waited so many years.

'Taking in the sights?' Charlie said.

'Yes. But the crush was horrific on the main road.'

'I'm meeting some people at the Cabaret Club,' Charlie said, 'but I'm not sure where it is. This place is huge.'

'The Cabaret?' said Desmond. 'They do revues in English and Chinese. Well worth a visit. I know the way. What do you say, Annie?'

'Yes, sounds fun.'

Desmond led the way, avoiding the crush of the main thoroughfare. He clearly knew the park well, and they soon found themselves in front of a flashing neon sign. Pictures of the glamorous stars of the revue lined the walls. Eddie Monteiro, the Filipino Bing Crosby, stood smiling between the alluring pinkly befeathered Yvonne Yip, *contortioniste extraordinaire*, and Loretta Ling, who was dressed in black with a scarlet boa. The Sikh doorman in a bejewelled turban did his job, and they went into the lobby. A slight Chinese man came forward and bowed.

'Welcome. Thank you for coming. Table for three?'

Desmond nodded and took Annie's arm. She looked around. The inside of the Cabaret Club was decorated in the style of a sophisticated Hollywood nightclub of the Thirties. At any moment, she thought, Lauren Bacall and Humphrey Bogart might walk in, in the company of Charlie Chan. It was abundantly clear that this club catered only to the upper echelon of Singapore's society. The newly wealthy or the old money that had managed to survive the war sought sophisticated and opulent surroundings amongst the top men of the colonial government. Outside it was hot and bustling, filled with the life of the people. Here it felt like taking a step back into the past.

Scantily clad Chinese girls were high-kicking their way through an upbeat version of 'There'll Always be an England'. Desmond ordered Champagne. When the music came to an end, the patrons clapped enthusiastically and the girls bowed charmingly, throwing kisses to the crowd. The orchestra began to play 'Smoke Gets in Your Eyes', and dancers filled the floor.

'Charlie! Darling!' an American voice called out.

Annie turned to see a woman in a red dress. With her were three men. She was the kind of woman, Annie knew, who always had men around her, like moons gathered in by her irresistible pull.

Charlie rose.

'Mickey,' he said. 'Where did Yu Li go?'

'Oh, she'll be along. Who are your friends?'

Charlie made the introductions. Mickey Blaine was the *New Yorker* correspondent; Nobby Styles was the *Reuter* correspondent; Roy MacCartney was from the *Australian Associated Press* and Tom Masterson was with the *Associated Press*.

A muscled, ginger-haired man approached them.

'Oh, this is Beaver,' Mickey said.

Beaver gazed coldly at the group. As his gaze fell on Annie, she saw the slight curl of his lip. She had seen it so many times that she had almost grown immune to it. She was not white and it offended him. He turned away, ignoring her. Desmond noticed and frowned. So did Charlie.

'Beaver, you say?' Charlie said

'Inspector Beaver of the Singapore Police,' Beaver said in the clipped tones of the English public-school boy.

'One of the Canadian Beavers?' Charlie asked.

Mickey, Tom and Roy laughed, and Annie and Desmond smiled. Beaver glared.

Mickey took Beaver's arm in hers.

'Bobby's Special Branch.' She patted him on the sleeve. 'It's just a little joke. Gotta admit it's a funny sort of name.'

'I certainly won't. It is an ancient name. It comes from the French, Beauvoir. We came to England with the Norman Conquest.'

'Foreigner, eh?' said Charlie with a smirk.

Pink spots began to glow amongst the freckles of Beaver's white skin. He looked closely at Charlie.

'I know who you are. You replaced Braithewaite. You a Commie sympathiser, as well?'

He raked his gaze over the other journalists. 'All you reporters are pinko bastards.'

'There are ladies present. Not the right place, I think, Inspector,' Desmond said, giving him a malevolent look.

Beaver scowled at Desmond and lit a cigarette.

Mickey smiled and winked at Annie. 'Don't worry about me. I'm no lady. But this is a farewell party, not an interrogation. Come on, Bobby.'

Mickey pulled him onto the dance floor. With an icy stare at

Charlie, Beaver took Mickey into his arms, her red dress swirling round her shapely legs. Roy and Tom drifted away to the bar.

Annie turned to Charlie and Nobby.

'Farewell?'

'Korea,' Nobby said, downing a beer.

'That's why I'm here. Basil was sent off and now Lane's gone,' said Charlie, looking glum. 'And I'm stuck here with no story and a bloody great house I can't afford.'

He glanced at Annie and blushed slightly. 'Sorry about the language,' he said.

Annie shook her head.

'That's all right. I'm not much of a lady myself. But I am a bit lost. Please explain.'

'Basil's the former correspondent here.'

'Yes, I see,' Annie said. 'What's this Korea place?'

Mickey laughed loudly as Beaver whirled her round the floor, and Charlie turned his head, attention diverted. Nobby smiled.

'Allow me, dear lady,' Nobby said. 'It is the firm belief of the news hounds of the world that war is about to break out on the Korean Peninsula, a bit of country stuck on the armpit of China.'

'Yes,' said Desmond. 'I think you're right.'

'More war?' Annie was dismayed.

'Yes, indeed,' Nobby said. 'War is our business. There's always a war and, with any luck, we get to cover it.'

Nobby signalled to a waiter.

'Mickey's going to Tokyo in a couple of days. All the Americans are there including Lane Cooper, *Newsweek*'s man. He used to share with Charlie.'

Charlie turned his head.

'Leaving me with a half-empty house. Lane's a great guy. Paid up to the end of June but after that …'

Charlie shrugged.

'The servants will have to go. Lane's a rich guy in his own right, and he paid for them. I won't be entirely sorry to see the back of Madame Wing, even if she does make life very comfortable.'

The dance came to an end. Mickey hailed a friend at another table, and she and Beaver wandered away. The dance floor fell into darkness and the noise of the crowd subsided.

'Ladies and gentleman,' a disembodied voice announced, 'the Chinese songbird, Miss Loretta Ling.'

The crowd applauded and the overture to 'It Had to be You' began. A spotlight flooded the floor, revealing the songbird in front of a microphone.

She was wearing a silky electric-blue gown that clung to her slender body. She began to sing in Chinese, her voice low and sultry, her hips swaying.

In the semi-darkness, Annie watched as a Chinese woman in a white chipao approached Charlie and put her hand on his arm. It was the woman from the cinema. Charlie turned to her and smiled. She put her fingers into Charlie's hair.

'It had to be you, wonderful you.'

Charlie took the woman's hand and put it to his lips.

The music stopped, the spotlight was cut and the house lights went up. Annie turned to the singer and joined the applause. When she turned back Charlie was gone.

The orchestra struck up a lively tune.

Desmond put his hand out to Annie.

'Shall we?' he said.

'I warn you,' she smiled.

Desmond was a good dancer, strong and confident. Annie knew she was more a shuffler than a dancer. Dancing had not been high on the curriculum at the convent. Ronald had never cared for it. Desmond made up for her clumsiness, guiding her through the steps until she relaxed.

The orchestra slid effortlessly into a slower number. He pulled her closer to him, running his hand around her waist. Annie let him, leaning her head against his shoulder.

The tune meandered into a melody. It was a Chinese song, 'China Nights'. She hadn't heard it in years. Her mind seemed to slide to another place as if the song had turned the tumblers on a safe to open.

There is a bedroom. The bed is hung about with swathes of white netting. A green and red light glows faintly through the shutters. The music is whispering out of a radio next to the bed. A woman's hand with blood red painted nails falls slowly against the white sheet.

Her feet became entangled in Desmond's and she pulled away.

'I'm so sorry. I warned you.'

He smiled. 'Champagne,' he said and took her arm.

5

'The Chief Justice, Mr Justice Murray-Aynsley, in the Singapore Supreme Court yesterday, granted a stay of his order made last Friday giving custody of 13-year-old Maria Hertogh to the Consul-General of the Netherlands, pending an appeal by her foster-mother, Che Aminah. His Lordship stated that the child was not to be taken out of the colony pending the appeal.'

The Straits Times, 23 May 1950

'To hell with the decision. We are asking that our child be returned to us. What is wrong in asking for our child to be with us?'

Adrianas Hertogh

Annie climbed the stairs to *The Mercury's* office and knocked on the door. She heard Charlie's footsteps echoing and then the door was flung open.

'Oh. Hello,' he said, and she stepped inside and looked around.

The office was big and quiet. One could feel that it was used to the whirl of news-gathering mayhem, the clicking of typewriters, the noise of voices raised in anger and of laughter in several tongues. Desks sat here and there, and typewriters were lined up along the wall. It was cavernous and forlorn. And hot.

'Tea?' he said and she nodded.

He wandered over to an ancient kettle. Dust lay around the kitchen cubicle, and she watched as he turned on a tap that emitted a series of sharp rattles before spewing water into the sink.

'Never mind,' she said. 'Listen, Charlie, I'd like to buy you lunch. Is there anywhere around here?'

'Toenails,' he said, and she laughed. He looked up from the sink. 'It's a bar.'

'Sounds delightful.'

'Decent food and fairly cool.'

'So, what are you doing in here?'

Charlie abandoned the kettle. A bank of filing cabinets lined one wall. Papers lay piled up on a desk.

'Deciding on what to keep and what to chuck. Orders are to keep stuff for the records, in case there's a letter from God Almighty or something.'

He pointed to two cardboard boxes, neatly filled with papers.

'That's keep. When I'm done, I'll post it off to Melbourne.'

'You're pretty thorough.'

Charlie poured irony into his hollow laugh.

'I am here until the lease runs out on this office. That's about a year away. In the meantime, I have to sort this lot out and sell whatever I can in the office, which as you can see isn't much. I get the feeling most of it has found its way to the black market after my predecessor left.'

Annie walked to the window and looked down at the jinrickshaw station at the end of the street. The wiry dark-skinned Chinese men were gathered there, smoking and drinking tea under the spreading leaves of a large tree. Charlie joined her.

'I'm expected to write stories of the human-interest variety. Everything else they get from the wires upstairs.' He saw her look of puzzlement and added, 'AAP or Reuters. Nobby, you remember, and Roy MacCartney.'

Annie nodded.

'Nobby, Tom and Larry from AP, Roy, the ABC guy and I are about the whole foreign contingent left here. 'Course they've got local staff and a load of stringers.'

'Stringers?'

'Local freelance reporters who work for them. Eight or so. Nice guys. I get all the news off the *Reuter* machine. We closed down the service here a week ago. I practically live in his office.'

Charlie sighed.

'My current story is the Hertogh girl's case and that's doing nothing for the moment. I found a man who juggles dogs though.'

Annie laughed, took a pack of cigarettes and offered one to Charlie. They sat by the window, smoking and staring down at the trishaw men, who greeted one of their own vociferously, laughing at some private joke. Their laughter wafted on the hot breeze.

'The court found for the Dutch mother of course,' Annie said. 'I read there's an appeal, but really what other decision could they make. I suppose that's what'll happen with Suzy.'

Charlie glanced at her but merely nodded, noncommittally, and blew a smoke ring. Annie was unsure how to raise the subject she had come for. She wanted him to stay put, and Madame Wing to stay put and she wanted to know more about Joseph and so many other things. She took a deep breath.

'Charlie, I've got a proposition for you.'

Charlie eyed her. 'Oh yeah,' he said and she laughed.

'Not that. Get your mind out of the gutter. I'd like to move into Peirce Road, take over half the rent.'

Charlie scratched his cheek and blew out smoke.

'I can take care of the servants too. Manage the house. All that sort of thing. What do you think? I'm a bit sick of living in a hotel.'

Charlie shuffled his feet for a moment or two, the movement clearly reflecting the turmoil in his head. She waited. Finally the feet stopped moving.

'Listen, Annie. I'm a bloke. I don't lead the life of a monk, you know.'

She raised her hand in dismissal.

'I don't care about that. The house is huge. You have your half, I have mine. It means you don't have to move out or look for someone else.'

Charlie stared out of the window for a minute.

'I don't want you trying to get into bed with me every night. I know something about widows.'

Annie laughed.

'Promise. Come on, I'll buy you lunch at Toenails. You can introduce me to some stringers.'

*   *   *

You need a different set of keys to unlock the Chinese face, Annie thought. It was so easy to say that the lidless eyes left it expressionless but that wasn't true. She just didn't know how to read it. She waited. It was imperative to have Madame Wing's complete agreement, or the house would be impossible to run.

'I will be responsible for the wages of the staff and for the general provisions.'

'Mr Cooper employed me. He was a gentleman. For an American, first class.'

'Yes, I know,' Annie said, putting on a sympathetic face. 'Mr Ransome's not out of the top drawer. But we have to make allowances. He's Australian.'

Madame Wing contemplated Annie and then nodded slowly, as if this suddenly explained everything.

'A women in the house will be more settling. Two men together, like that. Must have been very difficult. You've done a wonderful job.'

Madame Wing seemed to make up her mind.

'Yes. Well. I have the account books. When will you be moving in, Madam?'

'Please, Madame Wing, I should like you to call me Mrs Collins. I hope that we can discuss any problem as equals. I am not a white memsahib, and this is 1950. Would that be acceptable?'

I've gone too far, Annie thought as silence fell and the seconds ticked away. Then Madame Wing rose and Annie, too, got to her feet. Madame Wing inclined her head slightly.

'Yes, Mrs Collins, that would be acceptable. Thank you.'

Annie put out her hand and Madame Wing took it. Annie

thought that, as she turned away, Madame Wing looked pleased, but she couldn't be sure if it wasn't only a touch of dyspepsia. The woman was something of an enigma.

She moved in her meagre belongings the next day and began to take stock. Madame Wing had her own room on the ground floor, at the back of the house. She had one day, Sunday, off when she stayed with her family and returned on Monday morning. This was the arrangement she had made with Mr Cooper and Annie had quickly agreed.

Everyone else lived outside the main house. The cook, Ah Moy, his wife, Ah Lian, and their son, the cook-boy, Xiao Wen, lived next to the cookhouse. Ah Lian handled all the laundry with the help of a Malay girl named Salima and her mother, Jumairah. Salima's father and her brother were the gardeners, alongside two other Malays, both apparently named Ali. Mr Ali-One had a wife and a sister called Fatimah. They lived with their four children in the servants' houses at the back of the property.

Two Malay sisters cleaned the house and their parents also lived in the servants' block with their younger brothers. Two more Malay families occupied a ramshackle dwelling attached to the servant's block and were marked in the accounts as woodworkers and general staff. Some helped Ah Moy with the shopping and ran various errands.

Charlie had his own Chinese house boy, Ting, whose fifteen-year-old sister, Wei Wei, and sick mother also lived in the grounds. A very old wiry Indian man, Saahan, who had worked for the Traction Company, occupied one of the garages and looked after the bicycles and the car, with the help of two or three of the

Malays and most of the children. He also, she discovered, took care of Joseph. The Indian guard, Kumar, lived with his wife and two young sons in the guardhouse.

When she totted it up she found there were seven Chinese, counting Madame Wing, five Indians and thirty-five Malays. Annie wasn't sure this was the totality of everyone living there. When she totted up the wages in the account books and added to it the pilfering that she knew went on, she found that, excluding Madame Wing, all of them were living on the wages of a couple of Australian bank clerks. It seemed fair that fifty-seven people should live on a property so large and given the chronic shortage of housing, she left everything exactly as it was.

When the final tally was made, based on whatever identity paper each person could produce and on the names written in the register, the number actually came to fifty-three. Fifty-three people to take care of two. She added the four mangy dogs and the dozen cats to the total and called in the vet to treat and neuter them. Though they had been informed about what was happening, most of the children had, initially, cried buckets of tears and walked around with woeful and accusatory looks, but when all the animals eventually came out better than they had gone in, with sleek coats and no sores, Annie knew she would be forgiven. Joseph had been one of the boys who had remained dry-eyed, even though his favourite, Yellow, the dog that followed him everywhere, cried piteously on being taken away.

'It's only for a while, you understand, Joseph? The doctor will give him medicine and food and he will be well.'

Joseph had not even shrugged, merely walked away silently.

Annie wasn't sure he had understood. His English, whilst serviceable, was uncertain and consisted of stock phrases learned parrot fashion.

She then sent for a doctor to carry out health checks on every inhabitant. This was an absolute condition for letting them stay on. Doctor Chen, a young, smart, English-educated Chinese doctor with a Malay interpreter and an old Malay woman-chaperone, set up his temporary surgery in the second garage. A straggling line formed and each member of it passed through over a period of four days. Madame Wing was wholly in favour of these changes, having taken strongly to Mrs Collin's efficient and no-nonsense manner and her calm and pleasant personality. She organised the lines and her countenance brooked no breach of discipline.

The doctor discovered two cases of beriberi, ten of impetigo, two – amongst the elderly – of tuberculosis, one of heart problem, six cases – four amongst the men and two amongst the women – of syphilis, a dozen cases of scabies, and practically everyone had sores of one kind or another, even rat bites, and the children, like the dogs and cats, all had fleas and lice. Everyone was inoculated for everything despite a lot of grumbling. Dr Chen sent the tubercular cases to the quarantine hospital for isolation. Tuberculosis was a scourge and killed the elderly and the young with great rapidity. The woman with the heart problem, Ting and Wei Wei's mother, was also moved to Singapore General Hospital. The scabies carriers were isolated and painted with Malathion, pitifully miserable in their hut. Penicillin and antiseptic creams were prescribed and applied.

She ordered a section of the garden to be fenced and set the gardeners to show the children how to plant vegetables that were beneficial for their general health; this would also stop them from roaming around without purpose and getting into trouble.

Then came the clean-up. Annie recognised in this obsession for cleanliness the transmission to her of the missionary zeal of the sisters at the convent, of their mantra of cleanliness being next to godliness. In fact, she knew, whether she liked it or not, that the nuns had instilled at least half a dozen traits in her, none of them religious, which she now found impossible to shake off.

Her sense of order and organisation was one. Another was a tendency to high seriousness and lack of humour, which had been somewhat tempered by life in Perth with Ronald's more easy-going and increasingly dotty aunt. Annie, active and energetic, was perfectly suited for Australia's open outdoor life. She shared many Australians' dislike of authority but it went deeper than that and came from inside herself. She had leanings towards the nihilistic. In part this search was because she recognised within herself a pull towards indifference to life and even, on occasion, oblivion.

Now, though, the task before her was monumental, requiring all her organisational skills and attention. This suited her very well and she found peace and comfort in all these swabbings and sweepings. All the houses were washed out with gallons of disinfectant. The children were paid ten cents for every rat they caught in their traps and thus ended up making a good deal of money. All the old attap roofing, now swarming with fleas, was ripped away and burnt. The woodworkers were set the task of making all the dwellings waterproof and installing wood floors.

All bedding was burnt and new ones supplied. The old servants' quarters, meant only for some eight to ten people, were extended along the back wall in brick, and a bath house was added to them. In order not to put Ah Lian's nose out of joint, a wash house separate from the main laundry was also constructed with separate drying lines. She also supplied mosquito nets and cloth for new clothes.

She enjoyed shopping in Arab Street with the widowed Fatimah. Fatimah was a quiet but determined and clever young woman who had, like so many others, lost her husband in the war and been left to fend for herself with two small children. She and Annie chatted pleasantly together and though Annie improved her own Malay a little, Fatimah was almost zealous in her wish to practise her English, which she had been studying for four years.

Annie discovered that Fatimah wanted to work but her brother was against it. Strangely, she said, Malay women were encouraged by the Japanese to get out of the home and work during the Occupation. At the end, she said, they took all the men and pressed them into the army or made them dig trenches and bomb shelters. In their place they told Malay women to get out of the house.

'For me,' she said, 'it was a taste of a different life. Take off sarong, put on mompe, the trousers. Go to work.'

She smiled at Annie shyly.

'Nippon newspapers all come, take photographs. I was member of Malay Women's Public Service Corps. We farm and do factory work. Out of house, free and together with other women. Not with men. You understand, Miss Annie. I learned Japanese.'

'What was it like for you,' Annie asked, 'for a Malay family?'

'So terrible. Like everyone. They say we all equal, part of them, Asian people like them. Great East Asia Prosperity Sphere they say. The white man's time over.'

She lowered her eyes.

'But Malay girls were taken from kampongs for, you know, to be used and then murdered and the young men had to work for them in army. We soon find what promise means when there is no food and no medicine. My husband died because there is no medicine. The Japanese take everything. When they talk of prosperity they only mean for them.'

She glanced at Annie.

'You understand.'

'Yes. It was a lie.'

The women touched some of the material displayed in the Arab shops, richly textured and coloured. Saris, like colourful birds, drifted on the breeze. Some small children came up, their hands extended. Annie put her hand to her purse but Fatimah shook her head and looked scandalised.

'We shall be mobbed, Miss Annie. They have food at the public kitchens. They are run by street gangs.'

She shooed them away, speaking sharply in Malay. They turned out of the street and Annie hailed a taxi.

'Your English is very good, Fatimah.'

Fatimah smiled with pride.

'I study English very hard so I can work. Not just stay home, take care of children, cook.'

Annie nodded.

'With English I can work in government office, maybe the post office. I should like that.'

'Your brother would not approve?'

'No. But never mind. My children are not so young now. He is not my husband. I will never take again a husband.'

'No, you might be right.'

Annie laughed and Fatimah joined her.

'Perhaps Mr Pillai might teach English to all the Malay men and women on the compound? Separately, of course. Do you think the men would approve?'

'No,' said Fatimah wistfully. 'It would make trouble. It is better to be quiet. Many cannot read or write and are very ignorant but still they like to boss us around.'

Annie nodded. Fatimah was a determined woman. She would find a way.

The children, in any case, all had to go to school. Anyone who did not comply was to be threatened with expulsion. This included Joseph, who, she discovered, was around nine years old, the same age as Suzy. There was something about this little boy that tugged at her. He was so willing and sweet-natured despite a life of such adversity. Perhaps, she thought, we recognise kindred spirits and in this little orphan boy I find an echo of myself. Whatever it was, she wanted to know more about him.

Madame Wing arranged for her to speak to Saahan and she sat with him one day and shared a glass of tea. He spoke reasonably good English and had told them that he knew that Joseph was an orphan raised by the nuns at the Convent of the Holy Infant in Victoria Street. Joseph spoke of the nuns and remembered the building.

Saahan had first seen Joseph, begging, on the road one day, three years ago. He was part of a gang of beggar children that preyed on the squaddies and tourists round Raffles Hotel and the shoppers in Victoria Street and Bras Basah. Saahan had owned a stall selling cigarettes and drinks and had seen these kids every day. He had thus gotten to know Joseph and used to give him food. He had seen how the one-eyed Chinese man treated the kids, punishing them with beatings and slaps if they didn't bring back money. Usually the police ignored it but one day the social welfare must have got wind of it and there had been a police raid. In the confusion, Saahan had taken Joseph and brought him here. He had taken care of him ever since, he said. He was getting old. Would they take Joseph away now when he might need him most?

Annie assured him that everything was all right and he had departed but not, she saw, without concern. She was convinced that Joseph had probably simply been asked to continue begging on Saahan's account down on Orchard Road. She had a certain sympathy with the old man. He had probably treated Joseph better than the beggar gang leader.

'And on the seventh day, she rested.'

Charlie wandered in, a beer in his hand and threw himself into the chair of their shared living room. She hadn't seen Charlie for days. For long periods, he came in, in the early hours, like a tomcat slinking home, and left virtually wordlessly the next day. Annie knew it was the slight-figured, dark-haired woman she had seen flitting from his bathroom one morning. He seemed to be nutty for her.

'You've made such a paradise here, you'll have them clamouring at the gates.'

'I thought of that. Kumar has to do a head count every morning and night. He knows who they are. Anyone else has to leave. I don't like to do it, but otherwise you're right, we would be swamped.'

'Too right. It's a minor miracle though. Madame Wing no longer looks at me as if I'd crawled out of the primeval slime.'

She smiled and he winked at her.

'It's right, Charlie, though, isn't it?'

''Course it is. Fine by me. Whatever problems arise, you'll solve them.'

He went to the drinks cabinet.

'Drink?' he said and she nodded. Despite his absences, when they did speak they chatted like friends. She had, once or twice, seen the shape of that woman silhouetted against the light in his rooms. She wanted to ask him about it but didn't dare. They had an agreement. Most nights, in any case, she was so exhausted she often fell asleep over her book.

For the last two or three nights, however, he had spent the evenings with her, dining together in the long, formal dining room.

She looked around. The house was spotless. The furniture was a ragbag of colonial bits and pieces thrown together since the war, but it was clean and comfortable. The chick blinds needed replacing. They let in the more violent squalls but when the rain was driving and straight they did their job. The roof, at least, was solid. Lane Cooper, the *Newsweek* man, who had lived here for three years, had done two marvellous things, three if you counted allowing such a rag-tag crowd to live all around him. He had repaired the roof and insisted on indoor plumbing and a brand new septic tank. Anyone British, she had mused when she discovered this miracle, would have bumbled on putting up with such sorts of discomforts, but not so an American. A lack of indoor plumbing was un-American. God Bless America, she thought, and Lane Cooper III.

Now, in the blush of the tropical twilight, as the sun cast its last tiny glow onto the polished floors and the rich red cotton rug she had bought in Kampong Glam, she recalled her joy at living in a house like this, with its elegant symmetry, surrounded by the dense beauty of the forest trees.

Charlie dropped ice into a glass. Clink, clink.

There is music. Dance music. And talking, but not in English.

She shook her head. I can't understand, she said inside her head.

Ice clinking in a glass and laughter. A woman is wearing a silver dress, silk. A voice murmurs against her cheek. What is it saying? The laughter is too loud.

'You all right?'

Charlie was holding out a glass to her.

'Thanks, yes. I thought …'

She shrugged. 'Never mind.'

She heard the doorbell, and in a moment Madame Wing showed Desmond into the room. He'd been in Kuala Lumpur. He kissed Annie on the cheek and sat near her. Charlie poured him a drink.

'How's it going?' asked Charlie, 'the Briggs Plan having any effect?'

'Early days.'

Annie looked puzzled.

'You know I don't really understand what this Emergency is all about.'

'To understand that you have to understand the state of Malaya after the war.'

'Well I'm happy to hear about it.'

Desmond glanced at Charlie, who shrugged.

'Go ahead, me old matey,' he said. 'Don't understand it myself.'

'Where shall I start?'

Desmond lit a cigarette. Annie got the distinct feeling that Desmond rather enjoyed this schoolmasterly role. It was a side of him she hadn't seen up to now. She was surprised he didn't rise to his feet.

'Well, the war left Malaya in a mess. The British had destroyed most of the tin mines to prevent the Japs from using them. The rubber plantations were neglected. So the economy has been very slow to recover. But that's not the main problem. The ethnic divide is.'

'You mean the Malays and Chinese. That sort of thing.'

'Yes. The indigenous Muslim Malays are the biggest group. They accept British rule in theory but are loyal to the Sultans of the different states. There are over two million Malayan Chinese who might well be born in Malaya but are mostly loyal to China. Amongst them are about half a million Chinese squatters who've ended up here somehow or other before and since the end of the war. They don't own land; they just make a living on the edges of the forest and so on. Then there are about half a million Indians, mostly Tamils, working in the plantations. There are native people too who live in the mountains and hold no allegiance to anyone.'

Desmond rose and refreshed his drink. He took up a schoolmasterly stance before them both, legs akimbo. Charlie and Annie glanced at each other.

'The first British plan for independence was called the Malayan Union. Basically the plan would wipe out the power of the Sultans and take Malaya from a protectorate to a Colony, granting citizenship to anyone who had been born in Malaya in the last ten years regardless of race or ethnicity. Naturally all the Malays were up in arms. The Sultans didn't like to give up their power of course and, also, all the Muslims thought they would be swamped by the millions of ethnic Chinese and Indians living in Malaya. So the British came up with the Federation of Malaya Agreement in 1948. The Communists, however, had other ideas. They want a Maoist state.'

'That's when Chin Peng comes into the scene,' Charlie said.

He turned to Annie. 'Leader of the Commies.'

Annie nodded. She was interested in this. If Suzy was in Malaya she would need to understand what the lay of the land was over there.

'Right,' said Desmond. 'Actually Chin Peng had learned guerrilla warfare from the British. He was part of Force 136 and the Malayan Anti-Japanese Army that fought the Japs during the war. You know, we all knew they were Communists but, then, it was a matter of the enemy of my enemy being my friend. They're widespread, well armed and well organised. They hide in the jungle and employ hit-and-run tactics. They force the Chinese squatters and Chinese villagers to join them or help them by supplying rice, weapons, information. They're a nasty bunch and happy to murder anyone who won't comply. They have sympathisers of course, but they rely on terror to get the rural population to do their bidding.'

Desmond looked at Annie.

'Lt. General Briggs is the new director of operations. His idea is to cut the Commies off from food, supplies and new recruitment amongst those Chinese. He's ordered for them to be gathered into fenced and guarded villages where they are safer and can't get food to the rebels.'

'You mean prisons? Camps like we were in? Heavens, Desmond.'

'No, no, Annie. It's not like that. These people are victims. We need to isolate them.'

'You know, the Brits might call it an Emergency but some people say it's a civil war.'

Desmond said nothing, merely throwing a look of resentment at Charlie.

Charlie shrugged. 'Not sure the locals like being rounded up either.'

'The Malayan Chinese Association is working with us. They don't like these Maoists any more than we do. No reasonable man does.'

'But can they get out?' Annie asked.

'During the day, to work on the new parcels of land they've been given. Their own land. They have clinics and schools. But there's a curfew. At night the gates close.'

Desmond shuffled slightly.

'We have to stop such indiscriminate murder all over the country. This is one way. Strangling them.'

'And that's what you're doing, Desmond? Helping to strangle them,' Annie said.

Desmond looked her in the eye.

'They kill women and children, blow up villages, cinemas full of people just trying to rest from the day's work, cut off the heads of planters and tin miners. No one is safe, not white, Malay or Chinese. Until you've seen it, you have no idea. This is one way to stop it.'

He drank down the remainder of his glass.

'And actually that's not what I'm doing. I'm involved in the police recruitment drive. We're trying to get ex-service Europeans to stay on and get Malayan Chinese men into the police force. It's essential. The Emergency is Chinese-Communist driven and the Chinese are the key to solving it. And we have to look forward to a time when Malaya will be independent. They will need their own force.'

'And when will Malaya be independent?' Charlie asked.

'Eventually. But not like it is now. It's still too primitive.'

'Malaya too primitive for independence. Can I quote you?' Charlie said.

Annie saw Desmond's jaw stiffen.

'I don't mean that. I mean it's fledgling. It needs guidance.'

Charlie smiled. Annie frowned.

'Does it?'

She looked at Desmond.

'Yes, of course it does. Since the independence of Indonesia, the hot bloods in Malaya are even more gung-ho for armed struggle. Look where it's led. To this Emergency. Bloodshed and misery.'

'If the British got out it would be their own bloodshed and misery though, I suppose,' Annie said.

'The British are not getting out and leaving Malaya to utter devastation and ruin. Look at partition in India, with millions displaced, millions dead. Gandhi was right. A disgrace and a shame. The aim is to give the people of Malaya a good, stable base to grow from. With the Communists that's impossible. Perhaps when these rebels are crushed and this Emergency is over.'

'One man's rebel is another's freedom fighter,' Charlie said. 'Do you know, Annie, why it's called an Emergency and not a war?'

Annie shook her head.

'Because the lot with the rich rubber plantations and tin mines wouldn't have their losses covered by Lloyds if it's a war.'

'I can't see what difference that makes. It's bloody.'

Desmond threw a keen look at Charlie and seemed about to speak again. Then his face closed down. He turned away. Annie saw there was no point in pursuing this subject. She had done so only really in a spirit of mischief. Sometimes Desmond could be as pompous as Beaver.

The gong sounded. They made their way down to the dining

room. The table was set with a snow-white cloth and some crystal glasses Annie had found in the large dining-room cupboard filled with an assortment of crockery, none matching. A breeze had picked up, and it was pleasant to sit in the low lamplight with the shutters thrown back onto the cool of the night. Sandalwood incense went some way to keeping the mosquitoes at bay, though the moths fluttered constantly against the light. Ah Moy had made excellent Chinese food and several dishes were put on the table.

In addition he had made shepherd's pie with pork and sweet potato. Annie knew that Ah Moy had been presented with a cookbook by Lane Cooper, the 1939 *New York World's Fair Cookbook*, dedicated to 'the home economists of the United States of America'. Annie had spent an evening perusing this tome. Acknowledgements were made to the first Americans, who had possessed romantic names like the Narragansetts and Choctaws, and the book went on to discuss the regional varieties across the United States. How Lane Cooper expected Ah Moy to make anything of this book, she had no idea. However, certain recipes had been marked and on those pages there was a vast array of Chinese writing. Lane appeared to like crab, dishes from New England and apple pie. Where this shepherd's pie recipe had come from she wasn't sure but she guessed from inside Ah Moy's fertile imagination.

Charlie stayed away from further discussion of the Emergency.

'There's news on the Hertogh girl,' he said.

Annie looked up from her examination of the shepherd's pie.

'The Muslims are up in arms. The Muslim Welfare League has mounted a legal defence fund. They are appealing the decision.

She can't leave for Holland and the Dutch are up in arms too.'

'Oh, the poor girl. Where is she?'

'Stuck in the York Hill home, adamant she wants to stay with the foster-mother.'

That night her sleep was shallow and disturbed. What did this decision mean for her? She dreamt about Suzy, her little face constantly morphed now into Joseph's, and now into that of Maria, the little Hertogh girl. She dreamt about the sounds of ice clinking and laughter but now she wasn't sure whether it was laughter or sobbing.

She woke and tossed about a moment then gave up and turned on the light and took up her book.

Annie had made a pact with herself when she had come into Ronald's money. Her education in the convent had been so stultifying, confined to repetitive endeavours, domestic chores and religious studies, that she had felt a need to allow the air to blow into her mind. To that end she had chosen works to read that tested her imagination and her intellect.

In this way she had come across *Lycidas*, Milton's elegiac poem to the tragedy of youthful death. She opened it now. It was complex yet she found it strange and satisfying. It spoke of the space between semblance and truth, of death and rebirth, of grief and forgiveness. She struggled with the allusions and in many ways found the work contradictory, as if there were many voices speaking at once. It seemed at once a lament for death and Lycidas, as well as for the poet's own promise unfulfilled, his own intimations of mortality and then an uplifting rush to hope.

Look homeward Angel now, and melt with ruth.
And, O ye Dolphins, waft the hapless youth.
Weep no more, woful Shepherds weep no more,
For Lycidas your sorrow is not dead,
Sunk though he be beneath the watry floor,
So sinks the day-star in the Ocean bed
And yet anon repairs his drooping head,
And tricks his beams, and with new spangled Ore
Flames in the forehead of the morning sky

Mourn, it seemed to say, find sorrow and lament, then look towards the new day dawning.

She lay down the book. Well, she thought, whatever it meant to say, it spoke to her of all the contradictions about grief, hate, death, fear, hope and twisted memories that seemed to have found themselves inhabiting her both consciously and unconsciously. It was exhausting.

6

'This case is a product of circumstances quite beyond anything contemplated. It is the product of world upheaval. The position is tragic but no good will be served by keeping the child here.'
Kenneth Gould, Counsel for the Netherlands Consul-General
The Straits Times, 23 May 1950

Yellow and most of the other animals came back to the house. The children jumped and screamed and even Joseph, as Annie was happy to see, threw his arms around the dog's now clean neck. Fortunately this excitement deflected any questions about those animals that did not return.

Joseph proved to be a more difficult child than Annie had thought. She had imagined that his devil-may-care attitude and his easy smile were merely outward swagger but this proved quite wrong. He constantly played truant from the government school and went begging on Orchard Road. She had been to see his teacher, Mrs Bowyer, a young Indian woman whose looks were marred by a large red naevus on her forehead.

'He's never been to school, that's the problem. He's with the very little ones, learning his letters, and doesn't like it.'

'I see. What do you suggest?'

Mrs Bowyer had shrugged. 'It's not that he's not clever. Like for us all, his life was interrupted by the war. Almost four years of no schooling at such an age. It takes a toll. I was in college then. My own education was interrupted but it's easier for an adult to pick up the pieces.'

She sighed.

'We can't go by age, we have to go by ability and it's hard on the older ones to be sitting with six-year-olds and not picking it up so fast.'

Mahmoud drove her to Orchard Road to pick up some provisions from Cold Storage. Mahmoud had finally agreed to call her Mrs Annie, which he thought reasonably proper but, she noticed, he had resorted to not calling her anything at all most of the time now. However, it did feel like their conversations had become a little less stilted.

'Mahmoud, you are married.'

'Yes,' he said.

'And you have children?'

'Yes, two.'

'How old are they?'

'Twelve and nine.'

'And what happened during the war? About their education, I mean.'

'My wife taught them at first. Later they had a tutor, Mr Grey. He was an Anglo-Indian fellow from Rajnapur who came here to be a schoolteacher just before the Occupation.

He taught mathematics and literature and English, though that was forbidden of course. And they went to Japanese school and learned Japanese, though they have forgotten all that.'

'I see. A tutor. I see.'

Mahmoud looked at her quizzically in the rear-view mirror.

'Mrs Annie?'

'For the older children like Joseph, who don't want to sit with the six-year-olds.'

Annie settled back, satisfied. A thought came to her.

'Mahmoud, during the war, what did you do?'

'I was a driver.'

Annie frowned.

'For the Japanese?'

'For an Indian man, Mr Menon. He was arrested by the Kempeitai, then I worked for a Japanese, Mr Shinozaki.'

Annie retreated into silence. Why did she know that name? Shinozaki?

Cold Storage was cool and inviting. Ah Moy did most of the food shopping from the wet market, and Madame Wing handled household goods, but Annie liked to buy her personal items herself. She lingered at the soap and shampoo counter, turning a tin of bath crystals in her hand.

'Annie? Is it Annie Collins?'

Annie turned to face the woman who had addressed her. She was about thirty years of age, Eurasian, plump, with badly pitted skin. Annie knew who she was instantly and broke into a broad smile.

'Maria Coelho. Good heavens.'

Maria threw her arms around Annie's neck, and Annie hugged her warmly.

'My gracious, Annie. How wonderful to see you.'

'What are you doing now, Maria? Are you well?'

'I'm jolly well. I'm married and got three thumping great kids. It's Maria Shepherd now. My husband's a copper. Would you believe I married a policeman after doing all that prison time.'

'That's lovely. You look happy.'

'Oh happy as you can be on a sergeant's pay. You know.'

Her smile faded. Her eyes dropped to Annie's wrist.

'And you, Annie, what about you? Are you all right now?'

Annie looked down and nodded.

'Yes. You were very good to me. What about Jean?'

'Like me. Married an English captain. Medic. Lives in Buckinghamshire, wherever that is.'

A beleaguered looking Malay girl came up with a rotund screaming child on either hand.

Maria let out a long peal of laughter. Shoppers turned.

'These noisy brats are mine. Oh, it would be lovely to catch up, but I'd better drag them off home before we get chucked out. Give me your number. I'll give you a call.'

Maria produced a crumpled envelope from a bag bursting with odds and ends, and Annie wrote down her telephone number. The children jiggled and screamed and with a final wave Maria left.

She owed Maria Coelho and Jean Barker a debt of gratitude. When she had been so ill, like sisters, they had nursed her. She hadn't seen them since the day they had all been freed at

Sime Road Camp.

As they turned into the gates she saw Kumar standing with an old Malay man carrying a long stick. As the car swept past she recognised him as the Haji from Kampong Swettenham.

'Stop, Mahmoud,' she cried.

She ushered the Haji into the car and took him up the drive.

'Come inside, Haji,' she said, dropping her gloves and bag on the hall table.

Madame Wing emerged, looking askance at the old Malay.

'Lime juice, Madame Wing, please. In the garden.'

She settled the old man in a chair.

'You have news for me?' she said, looking at him intently.

He took the paper she had given him from his pocket, smoothed it and put it on the table.

'I have news.'

Annie's heart leapt.

Madame Wing walked across the grass, holding a tray.

'Nobody can recall the Indian driver or the gardener, but the housekeeper, she someone can recall.'

'Yes,' Annie said, leaning forward eagerly.

'There is a woman who worked in your house before the war, before you came. She remembers your husband, the English tuan besar. She sometimes came over to do laundry and other jobs. She was summoned when needed by the housekeeper, but she does not recall you. So perhaps you were not yet there.'

'Yes, yes,' said Annie, impatiently. Why did he take so long?

Madame Wing put the tray onto the table.

'This woman says the housekeeper was well known because

she was a kindly woman, more so than most who were serving the tuan besar, and because of her gold tooth. She says her name ...'

'Will there be anything else, Mrs Collins?'

Annie glanced up and shook her head.

'No, nothing, thank you.'

Madame Wing turned to leave.

'Yes, Haji. Go on.'

'It is on the paper. Her name is Mrs Loke.'

He tapped a bony finger on the paper and peered at it.

'Loke Swee Lin. That is how the Chinese say.'

Madame Wing came to a halt and turned. She approached the table.

'Excuse me, but are you looking for Loke Swee Lin?'

Annie rose from her chair.

'Yes, Mrs Loke. I knew her as Ah Lin. She was the housekeeper at my old house on Swettenham Road before the war. Do you know her?'

'Of course. She was a friend of mine. A devout woman.'

Annie's eyes opened wide and she stared at Madame Wing.

'Do you know where she is, Madame Wing?'

Madame Wing looked directly at Annie, with a barely imperceptible furrowing of her brow.

'I do. She has gone to our Lord. She died at Bahau in 1945.'

7

'Mummy (Aminah) is apt to get very upset when she comes to
see me. I will tell her not to cry so much the next time I see her.

I, too, will try not to cry.'

The Singapore Free Press, 3 June 1950

Annie felt disappointment like a knife thrust.

When the Haji had taken some refreshment, Annie
accompanied him back into the house and gave him some money.

'Thank you,' she said. 'You are wise. This money can buy
medicine and food. I leave it up to you. Please give some extra to
the woman who gave you the information.'

'Can I do anything more for you, Puan?'

'No. Thank you.'

Her eyes followed the old man as he made his way slowly
down the hill.

She climbed the stairs to her bedroom. This had been the
marvellous American's room. She had half fallen in love with
her own image of Lane Cooper. She imagined him a typical well-
fed General-Macarthur type, strong and forceful, a man's man,

taking charge with his American accent, full of confidence. He had whimsy too, though. She saw it in the bed he had bought: a beautiful Chinese four-poster bed, carved with fruit and bats and dragons. And he liked privacy for his quiet moments. He had had a door cut into the bathroom from the bedroom. The outer door remained resolutely locked, closing this room off to the outside, creating a haven. She half wondered what he looked like but didn't ask Charlie or anyone for fear that he was short and squat and middle aged with a large paunch and thick glasses. If she had a preference he would look like Clark Gable or perhaps Jimmy Stewart.

The day was still and hot and she ran a hand over her brow. She kicked off her shoes and padded into the bathroom.

She could spend hours in this bathroom. She dropped her package onto the chair by the window and opened the brown paper, arranging the soaps in the cupboard and putting the tin of crystals on the edge of the bath. The shutters were half closed, spilling sunshine into slats along the tiled floor.

She turned on the tap and poured in the contents of the tin, the small pink crystals bursting and swirling a rainbow of rose and lavender into the water. The air filled with perfume. She sat on the chair and began unbuttoning her blouse.

The bath is white. So is her skin under the pink frothy water. The crystals give off a heady perfume and she lies back languidly. A hand brushes her cheek. A man's hand. She takes it in hers and puts her lips ...

Annie rose from the chair so quickly it fell backwards with a sharp clack. The bath was practically overflowing and she turned off the taps hurriedly. How long had she been daydreaming?

'What's going on, Annie?' she said to herself aloud, as if by voicing her thoughts, an answer might come flying out of the air.

She picked up the chair and put it to rights. Fancies. It was the heat. She slipped into the bath, the cool water dousing her skin, washing away the sweat and the disappointment of this news about the housekeeper.

She rested her head against the edge of the bath.

Her lips brush his hand and he runs his strong arms around her, pulling her dripping from the bath. Her arms grip his neck, the pink frothy water running rivulets down his naked back. She runs her hand into his black silky hair and he drops his head to hers.

The telephone rang in the hall and her eyes flew open.

When Madame Wing knocked, Annie had towelled herself and put on a cotton housecoat.

'Telephone, Mrs Collins. Mrs Shepherd for you.'

'Would you mind taking a number please? I'll call her back.'

The idea of chattering to Maria at this moment held no appeal at all. She dressed in a fresh, loose skirt and blouse. She would have liked to have worn a sarong like the Malay women, like she had in the camp. It was the most sensible garment for the tropics. But Madame Wing would have been scandalised and probably given her notice instantly. It might no longer be the days of the Raj but it felt like it. White women, even one like her who was not entirely white, were still expected to keep up the side.

'Whatever side that is,' she said wearily to herself in the mirror, fixing her hair up for coolness.

She had made Wei Wei, Ting's sister, into her personal maid. The girl was quite hopeless but she could keep the clothes tidy and make sure the maids didn't steal everything that you left lying around. Not that Annie had very much one could steal. Annie was not one for adornments. She no longer possessed her wedding ring or engagement ring. Somewhere along the line those had gone, though she could not remember how.

She had sold the watch Ronald had given her for her eighteenth birthday in the camp to buy food from the guards. She recalled that quite clearly. At the end, when they put her into Raffles to await enquiries into Ronald's next of kin, her belongings, packed into a tiny leather case, had consisted only of the contents of a Red Cross parcel. Later, when she got to Australia, she had found, under the loose bottom of the suitcase, a folding fan wrapped in brown paper. It was a plain but pretty thing covered in black swirling lines. She had wondered if the suitcase was actually hers. She knew she had been ill in Changi. Perhaps it had belonged to one of the other women.

She found Madame Wing in the dining room putting fresh blossoms in a bowl on the sideboard. They had discovered they both had a great fondness for the champaca flower whose scent met you unexpectedly, like an old friend, carried on the breeze as you passed through the house.

'Madame Wing, may I ask you some questions about Mrs Loke?'

The Chinese woman put the last of the flowers in the bowl.

'By all means.'

'Would you sit?'

Madame Wing arranged herself decorously on a chair.

'You must have wondered why I am here, Madame Wing. Why I'm sharing a house with a strange Australian, running around having dogs and cats neutered and fed.'

'It is to your honour. A lean dog shames its master.'

Annie was momentarily taken aback. 'Yes, well ...'

'As for being here,' Madame Wing went on, 'well, in my experience, we are diverted unwittingly onto many unexpected paths in life.'

'Perhaps you wouldn't mind telling me a little about your life and something of your friendship with Mrs Loke.'

Madame Wing's expression didn't change but Annie sensed her reluctance. She went on quickly.

'It might be useful to tell you why I am here and why I am interested in Mrs Loke.'

Madame Wing inclined her head.

'I am here to search for my lost child.'

Annie knew she had caught the woman's interest.

When the tale had been told, from the orphanage in Ipoh to the present day, Madame Wing simply nodded as if this tale was no different to the myriad tales of woe that she had heard or experienced.

She gathered herself up and meditated a moment, her fingers on the gold cross, as if consulting a higher power on how to begin, then suddenly settled herself and allowed her hands to rest on her lap.

'Swee Lin and I were childhood friends. My father and hers were partners in tin in Malaya. We went to the convent school together in Kuala Lumpur. Just before her father died, Swee Lin was married at sixteen to her cousin, Loke Eng Boon, but Loke's financial imprudence forced my father to buy him out of the partnership. Loke died of malarial fever when Swee Lin was twenty-eight. His gambling and the Depression brought ruin on what fortune he had and he left Swee Lin penniless and with four children to raise. My father was a wealthy man and, as she was the daughter of his old partner, and of course, as we were all Catholics together, he helped her. It was then, I suppose, that she became a housekeeper. At that time I was living in Kuala Lumpur with my husband. We came to Singapore when the Japanese invaded Malaya. Of course all the British were put in prison.'

Madame Wing paused momentarily as if reluctant to take a further step into this memory room.

'The Japanese murdered my father and took over his tin business. They forced the Chinese in Singapore to pay reparations. Fifty million dollars. We had four large properties. We were forced to sell two for virtually nothing and, later, during the Occupation we sold the third in order to live. It was ruinous for us all.'

She looked at Annie.

'My husband died in 1947. He had spent two years in Outram Jail. It affected his heart, the harsh treatment, the lack of food. My children survived, both of them, thank the Lord. I had no idea what happened to Swee Lin until I found out through the church that she and her children went to Bahau. At that time, in 1944, all the Catholic Chinese were encouraged by Mr Shinozaki to leave Singapore and start a new life in Fuji-go, a village in Malaya. I would not go and leave my husband in the jail. And I am grateful

I did not. It was all a lie. The place was malarial and there was no good land for farming and, in any case, all those city people knew nothing about farming, so of course many hundreds died of disease and hunger including the Bishop of Singapore. He died too, of septicaemia, I think. Swee Lin and two of her children perished there. God rest their souls.'

Madame Wing made the sign of the cross and touched the crucifix to her lips, holding it there a moment, her face pinched.

Annie knew no words could give any comfort to this woman and waited for her to find her composure.

'After the British came back, I am sorry to say that the colonial government sought reparations only for damage to British property. My father's business was wrecked. My uncle had no health to set it up again and was forced to sell it cheaply. I took in Swee Lin's two surviving children. It was her dying wish. I had the care of my aged mother, my uncle, two aunts and four children. I needed to find work. I was fortunate to find this position.'

'I am very sorry.'

Madame Wing made a small movement of her head as if it carried the weight of loss and struggle and anything greater would be more than her tiny frame could bear.

'We must all navigate the bitter sea.'

'Yes,' Annie said and rose. 'We must all navigate the bitter sea. But I am most heartily sorry.'

Madame Wing rose too, arranging the chair neatly at the table.

'Mrs Collins, Swee Lin has a cousin. It is through him that I found out about Swee Lin and her children. He took care of the children for a little while after the war but it was too much for him. When Swee Lin understood she was dying in that terrible swamp she asked for her children to come to me. The cousin got in touch with me. Swee Lin spent some time with him during the war so he may know more of her life after the Japanese came.'

Annie smiled.

'Oh, yes. He might.'

Madame Wing eyes met Annie's.

'Or he may not.'

8

'Everybody who knows Maria loves her. She is a sweet
sensible child with an extremely happy nature.' This was the opinion
of Miss B.N. Tan, Superintendant of the York Hill Girls' Centre
who has watched 13-year-old Maria Hertogh closely since she
entered the centre a month ago.

The Singapore Free Press, 3 June 1950

'Joseph, pay attention. Read the letters please.'

Mr Pillai, the Indian tutor, clapped his hands together
sharply. He was a short, wiry man with round glasses and a
lugubrious countenance. Annie had engaged him to teach the four
older boys who were constantly playing truant.

'They are used to running around doing nothing all day so
they are having trouble settling into the routine of normal school,'
he explained to Annie. 'I suggest short lessons. One hour a day,
for a month and then perhaps more. We shall see.'

He stared at her mournfully.

'May I suggest giving the boys ten cents at the end of the
lesson? I have found that, in the event that you can afford it, it is

most efficacious for attendance.'

She had agreed and passed him the forty cents. He had shaken his head, his expression one of extreme misery.

'I am most hopeful,' he'd said.

Joseph threw a glance at Annie and stood to attention.

'Ayyy,' he began. She smiled.

She joined Charlie in the garden.

'Hope this leads somewhere,' he said.

'Where is this place?'

Charlie peered at the pencilled address on the top of the newspaper.

'Jalan Kayu, RAF Seletar. It's an airbase up woop woop.'

Annie half smiled.

'Woop woop?'

'Yes, you know. Beyond the black stump. Up country.'

'Well, how do we go?'

'Mahmoud takes us. I don't know where it is. We'll set off after lunch.'

Madame Wing had agreed to come with them, a necessity, she said, as otherwise they would never find his hut and it was more than likely that the fellow might run off.

Annie kept an eye on the lean-to that had been thrown up as a temporary school room. She could hear the steady hum of the children saying their alphabet. 'Beeeee, Ceeeee, Deeee.'

'I'm sure he'll make good progress now.'

Charlie looked up from the newspaper.

'He? Don't you mean they?'

'What?'

'He. You mean Joseph.'

Annie gave a dismissive wave.

'I want them all to do well.'

'Yes, but got a soft spot for little Joe, I think.'

Annie shrugged.

'He's an orphan. He has no one,' Charlie said.

'I have a child,' Annie said, her face shutting down.

Charlie gave up. Annie took up a file from the table.

'What's this?'

'The Hertogh file. I need to take another look. The issue is getting sticky. The Malay press is pretty numerous here. They're stirring things up, screaming racism. Pictures of the kid getting dragged screaming out of Aminah's arms, that sort of thing. The press in Holland are on it too, excited by the prospect of a poor white girl getting ripped from her good Christian family. *The Mercury* has asked for an update and a backgrounder.'

'Can I have a look? I never fully understood the details.'

'Be my guest. When's lunch? I'm starved.'

'Half an hour. Just wait.'

Charlie went back to the newspaper. Annie gazed at the lean-to a moment, listening – 'jaaay, kaaay' – then opened the file.

She read a typed note.

Maria and her foster-mother, Che Aminah, came to Singapore in April 1950 at the behest of the Dutch Consulate in order, Che Aminah was told, to officially formalise the adoption. Once here Aminah was offered money for Maria but refused. She subsequently received an order to hand the child over to the Social Welfare department. Despite all objections Aminah was obliged to hand Maria over and she is now in the Girls' Home in York Hill.

Annie flipped to the background. The first pages were headed simply 'Facts'.

Maria Hertogh was born on 24 March 1937 to a Dutch Catholic couple living in Tjimahi, near Bandung, Java, then part of the Dutch East Indies. Her father, Adrianus Petrus Hertogh, came to Java in the 1920s as a sergeant in the Royal Netherlands East Indies Army. He married Adeline Hunter, a Eurasian of Scottish-Javanese descent in the early 1930s. Maria was baptised in the Roman Catholic Church of Saint Ignatius at Tjimahi in April 1937, the third child of five.

When the Japanese invaded, Adrianus Hertogh was captured and sent to a POW camp in Japan where he was kept until 1945. Adeline was then pregnant with her sixth child, and gave birth to a boy in December 1942. She lived with her children and her mother, Nor Louise, a Eurasian, who had left her Scottish husband for a Muslim man. For many years Nor Louise had been friends with Aminah, an educated woman from Trengganu in Malaya, who had lived with her first husband for ten years in Tokyo and spoke fluent Japanese. After his death she moved to Bandung where she married a jeweller, Ma'arof bin Haji Abdul.

Maria went to live with Aminah binte Ma'arof in 1943, was circumcised according to Malay custom and given the name Nadra binte Ma'arof.

Annie looked up and over to the edge of the garden where the boys were starting a game. The girls were skipping on the path by the vegetable patch. This circumcision was something she had heard about in Ipoh, where the sisters quietly condemned it. She was surprised the press had made so little of it considering how barbaric most westerners considered it. The more particularly for a baptised child. She found the prospect of this having happened to Suzy so distressing that she rose from the table and walked to the hibiscus bush that spilled over the edge of the lawn, plucked a flower and waited for this feeling to subside.

Charlie looked up at her as she regained the table but she buried her face, once again, in the file.

Maria, or Nadra as she was now called, and her new family went to Jakarta for a period before moving back to Bandung, where Aminah worked for the Japanese military police as an interpreter until the end of the war.

In 1945, Sergeant Hertogh was released and reunited with his wife. They made enquiries about Maria, but Hertogh was a sick man and they returned to the Netherlands, after requesting Dutch authorities in Java and Singapore to trace the child.

In 1947, Aminah moved to her hometown in Malaya. At this point Maria spoke only Malay, wore Malay clothes and practised her religion devoutly.

Investigations were made by the Red Cross, the Indonesian Repatriation Service, the Royal Netherlands Army and the local police. In September 1949, Aminah and Maria were traced to the village where they were living.

'Ah lunch. 'Bout time. Good oh,' Charlie said, tossing the newspaper on the table.

Annie looked up. She had been engrossed.

Madame Wing placed the tray on the table, carefully folding

the newspaper and setting it to one side. Charlie grinned sheepishly at her.

'May I suggest that we leave at one? The drive is quite long and the roads are not always of the best.'

Annie nodded.

'Perfect, Madame Wing. Thank you.'

'Shall I be mother?' Charlie said, picking up the teapot.

'The case is interesting. The child had become entirely Malay by the time she was found.'

Charlie drank a cup and poured another, then tucked into the pork pie and salad.

'Yes, turns out that the bloke in Malaya who found her at some kind of sports day was appalled. She was tall and white so he'd noticed her of course. Found out that she was a Dutch girl who'd been adopted by this Aminah.'

Annie blew on the tea and read from the file.

'Right. The Administrative Officer was Arthur Locke. This Locke went to see her about a month later in the village. Quizzed her about adoption papers, which she didn't have, and her relationship with Adeline. Found out that a Dutch girl was being sought in Singapore and questioned the adoption with his boss.'

Annie picked at the pie and took a bite.

'Dumdy dum, blah. Oh yes, Locke came back later and told Aminah that she had to legalise the adoption. Hang on.'

She took a celery stick and crunched on it for a while. Charlie watched the children in the lean-to run outside and waved to them as they ran noisily off into the trees. Annie looked up as Mr Pillai approached across the lawn. 'Mrs Collins. Things went well. I shall see you tomorrow.'

'Yes, thank you, Mr Pillai. You've done a splendid job.'

He nodded and set off with a slow plod.

Annie closed the file.

'I can't make sense of what happened next. Need to read it more closely. Looks like Locke told her something about her needing to legalise the paperwork to get her and the girl to Singapore.'

They both tucked into the lunch and watched the boys play sepak raga with the rattan ball at the bottom of the garden. Charlie had tried this game that he called 'keepy-uppy' with them but had made a fool of himself. It required agility and swiftness of eye and years of practice.

Annie set Fatimah the task of making her son and all the boys write out their letters for the next day. If they could write their name by the end of the week she promised to bring Eskimo Pies from Cold Storage for all the children on Saturday. Since most of the children were hanging around listening, Annie was certain that mob rule would prevail.

They set out ten minutes later and headed into the northern reaches of woop-woop. The roads were in good condition for the most part and they arrived at Yo Chu Kang Road in good time. They passed a large cemetery, a mental hospital and a leper settlement on the right before arriving at the spectacular vista of the marshlands and river of the Punggol inlet. As they turned into Jalan Kayu, the road to Seletar Airbase, the lane became narrower and was lined with neat wooden and attap houses and all manner of shops. English men in casual clothes wandered along or gathered in clusters here and there.

Madame Wing directed them past a church, a variety of curry shops, an Indian cinema and the Ngai Sun Tailors to turn left at Lim's Photo shop. On the corner of this street was a milk bar and coffee shop with clean checked plastic tablecloths, and Madame Wing asked that they wait inside.

She set off down the dusty lane, an incongruous figure in her impeccable chipao. Annie and Charlie sat in the shade of the coffee shop and ordered iced Sinalco Orange. Children emerged from every side and stared at them for a while then meandered off. Foreigners were not an unusual sight here where men and women from the airbase were daily visitors. A few old Chinese and Malay men, who clearly occupied these spaces for hours at a time, stopped their game of cards and gazed at them in a desultory fashion.

After a few minutes Madame Wing returned with the cousin, Kiat Tiow. He was thin as a rail and dressed in ragged shorts. Annie had seen opium addicts in Ipoh and he had all the appearance of those boney men, though he seemed clean and otherwise healthy. Before the war opium was freely available everywhere. Now it was banned, she understood, but there were still dens in Chinatown and probably sellers and users out here in the kampongs.

He pulled his mouth into a toothless, mirthless grin. Madame Wing took a seat at another table and dabbed at her temple with a handkerchief.

'I am here to ask about your cousin, Loke Swee Lin.'

'I know that, Missus,' he said in squaddy's English. He had obviously spent a lot of his life around the mechanics of the airbase.

'It's about a baby.'

He took out a pouch of tobacco and began to roll a cigarette. Annie offered him one of hers and he took it and put it behind his ear and continued rolling.

'My baby was given to a Malay girl when the Japanese came in 1942. Your cousin would have known about it. Do you know anything about that?'

He lit his cigarette and pulled some loose tobacco from his lip.

Madame Wing tossed some Chinese vowels at him and he waved his hand at her dismissively.

'I dunno.'

He looked around the shop. Everybody was staring at them.

'Look,' began Charlie, but Annie put her hand on his arm.

'There's a reward.'

'I tol' you I dunno nothing. My cousin here for a while then she go Bahau and she die there, children die there. Mistake to go. Mistake.'

He paused, his face working through a hidden grief, then he looked up.

'I work for Japs. Now I work for English again. I dunno, Missus, I dunno.'

He rose abruptly and moved off, his raggy shorts flying round his skinny legs. Madame Wing rose but did not follow him, her face filled with the sorrow of it all. The other patrons murmured amongst themselves.

'He knows something,' said Charlie softly. 'His whole attitude was strange.'

'I'm sure too. All I can glean about Mrs Loke is that she was a good woman, a Christian woman. She wouldn't have left a child like that, a baptised child. If Ronald gave Suzy to the ayah, Mrs Loke would have known and done something about it. I'm sure of it. Madame Wing is sure of it too.'

Annie took a notebook and wrote her name, Charlie's name, the address of *The Mercury* and their telephone number on a paper. She took a pin from a noticeboard by the bar and stuck the paper with it and addressed the impassive faces of the old men around her.

'A baby,' she said, 'when the Japanese came. There's a reward.'

She spread five fingers into the air.

'Five hundred dollars.'

The faces stared blankly back.

9

'I have five other children but even if I had twenty-five, I would move heaven and earth to get Maria back.'

Adrianas Hertogh in *de Telegraaf*, 20 May 1950

'J-O-S-E-P-H.'

Annie pointed out the letters to him as he read.

'Very good. Oh, very good, Joseph.'

Annie took the boy on her knee and hugged him. He threw his arms around her neck and she felt the vulnerability of his little bones. All the boys had written their names and all the children had eaten their Eskimo Pies, the ice cream melting down their faces in the heat. Joseph had come back, sticky, and presented her, proudly, with his paper.

'I shall put it in my room,' she said smiling at him.

He nodded seriously, then got off her knee and raced away into the darkness. Annie rose and turned into the house. The smell of stewed cabbage came from the back-kitchen area and she frowned. She had asked for more variety in the vegetables and Ah Swee had interpreted this as a desire for western recipes. So far he had served a watery turnip soup and an insipid carrot and long bean stew, neither of which had been a great success. Tonight there was to be stewed cabbage and ham. Tomorrow she would ask him to return to the wok.

She went to the upper-verandah living room and poured herself a gin and tonic, then picked up the phone and dialled.

She watched the hawks circling in the last light of the darkening sky and heard the bullfrogs begin their chorus. A bird gave a mournful cry. It reminded her of something. Crying.

'Hello,' a voice said on the phone.

'Maria,' Annie said. 'It's Annie.'

'Hellooo, my dear. I thought you'd forgotten me.'

'Sorry but I got all caught up in things. Look, how about coming to see me for tea next week? Are you free?'

Maria laughed gaily and loudly.

''Course. What about Wednesday? Two at school and the girl can take care of Willy.'

They chatted a little longer and Annie gave Maria her address and she rang off.

Annie took her drink and sank into the cushions of the rattan chair. She took up the file on Maria Hertogh. Her sympathies were very much with the poor child locked up in the Girls' Home like a criminal, only allowed to see her foster-mother once a week. Aminah was clearly devoted to this child. The mother from Holland had not come out because the family was not well-off. They were waiting for the appeal to be over and for the Dutch government to send Maria home to them. They were all waiting, they said, desperate to welcome her to Holland.

She opened the file and turned to the section marked 'Disputed Versions'.

The first section was by Adeline Hertogh.

Adeline Hertogh claimed she was persuaded by her mother to allow Maria to go and stay with Aminah in Bandung for three or four days whilst she recovered from the birth of her sixth child on 29 December 1942. Aminah arrived on 1 January 1943 to fetch Maria. When the child was not returned, Mrs Hertogh borrowed a bicycle on 6 January and set out to retrieve her daughter. She claimed she was arrested by a Japanese sentry on the outskirts of Bandung as she did not possess a pass and was thereupon interned.

From her internment camp, she smuggled a letter to her mother, requesting her children be sent to her. This Nor Louise did, but Maria was not among them. So Mrs Hertogh asked her mother to fetch Maria from Aminah. Her mother later wrote and told her that Aminah wanted to keep Maria for two more days, after which she herself would bring the child to the camp. This did not materialise and Mrs Hertogh did not see Maria throughout her internment. After her release, she could find neither Maria nor Aminah.

The second section was by Aminah.

Aminah rejected Adeline's story. She claimed that Adeline had given Maria to her for adoption in late 1942. She said that she, without offspring of her own, told Mrs Hertogh then that she would regard Maria absolutely as her child, whom she would bring up in the Muslim faith, to which Mrs Hertogh had agreed.

Aminah also contested the truth of Adeline's internment by

the Japanese. She testified that she and Mrs Hertogh continued to visit each other frequently after the adoption until the latter left for Surabaya to look for work about the end of 1943 or the beginning of 1944.

It was hard to understand what could have happened or who could be believed. Had Adeline, with six mouths to feed and a husband who could well be dead, made the decision to give one of them away? But could one give away one's children? Ronald had done so. But could a mother? Annie shook her head. Out of desperation one could do anything of course and the war made you desperate. On the other hand, if Aminah had wanted a child badly enough, and had fallen in love with Maria, perhaps she had simply not been willing to give her up. Her thoughts rested momentarily on Joseph. An inkling of how one could love such a child was coming to her.

She closed the folder as the lights of a car flitted like fireflies between the trees. She went to the edge of the verandah to watch it come up the drive. Fireflies, she thought. Wasn't there a poem about fireflies?

The thought flew away. She hadn't expected Charlie this evening. He'd been coming back very late. They'd almost not seen each other for several days for he rose late and left instantly. She'd taken to pottering in the kitchen garden. She wasn't sure the Malay gardeners were very delighted or thought it entirely appropriate, but they made her welcome and showed her very kindly how to do things. Desmond had been away. The troubles in Malaya took up a lot of his time and she had to admit to missing his company.

She heard footsteps on the stairs and Charlie burst into the living room.

'Sit down, Annie. I've got news.'

* * *

She closed the mosquito net firmly around the bed. The smell of the sandalwood incense floated in from the verandah. Sandalwood was supposed to keep the mosquitoes away and trays of it were placed under every window and by the doors, but some always found their way inside, zinging and buzzing throughout the night. The shutters were always thrown open at bedtime to catch the evening breezes and when the dusk swarm had lessened.

She lay back on the snow-white pillows under this serene canopy of netting. The ceiling fan moved the material about like foam on the sea.

Charlie had talked and talked and she had sat, silent and nervous through it all, hardly able to believe what he was telling her.

He had been sorting files as usual, Charlie had told her, when a knock had turned his grateful attention from 'waste management policies post-war' to his visitor. 'An old Chinese fellow appeared and said he'd been a journalist himself, worked for the Aw Brothers way back.

'Which was all very interesting but I was getting a bit worried that the poor bloke simply had too much time on his hands. Then, he told me he had come to tell me about some babies.'

The old man, called Mr Ong, had turned out to be a friend of Kiat Tiow. He had told Charlie a terrible tale of Kiat Tiow's experiences in the Occupation. 'Kiat Tiow was rounded up with scores of others and driven to the beach at Changi and machine-gunned. He survived where all the others had perished. Wounded and bleeding, he nevertheless managed somehow to find his way back to his father's village.'

Charlie had shaken his head.

'Anyway Ong said that when the Japanese had invaded, everyone, who could, got out of the city and into the countryside.'

That included Loke Swee Lin who had turned up in that village with her four children, a Malay girl and another Chinese woman named Rose Lim. Also three babies, brown babies, Eurasian babies.

'Kiat Tiow told Ong that his cousin Swee Lin and the Chinese woman had taken in the babies, which had all been abandoned when the Japanese invaded.'

Mrs Loke, the Malay girl whose name no one could remember and Rose Lim had stayed at the kampong for six months. When the Occupation settled down, the Japanese had called for the populace to return to their old jobs. Kiat Tiow, recovered from his bullet wounds, had been forced to return. Everyone had had to make a living in this new world of Syonan-To, the name the Japanese had given to Singapore, and he had to bury his memories and work for the men who had tried to kill him.

When Kiat Tiow had returned to Kampong Kayu, he had found many abandoned houses. People had either been murdered or had fled in fear. He had sent for two of his brothers and his cousin to join him and they had occupied three good houses on the bank of a fast stream, one of the myriad waterways that flowed into the Punggol River.

He and his brothers had gone to work at the airbase. Mrs Loke had also gotten a job at the Japanese commander's house as a housekeeper and the Malay girl had become a maid. Rose had taken care of all the children. The shopkeeper clearly recalled the four children of Mrs Loke and the three babies. The babies' names were Mary, Joan and Theresa.

Annie brushed a tear from the corner of her eye. The thought that Suzy had been taken in and cared for by these loving women was overwhelming. Perhaps her childhood, surrounded by other children whom she thought of as brothers and sisters, playing on the river bank, barefoot and free, perhaps that childhood was a good one and she had been happy. This thought, though it might be illusion, comforted her.

In the middle of 1944, as the Allies grew stronger, the Japanese had begun winding up for a prolonged campaign to defend Singapore. Everyone knew the ruthlessness of the Japanese. They would kill everyone in Singapore before they surrendered. Living so close to the airbase was no longer safe and when Bishop Devals, the Catholic Bishop of Singapore, had called on the Chinese Catholics to join him and the Eurasian community in the new enterprise of Fuji-go, Mrs Loke, Rose and her new husband had packed up all the children and left for Bahau in Malaya.

Annie lit a cigarette and watched the smoke float through the netting like mist through cobwebs. It hung momentarily until a zephyr snatched it away.

They had gone from the relatively healthy life of Kampong Kayu and died in the barren fields and mosquito-laden swamp of a death camp.

When the war ended, Rose Lim's husband had returned to his old home of Kampong Kayu with Swee Lin's two children, his own baby and one little girl, the three-and-a half-year-old Joan. Rose, Mary and Theresa had died of disease, along with Mrs Loke and two of her children.

Kiat Tiow's brothers had drifted away but Kiat Tiow had stayed to work for the British and, for a while, had care of his cousin's children until Madame Wing had taken them. Rose Lim's husband with his own child had left, leaving little Joan in the care of the church.

Despite the fan, the night was warm. Annie took a drink of the water placed beside her bed and wished, as she'd wished a thousand times, that she had a photograph of Suzy. Ronald had not celebrated the birth of this little girl. Her colour had been a shock to him. He had made no attempt to disguise it. He had looked from Annie's face of light skin to that of the child, back and forth, as if attempting to make sense of the irrational. She had been unable to offer explanations. She had no idea what peculiar mixture of cells constituted her own body, what mingling of blood ran in the veins of her unknown mother and father or why she had been born so light and Suzy so much darker. No photographs were taken, no announcements made. Suzy was baptised with only herself and Ronald present, a hole-in-the-wall event of which Ronald ought to have been ashamed. Annie wasn't ashamed though. She loved this baby and had been glad to put the little gold engraved cross tenderly around her neck and see her welcomed into the arms of God. A month later the bombs and shells had begun and hadn't stopped until Singapore fell into the abyss.

But surely she would know her own child. Surely when they met she would sense it. For now she knew she would be able to meet this child. A man had come to Kampong Kayu, six months after the war ended, and taken Joan. A man that Mr Ong and, now, Charlie knew.

She turned out the light. The bowl edge of the waning moon was caught in the window, its sliver of silver a smile in the dark.

10

'The Dutch Consulate-General has not given up the fight
over Maria Huberdina Hertogh (Nadra binte Ma'arof) who,
under a Court of Appeal judgement delivered in Singapore,
goes back to her foster-mother Che Aminah.'

The Straits Times, 30 July 1950

Annie wandered into the garden. She sat and took up the newspaper. The Korean War had broken out and Charlie had chafed about it at length and, Annie thought, rather boringly. If he wasn't moaning about his terrible life of missed journalistic opportunities, he appeared to be lovesick.

She had wanted to talk to him about this extraordinary development, but this morning he had taken off like a rocket. Something was happening and whatever it was it had, at least, made him smile.

She heard the phone ring in the house and ran to pick it up.

'Annie,' Charlie said. 'Hertogh story. She's been given back to the foster-mother. Legal stuff.'

'Heavens. The parents in Holland will be shocked.'

'Yes. Got a feeling this is going to run and run. Finally I get to write some news.'

'Charlie, about this man and the girl, Joan.'

'Yes, I know. Look I need to talk this through, all right, with people who know what they're talking about.'

'But why can't we just go …'

'Annie, trust me. We have to tread lightly. We'll talk about it tonight. The kid's not going anywhere.'

She heard the impatience in his voice. She let him go. There was nothing else to do. She needed him and she wanted to speak to Desmond. She picked up the phone. He was back in Singapore and had left her a message but she hadn't wanted to talk to anyone last night. She had wanted to digest the news as calmly as possible.

'Annie, lovely to hear from you.'

'You all right? How are things in Malaya?'

'Not so good. Look, what about getting together?'

'Yes, I'd love that. Actually something's come up and I really want to talk to you about it. Come to dinner?'

Desmond agreed and made nice noises down the phone about missing her. She hung up. She had missed Desmond's pleasant and attentive company but nothing more than that. How long he would hang around when he realised there was absolutely no chance of anything more between them, she had no idea.

Annie had recently realised something about herself. She was twenty-six years old and had never been in love. She'd got a job in a Greek doctor's office in Perth and men had paid court for a while. She'd liked them, had enjoyed going out, but eventually she had just stopped seeing them, or they had found out she wasn't totally white and had dropped her. When the money had come through from Warne she'd stopped work and devoted herself to Aunt Mabel's final months. She had come to love the old woman as much as a daughter might a mother. So she knew she was capable of love. She just couldn't find the answer to why she found so few men worth the bother.

She shook away these thoughts as she heard the children leaving their lessons. She went outside. Joseph raced across the lawn when he saw her and she pulled him up into her arms. Mr Pillai plodded towards her, wiping his brow with his big polka dot handkerchief.

'Good progress?' Annie said.

She released Joseph to the ground with a kiss and waved to the other boys as they raced off to play.

'I think this formula is proving effective,' he said. 'Next week I will bring my daughter-in-law who is a fine player of the accordion, and add one half hour to learn a song. Would that be acceptable? She will not cost a great deal, five or six dollars only. Learning the words of a song is good for their memory and music is so enjoyable for all the children, do you not think?'

Annie agreed and, at the house, she paid him. She spoke to him of Fatimah, about her English. Mr Pillai said he would find some books. Perhaps Che Fatimah could be his assistant with the children, here where the brother might have fewer objections. Annie smiled. Clever Mr Pillai. She felt like hugging him.

'On the quiet,' Annie had said.

The day was slow. The thought of the man who had taken Joan continued to nag at her. The cinema would distract her. There was a new picture at the Cathay called *Asphalt Jungle*.

She picked up her hat and bag and walked quickly down the drive. She could have sent one of the boys but she was happy to stretch her legs. There was always a gaggle of trishaw men hanging around, drinking coffee in the makeshift village of provision shops, souvenir and hawker stalls, which had set itself up in an open space at the bottom of Dempsey Road where it bordered on the barracks. Before the war, in Ipoh and in Singapore, the rickshaw was the most ubiquitous vehicle on the road. She couldn't recall even having seen a trishaw then. She liked it better than the rickshaw. It was a smoother faster ride, and one had less sorrow for the poor puller. In Ipoh, when she was young, she had always felt the hardship of the hollow-chested rickshaw man, his muscles straining to drag along some fat businessman three times his size.

She sat back under the canopy to enjoy the ride. The legs of the trishaw man turned circles smoothly and, in the dappled sunlight, the shadow lines of the trishaw flitted along the road.

Their legs touch. His hand is in hers. It is night and the rain is beginning to form puddles in the street. He puts out his hand to the trishaw driver and they come to a halt. He leaps out and takes her by the waist, lifting her from the carriage into the neon light. He smiles, his mouth tempting, and she puts her lips to his.

Annie stared at the passing trees. What were these flitting daydreams? Glimpses into a mirror covered in dust. But what had they to do with her?

11

'Che Aminah, foster mother of Maria Hertogh, was the happiest
woman in Singapore yesterday. "Allah has answered my prayers,"
she told *The Straits Times*.'

The Straits Times, 29 July 1950

'You must be joking!'

Desmond lit a cigarette and contemplated Charlie.

'I don't care who he is,' Annie said vehemently, and Nobby
threw her an understanding look.

The discussion had been going back and forth, with Charlie
and Desmond getting more and more hot under the collar.

'Let's re-examine,' Nobby said when the two men retreated
into a sulky silence. He poured a large tot of Lane Cooper's rye
whisky.

He swirled it around the ice in the glass and sipped it.

'This stuff's not half bad,' he said. 'Good old Lane, leaving a
nice supply.'

Charlie sniffed at the bottle. Nobby leant back.

'Let's recap. Sir Christopher Tan is a wealthy lawyer, leading light in the Progressive Party and elected member of the Legislative Council. It is very likely that he will one day be the first Prime Minister of an independent Singapore. He is a war hero and has the full support of the British government. He is a personal friend of the Governor and was knighted one year ago by the King of England. This is the man whose family you propose to disrupt.'

Annie leaned forward.

'I don't propose to do anything but ask him if I might meet the girl he took out of a village in the jungle and made into his daughter.'

'Remind me again how we know this.'

Charlie put down the whisky and went on with all the eagerness of a reporter's zeal.

'The man who turned up in Kampong Kayu in 1946 stepped out of a 1925 Rolls Royce Phantom, a car of extraordinary distinction, I'm sure you will agree. It was used by the head of the Kempeitai during the Occupation but had belonged, before the war, to Tan's family, most of whom were murdered. There is exactly one such car in the Colony of Singapore and, according to my sources, it is still owned and occasionally driven by Tan.'

'Your sources,' Desmond said, smoke filtering from his curled lip.

'Look,' Charlie began.

'All right. That's enough,' Annie said. 'Let's have some coffee before you two resort to fisticuffs.'

She rang the bell and Ting arrived. Ting and Wei Wei were on serving duty as Madame Wing had gone home to see her family.

Annie put a record on the gramophone and turned it down

low. Something soothing was required. She waited until coffee was served before bringing up the subject again.

'Desmond, I don't propose going and banging down Sir Christopher's door. All I'm asking is that you arrange to get a letter to him. A letter that will come through someone high enough up, the Governor for example, that he will sit up and take notice. A letter that will set out the salient facts and ask for a meeting with him and his daughter.'

Desmond shook his head.

'Annie, I want to please you, but really. Sir Christopher is a man the government values. He is pro-independence but is seen as a steady hand whilst hotter heads are rushing around and whilst the Communists are turning Malaya into a battlefield.'

He met Annie's eyes.

'And you have no idea if this child is not his. On what grounds can we challenge this?'

'If the child is his, what does he have to lose by letting me meet her and discover his side of this story?'

Desmond shrugged.

'I can only propose speaking to the Commissioner, and asking that he speak to the Governor. Will that do for now?'

Annie frowned.

'It will have to, won't it?'

She looked around at the three men.

'Goodnight.'

She left the room. Desmond looked appalled.

From the verandah outside her room, Annie watched Desmond's car make its way slowly down the drive. She'd been harsh on him. But he'd acted like such a cringeing diplomat. Tan lived in a house in Nassim Road, not more than a short trishaw ride away from here, and she had nothing to do tomorrow.

*   *   *

Nassim Road was an old street, with old trees, old houses, old money, reeking of elegance and privacy. As the trishaw turned from Tanglin Road she counted the numbers and saw a sign that indicated that the Tan house stood alone on a lane off to the right. The trishaw driver was struggling. Nassim Road was a street that rose gradually to a leg-pumping height and the turn to the Tan residence itself rose suddenly into a steep incline. She paid him and got out.

She wandered along the road, walking through the silence of the high rain trees. No sound came from these huge privileged places, not a glimpse could be seen of the house beyond the trees. She saw the gate, an elegant flamboyance of wrought iron. By the steepness of the drive, she knew the house must stand on a small eminence, giving a view down over the surrounding area. She knew, without seeing it, that it was beautiful. The road ran into the jungle thirty yards further on and she turned and retraced her steps. From this angle she could see there was a guardhouse some ten feet inside the grounds and that the side gate had a bell. The driveway curved away out of sight.

The bell held her gaze. She could cross the road, present her card and ask to speak to Lady Tan. She knew nothing about this woman other than that she was a Eurasian, like herself.

Charlie had dug up a file photograph of this couple taken at some glittering event two years ago. She was tiny and frail-looking. He was strong, handsome, every inch the powerful and successful Chinese man.

She hesitated, filled with indecision. A dog barked suddenly from behind the gate and the guard, a tall Sikh man, came forward and looked at her.

She took a deep breath and went forward, drawing a card from her bag.

'I should like to see Lady Tan,' she said, passing her card to the man.

An expression of surprised wariness came over his face. That a mem should be walking around the streets without a car or a driver was as unusual, in his experience, as an honest shopkeeper. He glanced at the card.

She had an English name, a proper address in Tanglin and a telephone number so, though she did not look entirely English, he dared not send her away.

'Please wait,' he said and Annie nodded.

He picked up the telephone in the guardhouse. A short conversation ensued, the guard hung up and opened the side gate.

'Ma'am, please come inside.'

She went through and he locked the gate behind her, walked quickly to the guard house and produced a rattan chair.

'Please,' he said, smiling, and Annie sat, mopping her brow. The day was so hot even the crickets seemed too worn out to sing.

A high-pitched sound grew gradually louder and she rose as a bright yellow three-wheeled motorised vehicle with a canopy came around the bend like a buzzing bumble-bee. The young Malay driver leapt from it and ushered her aboard.

The cart, because she couldn't think what else it could be called, turned a smart neat circle and headed up the driveway through the dense trees on either side. A wide-spreading, perfectly manicured lawn came into view and, as they passed through the array of hibiscus shrubberies on either side of the path, so did the house. It was, as she had known it would be, magnificent. It was a very large turn-of-the-century porticoed building occupying the crest of the hill. It was given lightness by the extraordinary quantity of lacy fretwork that embellished its eaves and verandah balustrades and by the expanse of its gardens, so that it stood like a crowned queen surveying all her domain. It spoke of great wealth and good taste and an elegance that the war had swept away, possibly forever.

The cart drew up at the porte-cochere and an English butler approached, bowing slightly, and though his manners were quite impeccable, Annie saw the momentary look of disdain he gave her as his upright form guided her through the cool hall of the house, an elegant drawing room and out to a wide covered verandah with an extensive view over the treetops.

The woman seated there was probably only thirty-five years old, but she rose with difficulty, clutching a silver topped cane. Annie recognised Eileen Tan but had not realised how thin and frail she was.

'Please don't get up. I am imposing,' she said, suddenly ashamed of this rash intrusion on a woman so obviously ill.

Eileen Tan regained her seat and waved a hand at Annie.

'Not at all. It's rather nice to have something spontaneous happen to me. I don't get out as much as I'd like.'

A servant appeared quietly on the terrace and Eileen ordered tea.

'Unless you would like coffee,' she said graciously.

'No, thank you. Tea is lovely. You are very kind to allow me to see you like this.'

Eileen smiled. She was as pale and delicate as a moth, her skin like translucent wings. But her voice was surprisingly strong.

'My man said a young mem had turned up at the gate. It was rather intriguing.'

'You may not wish you had let me in when I tell you why I've come,' Annie said, wishing to get straight to the point.

Eileen laughed. 'Have you come to steal the silver?'

Annie laughed too and allowed herself to relax slightly.

'No, Lady Tan, I have come to tell you a story, a tale of woe. One with which you are probably quite familiar, but it is my tale of woe and you are connected to it.'

Annie told her story, pausing only when the silver tea tray arrived. Eileen said nothing, listening intently. Annie wanted very much to gain this fragile woman's trust.

'Your husband tried to kill you. Perhaps he thought to spare you the horrors of the Japanese victors.'

'It wasn't really his choice, was it? Anyway, it doesn't matter now. I can't ask him. He is dead. I can't forgive him for giving away Suzy.'

Eileen sipped her tea and looked out into the cloudless sky.

'You believe that my daughter is actually your daughter. Is

that it?'

'I don't know. When I found out that one baby, Joan, one of the three had survived, I couldn't just walk away. You can see that.'

A sudden commotion sprang up inside the house, a man's voiced raised in anger. Annie turned to see Christopher Tan emerge from the French windows of the house.

'Who do you think you are?' he said, advancing on Annie. She felt a shock of fear. His face was distorted by sheer rage and he looked violent.

Eileen put up her hand. 'It's all right.'

He ignored her. Annie realised he was going to physically remove her. She grabbed her bag and turned to Eileen.

'Lady Tan, please believe me ...'

Annie felt her arms being grabbed and herself being lifted from the seat. It took the wind from her lungs and she couldn't finish her words. She had time only to throw a glance at Eileen's distressed face before she was propelled through the house.

'Stop,' she protested. 'I have the right ...'

He thrust her out of the front door and dumped her into the cart, turned back into the house and slammed the door. The embarrassed driver carried her rapidly away.

12

'Don't ever call me Maria. I am done with the Hertogh family
and my real Muslim name is Nadra.'
The Straits Times, 30 July 1950

'How could he know so quickly?' Charlie said at the bathroom
door.

She'd explained the scenario to Charlie when he had got back
the next day. He'd followed her up the stairs.

Annie examined her arms in the mirror. The marks of Tan's
fingers were livid on her flesh and the beginnings of a purple
bruise were appearing.

'Bloody animal. You shouldn't have gone,' Charlie went on.
'Ong said Tan was a dangerous man. I didn't tell you that. A
dangerous man.'

'Perhaps you should have. Anyway, why is he so dangerous? I
thought he was a lawyer, much beloved of the British authorities,
an upstanding and outstanding citizen.'

'Ong says he has friends, strange friends, triad friends.'

Annie pulled down the sleeves of her dress.

'Ong says, Ong says. Why doesn't Mr Ong pay us a visit. Doesn't he want his damn money?'

Annie pushed past Charlie, her arm brushing his chest. He put his arm on the door frame to stop her and she looked up at him, reading the concern on his face.

'I'm all right, you know. I got a fright and my pride's a little hurt. He chucked me out like a bag of rubbish.'

'Don't go off doing things like that without telling me. All right.'

Charlie threw himself into the chair by the window.

'Someone must have told him we'd been in that village. God, how paranoid can you get. Five years after the event.'

Annie ran a brush through her hair and began to arrange it in a clip.

'Must be a mighty careful man. I reckon the snooty-nosed butler gave him a call too.'

Charlie made a face.

'Creep.'

'She's nice though, his wife. Eileen. Lovely woman. She understood.'

She put down the brush and turned to face Charlie.

'I think he loves her very deeply. She's frail and he protects her. I think their story of woe is very terrible too, but I didn't get a chance to hear it.'

The telephone rang. Charlie sprang up. He wagged a finger at her.

'Promise you won't go off half-cocked again,' he said as he moved to the door.

'I promise to talk to you first, that's all.'

When Annie appeared in the hall, Charlie had just hung up. She looked at him quizzically. He shook his head.

'Not about Tan. Just Nobby. The Hertogh family is furious and the Dutch press is having a field day slamming British justice. The Catholic Party's up in arms and the Ministry of Foreign Affairs has protested to London.'

Charlie rubbed his hands.

'Come on, drinkies.'

'That poor kid,' Annie said ruefully. 'I hope this is an end to it. The only mother she knows is Aminah. What's the point?'

Charlie put his head to one side and contemplated her.

'Really? What's the point? And if the Tan girl turns out to be yours?'

Annie looked at him sharply and turned away.

Charlie raised an eyebrow and set out for the living room when the phone went again. Charlie picked up. Annie went to pour herself a gin and tonic and asked Ting to get a Tiger for Charlie.

'Desmond, hello, old boy,' he said putting on a drawling British accent, 'what's …'

Charlie listened, not speaking, glancing at Annie from time to time.

'OK, thanks.'

He hung up, joined Annie and drank half the beer.

'Desmond. He's pretty pissed off. He says the Governor has conveyed an official protest from Sir Christopher Tan to the Australian Commissioner. He states that you trespassed on his property, harassed his wife and that *The Mercury* has to answer charges of unlawful investigation into his private life.'

Annie stared at Charlie.

'I trespassed? I was invited in. Actually he assaulted·me.'

'Bloody oath. Cheeky sod. What's his game? Why the big guns?'

'What's unlawful investigation?'

'Nothing. Ridiculous. The man's rattling sabres.'

Charlie touched the side of his nose craftily.

'I reckon the kid isn't his. Is that it, do you think? He's scared we'll find out.'

'What to do?'

Charlie shrugged and finished his beer.

'Have another drink. What's for dinner?'

'Seriously.'

'I'm serious. We've done nothing illegal. I want a photo of those arms of yours. Do one tonight. We'll accuse Tan of assault.'

Annie was dubious.

'Really, that seems dangerous.'

'Don't worry. That's what big shots do. They bully and expect everyone to be terrified.'

'Can I be asked to leave, do you think?'

Charlie made a face and spread his hands.

'No. Don't worry about it.'

But Annie did worry. After dinner Charlie produced a camera and took several shots of her bruised arms. She went to her room and tried to sleep. She felt she'd kicked a hornet's nest.

13

'It was Hari Raya all over again in a little shophouse in
Rangoon Road, Singapore, yesterday as 14-year-old Nadra
binte Ma'arof, better known as Maria Huberdina Hertogh, spent
her first day home with her foster mother, Che Aminah.'

The Straits Times, 30 July 1950

'They've married off the kid,' Charlie said.

He dropped several newspapers in front of Annie.

'I need a bath. And then a drink.'

He grinned at Annie. He was as happy as a puppy with his
news story and she heard him hum as he left.

Annie picked up the *Singapore Standard*.

On the front page was a photograph of Maria and a long-
faced serious-looking man called Mansoor under the heading
'Bridal Smile' and a bold-type headline 'Maria marries a Malay
teacher'.

*The marriage took place four days after Maria's return to
her foster mother, Aminah binti Mohamed, following a High*

*Court decision which had set aside an order that the Netherlands
Counsel General should have custody of the child.*

*'It was love at first sight,' said the newlyweds last night.
Mansoor Adabi, a Kelantanese youth, is a teacher at the Bukit
Panjang Government School.*

*'Nadra is like a diamond to me,' Aminah said, 'but I am
happy now that she is married to the man she wants.'*

Annie touched the face of the young girl in the newspaper
photograph. She was pretty. Somewhat well developed and
precocious for her age, whatever it was. She looked happy. She
turned to the *Straits Times* editorial.

*In the aftermath of the Japanese Occupation of Malaya there
has not been a more tragic case than that of Maria Hertogh,
whose marriage – at the age of thirteen, according to her parents,
and fourteen and a half, according to her Malay foster mother –
to a Malay school teacher in the Colony last Tuesday night is the
main topic of conversation in the Colony and will become so in
every kampung in the Malay Peninsula as soon as the facts of this
case spread throughout the country.*

*The news of Maria's marriage has caused very unfavourable
comment among all communities, and not least among responsible
elements of the Malay public opinion. Evidence is already at hand
that the tone of Malay comment is as critical in Johore Bahru as
it is in the Colony.*

It went on at length about the age of marriage being sixteen in Europe and in newly independent India. The trend, it said, amongst educated Asians was for later marriage. It questioned the wisdom of a Dutch girl marrying a Malay in any case, especially one so young, as well as the actual legitimacy of the marriage.

'Drink,' said Charlie coming back into the room.

'G & T,' she said. 'I can't make sense of this sudden marriage. The child's back with the foster mother. Can it be genuine?'

Annie felt distress for this child, a quiver of hopelessness. Maria and, perhaps, even Aminah were turning into pawns in this chess game played between East and West, Muslim and Catholic. The child's welfare seemed to have been forgotten.

Charlie handed her a glass.

'Don't reckon so, but it is a great story.'

That night her sleep was unsettled. She woke in a sweat, her temples pounding. The dreams were vivid. Dreams of a child crying, a child laughing, a child accusing, faces melting into each other, the images tumbling in her head as she tossed on the sheets.

Charlie's words had wormed their way into her brain. If she thought this child was hers, this little Joan, then what? Was she going to make a hue and cry, demand her return? And what about the distress to the child who knew no other mother than Eileen, no other father than Tan; notwithstanding his violence to her, Tan was clearly a loving and protective father.

When she finally slept, she slept deeply and she rose late.

She walked towards the little lean-to schoolroom. A myriad of yellow eyes stared down at her. The cats were gathered on the shady soft attap roof where they could sport with insects or wash their fur. These cats with their distorted, bent tails standing upright like raised flags stalked the garden like a silent army, spreading a hecatomb of killing. Annie was always finding half-eaten birds or mice in unexpected places. She had never cared for cats. Their soft exteriors and quiet mews concealed a terrifying and savage nature.

The children had finished lessons and were doing their garden duties. She could see their heads bobbing together as they dragged large watering cans between the rows of long beans, kangkong and tomatoes, with Yellow and the other dogs at their heels.

She smiled at Fatimah who was arranging the books and preparing the next day's lessons. Her brother had made some mild objections but in the end had relented. The small amount of pay Fatimah was earning had motivated her liberalisation.

The children had all progressed to sentences and had learned lots of English words. Mr Pillai was lugubriously delighted. He had left a sentence on the blackboard – 'Baa Baa Black Sheep'. It seemed incongruous. The children would never have seen a sheep of any colour. Perhaps he had brought pictures. Then she recalled her own childhood in Ipoh singing 'The Skye Boat Song' and 'Rule Britannia'. Perhaps it didn't matter. Those songs had never convinced her that she was English. The Eurasian nuns had taught them, themselves caught confusingly between the desire to impart the civilising culture of a country they knew nothing about and their own doubts about a motherland to which they could never belong. The abandoned half-blood orphans, of whom she was merely one, were reminded obliquely in droning sermons of their need to overcome their inferiority and find a refuge in obedience to God and the King.

Madame Wing met her as she turned back towards the house. The two women had fallen into a formal but pleasant, easy relationship and Madame Wing smiled.

'The baker's van is here, Mrs Collins. Would you like to make a selection?'

Annie ran a handkerchief across her brow.

'Have I forgotten something?'

'I believe you have a visitor for tea.'

'Oh, my goodness. Yes. Thank you.'

She suddenly remembered Maria Shepherd. Wei Wei was nowhere to be found. Annie suspected that sixteen-year-old Wei Wei had a boyfriend somewhere. Her mother, a dignified quiet woman, was still in hospital and the girl did as she pleased. She had been ten when the war had ended and Annie was sure she had not gone back to school, which meant the girl had attended only one year of schooling. She could neither read nor write. The family had lost the father, a manager on a rubber estate, to illness in the Occupation and lived hand to mouth for years until Ah Moy's wife had recommended Ting as houseboy. Ting was now twenty so had at least had time to get a half-decent education, but the family, which would have been considered educated and well off before the war, had been brought down by its extended miseries.

Annie ran her bath and sprinkled the bath salts but on this occasion they brought no sudden and peculiar imagery to mind.

By the time she had bathed and changed, the hour for tea had come and Annie went downstairs to the verandah. The table was laid with a snow-white cloth and the English tea set that Annie had recently purchased at John Little especially for this occasion.

The rattle of a motor came from the drive and Annie went through the house to watch the yellow-top taxi pull up under the porte-cochere.

She opened the door for Maria.

'Annie, lovely. Gosh, this is all right, isn't it?'

'Welcome, come inside.'

They sat at the verandah. Maria removed her gloves and cast an appreciative eye over the gardens.

'Very nice. All yours?'

'No, I share with an Australian journalist.'

'Do you?' Maria laughed and winked. 'Nice-looking?'

'Nothing like that. Convenience, that's all.'

'Gosh though, sharing a house with a man. What would your mother say?'

'Haven't got one.'

Maria stopped smiling. 'No, sorry. 'Course not.' She changed the subject quickly.

'Gosh, what about this Hertogh girl then?'

'Yes, seems a bit hurried doesn't it.'

'Hurried! It's a damn scandal. She's thirteen. The kid's white and she's been married bit too pretty damn quick smart it seems to me. You know they can divorce them at a click of the fingers. It's primitive.'

'I feel sorry for the girl.'

'Me too. White girl like that raised amongst those savages.'

'Well, I wouldn't go so far …'

Maria waggled a finger at Annie.

'Sooner the government does something about it the better. My Stanley says he'd like to go and knock their blocks off, treating a white girl like that.'

'Well, that's a bit harsh. The foster mother seems a good sort.'

'She's the nurse or something, I thought. The ayah, for heaven's sake.'

Annie decided not to pursue this any further. She could see that feelings were running pretty strong in the Shepherd household and, fortunately, Maria's attention was diverted from the subject by the arrival of the teapot and a three-tier tray of cakes.

They discussed Maria's domestic arrangements for a while, the lack of good help, her children's schooling, the rising cost of living and Stan's firm opinions on the death of three Malay policemen in a Communist attack at a road block.

'After Stan's tour is done in a couple of years, he has plans to go back to England. He comes from Twickenham. I'm not so sure. Must say I've no idea what England's even like. Do you?'

'Crowds of something daffodils, isn't it?'

Maria smiled. 'Golden. Wandering over hills and dales.'

'Isn't that clouds?'

'Oh yes, maybe.'

They both laughed.

'I live in Australia. No daffodils. After the war I went to Ronald's Aunt Mabel in Perth. I suspect England's a bit like Perth but rainier and with more people.'

Maria took up another cream cake.

'Ronald?' she said. Cream squished out the sides of the cake.

'You know, my husband. He died in the war.'

Maria wiped her mouth and looked at Annie with surprise. 'Really? I didn't know that you were married.'

Annie frowned. How could Maria not know that? She couldn't recall actually telling Maria or Jean about Ronald. Perhaps she hadn't.

'Yes.'

'Gosh. Well. That is a surprise. You were so young.'

Annie refreshed Maria's cup. Had she told these women about Suzy?

'What did I tell you then? I can't remember.'

'Nothing. Of course you were pretty bad for a long time. What with the head injury. You've probably lost bits along the way. We all do. I can hardly remember the time there now. All boils down to fear, sickness, bickering and boredom. And hunger.'

She finished her cream cake and surveyed the rest of the confectionery.

'Did I have a head injury?' Annie asked, perplexed.

Maria put three lumps of sugar in her tea.

'What? 'Course. Shocking. Dr Worth wasn't sure she'd pull you through. Gosh, she was marvellous though. Got extra rations. And even penicillin. I think it must have been smuggled in by the Chinese or the Malays. You know they were marvellous, some of them. They did so much for us even when things were terrible for them and it meant certain death. Can't you remember?'

Annie shook her head and turned her scarred wrist up.

'I can't really remember doing this either.'

Maria put out her hand to Annie's and gripped it a moment.

'Luckily Jean got you in time. She found you covered in blood but you didn't do a good enough job. Look, everyone felt like slitting their wrists. Some succeeded, some didn't.'

Both women fell silent, each to their thoughts. Annie didn't mention her reason for being in Singapore. It would lead down avenues she didn't want to visit, at least with Maria, right now.

Finally Maria picked up a scone and the conversation.

'Can you remember anything now about the head wound? You couldn't inside. Obviously it hasn't come back to you.'

'Come back? What do you mean? I got the head injury in Changi.'

Maria piled strawberry jam on her scone.

'No. Gosh, you have gone loopy. You came in with it.'

'Did I? But how could I? Unless something happened on the way.'

'On the way?'

'Yes, the march into prison. After the Japs won.'

'My dear Annie, you didn't come into Changi when the Japs first came.'

'Didn't I? What do you mean?'

'You came into Sime Road Camp on a stretcher. In May of 1945.'

14

'I accompanied Aminah to the York Hill Home. When I looked at Nadra, I knew at once she was attracted to me. She looked elegant in her Malay baju kurung. She was a little plump with a bright round face. I, too, was attracted to her.'

Mansoor Adabi, Trainee teacher at the Bukit Panjang Government School (August 1950)

'I can't promise anything, Annie.'

Desmond tossed back the brandy and put the glass on the table.

'But you will write?'

'Yes.'

'An official letter. I've got that right?'

'For heaven's sake. Nobody has any rights. There's an Emergency on. It's up to the Commissioner and the police.'

'This has nothing to do with Communists. Surely I have the right to be heard.'

Annie leaned forward and put her hand on Desmond's arm.

'I want to make a formal complaint of violence against me.

He had no right to manhandle me. I was invited onto his property by his wife. She can verify that surely, and the butler and the driver …'

Desmond put up his hand.

'Yes, Annie. All right.'

'The whole story. The truth. The way he found his daughter. My doubts. I demand to speak to him about this.'

'Annie.'

She rose, filled with nervous energy and began to pace in front of the doors of the dining room.

'Or I will bring a court case against him. There's a man I've heard about here. Marshall, a lawyer, a brilliant lawyer. I have money. Perhaps not as much as Sir Christopher but enough.'

Desmond rose and went to her. He took her hand.

'I'll do everything I can.'

He put Annie's hand to his lips and kissed it. Annie gazed at him and felt the fizzing of adrenaline, the shivering imperative to pace, recede.

Since the news that Maria had given her, it was if she was kindling, filled with crackling flames of confusion. She couldn't make sense of her life.

She let Desmond hold her hand, allowed him to press her to his chest and run his arms around her. She folded against him, entering the protective girdle of his arms. She needed to feel a man, his strength, his sinew, his beating heart. Nothing made any sense.

Desmond put his lips to hers and she allowed herself to be kissed. She felt nothing for him, but the passionate strength of his embrace was a comfort. Nothing made any sense. When he became too insistent, his lips too strong, his grip too demanding, she pulled away. This made no sense either.

Desmond released her.

'Annie, I …' he said.

'I'm tired,' she said, quickly interrupting him, unable to cope with any professions of affection. 'I found out some strange things about myself today.'

Desmond gazed at her, his look full of concern and puzzlement. I mustn't use him merely for my comfort, I mustn't encourage him. It's not fair.

'You should go.'

She could tell by the fall of his shoulders that Desmond was disappointed.

'Of course. May I see you tomorrow?'

She walked him to the hall and opened the door. His car was parked under the porte-cochere. At the door of the car he turned back towards her, his body signalling reluctance.

'I'll call you,' she said and he smiled.

She watched him drive away, the lights of his car flicking between the trees.

Charlie wasn't home. Mahmoud had brought the car back at six o'clock and Annie knew he was probably going out on the tiles, ending up who knows where. There was no one to talk to so she retired to the sanctuary of her bed and pulled the mosquito nets around her.

The insects pinged into the fan or flapped and buzzed like demented djinns against the curtain, flitting in and out of the proximity of the light, sometimes tiny, sometimes monstrous shadows. Her mind felt like that, filled with hallucinating ever-changing ungraspable shadows.

What on earth was I doing from February 1942 until May 1945, for almost the entire duration of the Occupation?

She had had a vision of herself as a noble prisoner, swept into vicissitude by the winds of war, though she had barely a memory of it. She remembered the Sime Road camp but had imagined she had spent the entire war in Changi and had been moved there with the rest of the women.

She furrowed her brows as if by so doing she could oil the machinery of her mind, set cogwheels of remembrance spinning, casting light into this darkness, but nothing emerged.

And why was I interned then, at that moment and not another, and with a terrible head injury?

She had interrogated Maria to the point of exhaustion. Maria had told her everything she knew, getting into the swing of this stroll down memory lane, enjoying piecing it together like a detective story.

Maria Coelho, herself, had not gone into Changi with the British civilians during the first week of the Occupation. When the Japs had begun publishing the newspaper again they had issued edicts, one of which was to order all Eurasians to gather at the Recreation Club on the Padang. After being harangued by a strutting, American-accented Jap, they had passed along in the hot sun for hours getting registered. Anyone with a British or Dutch husband was sent into imprisonment. Anyone from Malaya was sent back. The rest of them, including her, her father, a Portuguese banker, her mother, an Irish/Malay, and her two younger brothers, had been sent about their business, called on, whenever out of the house, to wear the red arm band of the 'enemy alien.'

Maria's father worked for Shinozaki, the head of the Social Welfare Department of the Japanese military administration. Maria, who had been twenty, got a job at the office of an Indian dentist and, for the most part, the family kept themselves to themselves, learning the tricks needed to get along with these new masters, grateful merely to be left alone, and waiting, like, she supposed, almost every citizen in Singapore, for the British to return.

'Who's Shinozaki?' Annie had asked, that name coming back to her. She'd heard it several times now.

Maria shrugged. 'He was quite a good sort of Nip. He issued thousands of good-citizen passes to stop the Japs taking you off randomly and shooting you. He took care of welfare, organised associations, that sort of thing. He was the decent, go-to man if you had troubles. Thank God for him really.'

'Is he alive, do you think?' Annie had asked, writing this down in an exercise book she had grabbed from the store in the pantry.

'Good heavens, I've no idea.'

Maria had gone off in a gale of laughter as if Annie had asked her to explain atomic theory.

In October of 1943, the Japanese had suddenly become paranoid. Maria now knew that it was because of an attack on Singapore harbour, which had blown up six oil tankers and which the Japanese had attributed to an internal spy-ring run out of Changi prison. In fact it had been orchestrated by the Australians and had nothing to do with anyone in Singapore.

'But we paid for it,' Maria said. 'They rounded up anyone they didn't like. That's when my brothers and I were arrested. We were held for months.'

Maria had poured a cup of tea from the fresh pot Madame Wing had brought.

'It wasn't very nice. I don't want to talk about that.'

Tears had sprung to Maria's eyes and she sat, staring into the cup of tea.

Annie waited. She remembered that Maria had told her that one of her brothers had died of torture and she and her other brother had been sent to Changi. Maria gulped down her tea.

'It was all random and incomprehensible. That's when Jean came in too, about a month after me.'

She and Jean, a nurse, had formed a close friendship. Jean was a Eurasian whose husband, a member of the volunteer force, had been killed as the Battle for Singapore reached its crescendo. That association meant she was always suspect.

'We weren't very many Eurasians in there,' she said. 'Deprivation is a great leveller. 'Course the snootiest ones fell hardest. Eating cockroaches will do that to you. But there was still this skin-colour hierarchy nevertheless.'

In 1944 the civilians were moved out of Changi to Sime Road Camp. In 1945, along with hundreds of other Eurasians, Annie had come in, unconscious, with the bandaged gash on her skull, and had, for a long time, been either delirious or asleep. Dr Worth had treated her with the penicillin, which had probably saved her life. She had tried to cut her wrists with a kitchen knife, done a botched job and survived. After a while she had improved enough to get up and walk around, and work in the Japanese military clothing factory that had been set up. She talked with Maria and Jean, although not about much.

'Then the bloody marvellous Americans dropped the bomb. Gosh, it was wonderful. The planes came over dropping leaflets, telling us it was over and they were coming. God, what a feeling. No one can ever know what that feeling is like. Disbelief mixed with euphoria mixed with hate at what you had to endure, then the joy again.'

'I remember that. The joy of liberation,' she'd said. 'Did I?' she'd thought. Actually her most intense memory of internment was being told never to complain, to rely entirely on oneself and read anything you could lay your hands on. She remembered quite distinctly reading the Bible from cover to cover. She must have been forced to read it in the convent and she remembered enjoying it infinitely less the second time. She had not enjoyed the first time at all.

''Course it was a bit subdued after that. We got food drops and were told to stay put but Jean and I walked out and went back to our families, what was left. You were stuck there, of course, which was a bit of a disgrace, but I came back once or twice, do you remember and we went off to the Dutch Club. For the dances. Gosh all that was the most marvellous feeling.'

Annie hardly remembered that at all. The days at the camp seemed to have gelled into one long day, none distinguishable from the other. Now that Maria said it, though, she recalled hanging around until the British soldiers came. After the leaflet drop and news of the surrender nothing much had happened. The Japs walked around looking sulky and bursting into tears. They'd handed over the key of the rice store. Food and medicine suddenly became plentiful and all the prisoners realised that there had always been food, plenty of food, whilst they had died of starvation. The men planned reprisals but the Japs warned them to sit still; they still had their weapons. Then one day they faded away and four strapping paratroopers walked into the camp bursting with health and vitality.

The Union Jack had been hoisted and they'd all sung 'God Save the King'. A wireless was put up and 'This is London Calling' had come over the waves. She remembered that now but in snatches. The camp had been flooded with visitors, husbands looking for wives, families looking for daughters, nieces and mothers. Local people came, anxious to see their teachers or pupils, servants came too to see their employers. Food came into the camp, rice from those people, tinned fruit and meat from the army, quantities of vitamin pills, bread baked daily by the cooks of HMS *Sussex*.

She remembered most vividly the huge parcel she had received from the Australian Red Cross. The woman who had packed that deserved an OBE at the very least. It contained nearly everything one could possibly want, from toothpaste and toothbrush, face flannels, safety pins, pens and writing paper, brush and comb, soap and underwear and even a book for the voyage home. She had been given a dress by a young Eurasian woman who had come with her mother to the camp and given out clothing they had gathered in town for the internees.

They'd been given money. The 'freedom fiver', Maria reminded her, except the Eurasians only got half. Not much, she'd said, had changed, had it. Even Lord Mountbatten had turned up to visit the camp and make speeches but Annie could not remember that at all. It was for the grateful British prisoners, not for them.

Two weeks after the British soldiers had arrived, the camp emptied, the sick went to the General Hospital, those with families went home, the white women were moved out. Women, like Annie, who had no relatives and nowhere to go simply stayed in the camp. The soldiers improved the sanitation but, still, they had been left in this internment camp, in these huts. The talk had been that the military had taken over homes and the internees were stuck because of it.

Then, with the help of the refugee liaison officer, the handsome Lieutenant Wilkinson, she'd filled out all the forms with Ronald's particulars. When they had found Aunt Mabel and verified that Annie had been married to a British man, she was moved to the Raffles Hotel to await permission to go to Australia. That still left scores of women in that camp. What became of them she had no idea.

She recalled that time more vividly, perhaps because some sort of future had opened for her. Robin Wilkinson had paid a great deal of attention to her but nothing had come of that. He'd expected that, since she was not white, the usual British morality didn't apply to this half-blood, destitute waif of empire, and been bitterly angry that his moneyed attentions had been ungratefully rejected by such an inferior creature.

Annie smiled. 'Plus ça change.'

She turned out the light, casting the insects into darkness. She could still hear the pinging of insect bodies throwing themselves against the fan. She drifted.

The phone rang downstairs, its jangling voice shattering the serenity of the night. Annie woke, turned the light on and looked at the clock. It was three thirty.

'Mrs Collins!' Madame Wing called urgently. 'Come quickly. Mr Ransome's in hospital.'

15

'"I may have been small but I still remember the time when
my mother in Holland gave me away to Che Aminah in Java."
Nadra, or Maria, said that she has ignored several letters from
her family in Holland. She did not intend to reply to them either.

"What's past is past," she said.'

The Singapore Free Press, 29 July 1950

Annie swung the car down the drive.

She'd learned to drive in Perth at an age when such things could be nerve-wracking, but even the overbearing instructor had not deterred her. A car, in Western Australia, she had discovered, was an absolute imperative.

Women in Perth who didn't drive, she knew from the living examples of Aunt Mabel and the women of the neighbourhood, were effectively prisoners of the wide suburbs, reliant on infrequent buses that took you only into the tiny city. If you wanted to go anywhere else you had to call a taxi. On Annie's first taxi ride, she'd made the terrible faux-pas of opening the door to the back. The driver, his gut over his belt, one hairy orange arm bent out of the window, had given her a queer look.

'What's a matter, Love?' he'd said, a cigarette dangling from his lips, 'front seat not good enough?'

Her first lesson in the Australian version of equality was that one did not sit behind the driver as if he was, well, the driver. It was offensive. He had been scary, sweaty and smelly, drawling non-stop and giving her the eye. She had never taken a taxi again and had made sure to get her driver's licence on the first attempt.

As she drove through the quiet night, she digested what little Nobby had told her. Charlie had been found out cold and the police ambulance had taken him to Singapore General Hospital. Based on his reticence Annie knew Charlie had probably been hanging around somewhere unsavoury. It didn't matter to her but she twigged that Nobby was sparing her blushes. He'd told her not to come as they wouldn't let anyone in until visiting hours the next morning but she couldn't sleep anyway.

She found Nobby in the waiting area and he looked relieved to see her.

'How is he?'

'Sleeping. All right. Bruised ribs, bashed head. He'll feel it tomorrow.'

She sat down next to him.

'Tell me.'

'Well I got a call from the cops. When they found from his ID that he was a foreign journalist they called me. We wire-service types have the biggest office here and the coppers know us.'

'Where did they find him?'

Nobby made a detailed search of his hands.

'Nobby, I don't care what Charlie does. I'm not married to him.'

'No, course not. Sorry. Round Bugis way, behind the toilet block there, where the trannies hang out. Sorry.'

Annie thought she almost detected a blush on this hardened newsman's face.

'Trannies?' Annie frowned. 'You mean a transvestite. Do you think he was with a transvestite?' Despite herself Annie was shocked.

Nobby shrugged.

'Probably not but, well, you know how it is. Loads of single men, heat and alcohol. The trannies put on quite a show. They say that all the really beautiful women in Bugis are transvestites.'

Nobby glanced at Annie.

'Look. We all go down there from time to time, drink a bit, have a look, you know. Harmless. I wasn't there this time, so ...'

'He was beaten?'

'Seems so, kicked and punched the docs say. That's pretty rare round there. Sometimes the squaddies or the sailors get into a punch up or the trannies have a cat fight but usually it's pretty good tempered.'

'Could he have rubbed someone the wrong way, do you think? A sailor or something?'

Nobby shrugged.

'Can I see him?'

'They won't let us. No next of kin and so on. We'll have to wait until tomorrow morning. It was good of you to come, but there's nothing you can do.'

'Are you going?'

'No. I'll stick around. I like the kid.'

Annie smiled. 'I like the kid too. I'll stick with you.'

She looked at her watch. Six o'clock. 'Shall we go and get something to eat?'

Annie and Nobby checked with the nurse that Charlie was all right and sleeping then headed out to Chinatown. The dark night had gone and the dawn was waiting behind the horizon.

They scouted out the hawker stalls, finally settling for one that wasn't too filthy and where the noodle soup broth was boiling. They ignored the various stomachs, fish eyes and frogs and opted for chicken.

'Shouldn't kill us,' Nobby said.

Annie couldn't remember exactly what the area had been like before the war but knew it had always been crowded. Now it was a slum, there was no other word for it. A picturesque slum with its cracking, crumbling, sprouting shophouses, its vibrant colour, its noisy Chinese signs, washing flags and its lively, raucous people, but a slum nevertheless. The wafting smell of effluvia came to the nostrils from time to time. If you ignored it, the soupy noodles with green chillies and an assortment of spices were delicious and they both ate with gusto.

'Must be a hundred to a shophouse,' said Nobby, looking round and wiping his mouth. 'I've been in one. They live in cubicles not much bigger than a couple of beds, whole families. The overcrowding is horrific. That's why the smell and the disease.'

'It's Victorian London,' Annie said.

'Like that. The economy hasn't picked up, and they have

hundreds of thousands of squatters pouring in from Malaya and kids, kids, kids. It's tough.'

Nobby threw some coins onto the table and rose.

'Rich pickings for the Maoists. Poverty and dissatisfaction. Oddly enough I think Malaya might be the big beneficiary from the Korean War if it goes on long enough. Think of all the tin and rubber a war needs.'

'But will it go to the people who need it?' Annie said and Nobby smiled.

'Spoken like Chin Peng. Beaver will be after you.'

To their amazement they recognised the ginger features of Inspector Beaver as they re-entered the visitors' room of the hospital.

He was standing with another policeman and a doctor. He turned his sharp gaze on them as they approached.

'Ah, the friends,' he said.

'Morning, Beaver,' Nobby said cheerfully. 'What brings Special Branch to this neck of the woods. Reds under the beds?'

Nobby smiled benevolently. Beaver curled his lip.

'Perhaps so,' he said and raked his gaze over them both.

Oddly, Annie felt cold and guilty, as if her comment in Chinatown had been heard and Beaver was here to arrest her. It was the irrational power of authority, and the police here, in the Emergency, had powers that entitled them to do virtually anything. Nobby appeared unfazed. He took a notebook and pencil out of his jacket pocket and stared at Beaver.

'What's the story, Inspector, on the record?'

Beaver and his sidekick exchanged a slow glance. Beaver

raised his hand and pointed an accusing finger at Nobby.

'If I find that Charles Ransome has been consorting with Communists, there'll be a story all right.'

Beaver turned on his heel and the two men left the room. The European doctor gazed after them.

'Man's bonkers.'

'What's going on, Doc?' Nobby said.

'Turned up wanted to see your friend. Told him he's sleeping, which was true but probably isn't now. Interrogated me about his arrival, his wounds, all that sort of thing.'

The doctor shrugged.

'Suppose they have to investigate the beating of a European, especially a journalist. Doesn't happen much. Perhaps it looks suspicious. Sure your friend wasn't involved with shady characters?'

Nobby laughed. 'No,' he said, 'but that's a press man's business. We're always dealing with shady characters and most of them are coppers.'

The doctor smiled.

'It's not visiting hours, but you can see your friend.'

Charlie was propped up on pillows, his head bandaged, his lips and one eye swollen like a puffball. He tried a smile when he saw them.

'Awwrh,' he said, and his face resumed its battleground appearance.

Annie went to his side and took up his hand. It was scraped and raw, covered in brown iodine.

'Can you talk?'

Charlie emitted a groan. He looked out of his one good eye at Nobby who raised an eyebrow.

'Don't talk, Mate,' Nobby said. 'Beaver was here. Thinks you're involved with the reds. Just raise one finger if that is not true, two if it is.'

Charlie raised a finger.

'Right, that's what I figured. Doc says you've got bruised ribs, nothing broken, bit of a bash on the head. Looks like you had a go too. How many?'

Charlie raised two fingers.

'Right. Any reason you can think of. You muscling in on someone else's territory?'

Annie looked at Charlie who raised his one good eye to the ceiling.

He waggled a 'no' with his fingers then groaned.

'OK, let's go, Annie. Let the man get some rest.'

Annie made to withdraw her hand from Charlie's but he gripped it surprisingly tightly for someone with his injuries. She rose and kissed his cheek.

'It's all right. I'll be back this afternoon at visiting hours.'

He held on to her hand and emitted a low groan. Nobby drew near to the bed. Charlie looked at him and pointed to his pocket. Nobby looked down at himself.

'Awher,' Charlie muttered and pointed to Nobby's pocket again.

Nobby took out his notebook and his wallet. Charlie took the notebook.

'He wants to write something,' Annie said and Charlie let go of her hand.

Nobby put the pencil in Charlie's hand and the latter scrawled on the paper: 'Think Tan's men. Careful Annie.'

Annie's eyes flew to Nobby's then back to Charlie's. 'You think Tan had you beaten up. But why? What for?'

Charlie scrawled: 'Warning for you?????'

Charlie's neck had been leaning forward with the effort of writing. Now he collapsed back against the pillows.

'Come on, Annie,' Nobby said. 'It's all right, Charlie. I get it. I'll take care of her.'

He signalled to Annie as Charlie closed his eyes.

Outside the hospital Nobby turned to Annie.

'You understand? He thinks you're in danger. What about moving into a hotel for a while?'

Annie shook her head.

'No. It's ridiculous. We don't know it's that. We don't know Charlie's read the situation right. I can guess what he was up to down there.'

Nobby pursed his lips, avoiding that subject. 'Charlie's got a decent head on his shoulders. He wouldn't say it if he didn't think it.'

Annie had had enough.

'Sorry, Nobby. I'm tired and I'm going home.'

Nobby made a few noises but she got in the car and, with a wave, drove out of the gates. Tan was sending her a message? It was outlandish. Beating up Charlie to send her a message? Charlie was ashamed of what he was up to down there; that was it. Hanging around with transvestites. Men were strange creatures.

She looked into her rear-view mirror as a dark-glassed car swung out of the gates behind her. It turned when she turned, and she frowned. She slowed to allow it to pass but it stayed put, dogging her. She flicked her eyes to the road and back to the mirror. The car was still there. She saw a petrol station ahead and put on her indicator, turning into the forecourt. The dark car sped by. She put her head on the wheel. Damn them. Her imagination was going into overdrive.

16

'The Dutch Foreign Minister Dirk U. Stikker told Parliament here
today he would "do everything possible" to have 13-year-old Maria
Hertogh returned to her parents in Bergen op Zoom, Holland.'

The Straits Times, 23 August 1950

Mahmoud's face showed the underlying emotions he
was experiencing. He'd found out about Charlie from
Madame Wing when he had turned up for work at eight o'clock.
Annie had found him sitting despondently outside the garage.

'He's all right,' she'd said, exhausted now with the rushing
ebbs and flows of her own imagination.

'Look, it's nine-thirty now. Visiting hours are eleven to twelve.
You can go and see him if you like. I'm going to bed. Come back
and tell me later.'

Annie told Madame Wing to wake her at four o'clock, took
a bath and went to bed, drifting off to the boys reciting 'Yes, Sir,
yes, Sir, three bags full.'

When she awoke, she lay back, with a cup of tea that Madame
Wing brought her silently, and thought about this again.

Tan was certainly not going to answer any letters, even if Desmond succeeded in getting one sent. The man was clearly, whilst he served the British government's purposes, above the law, especially in a matter as trivial, for them, as a hysterical woman being a bloody nuisance.

She desperately wanted to see this little girl. Perhaps she would be so very different from Suzy that all this would be a waste of time. Perhaps she would just know it was her or wasn't her. By the time she had finished her cup of tea Annie had convinced herself of this. She had to find out where the girl went to school.

She dressed and went downstairs. Mahmoud was talking to the newly engaged Indian mechanic-wallah. Saahan, Joseph's guardian, was ill and Madame Wing had sent him to the doctor in a trishaw.

'How's Charlie?' she said.

'He is not looking very good.'

Annie smiled. 'No, but he will be all right.'

Mahmoud nodded miserably.

'Why did he go there? It is a very bad place.'

Annie shrugged. How he had found out where Charlie had been she did not know. Perhaps one of the nurses had gossiped about the white man and his habits. She had no wish to discuss Charlie's personal morality.

'Come to the garden will you, Mahmoud? I'd like to talk to you, please. It's too stuffy in here.'

Mahmoud followed her stiffly around the house to the verandah and she finally convinced him to sit down. Madame Wing, disapprovingly, brought some lime juice. Annie ignored her.

'Mahmoud, I need to ask you to do something for me.'

Mahmoud nodded.

'Mr Charlie believes that he was beaten by the man Tan's thugs because I am searching for my daughter. I think you know about all this. I know that the servants talk.'

Mahmoud examined his hands.

'No matter. I need to see the girl, the daughter of Tan. I need to know where she goes to school.'

Annie pushed the untouched glass of lime juice towards him.

'Please drink. You are my guest at this moment.'

Mahmoud, she thought, was probably searching through the pages of his book of Sikh as well as of servant etiquette, struggling silently. He must have then found the appropriate passage – it is rude to refuse hospitality, perhaps – for he took the glass.

'I am asking a lot. I want you to follow the car that takes this girl to school and tell me where it goes. Would you do that?'

Mahmoud sipped at the glass and put it back on the table. Finally he spoke.

'This man. I heard that he hurt you also.'

Mahmoud glanced at Annie as if he had spoken of something horribly inappropriate and begged to be forgiven.

'Yes, that is right. I am fine now. Thank you for your concern.'

Mahmoud inclined his head.

'I will find out where the girl goes to school, Mrs Annie.'

'Thank you.'

Mahmoud rose and they walked back around the house.

'Visiting hours are eight to nine-thirty. Will you drive me? Seven-thirty?'

Mahmoud nodded and disappeared. As she regained the house she saw the car disappear down the drive. She felt a moment of guilt at involving Mahmoud in something underhand but she shook it off. She needed to know and something told her that Mahmoud was angry at this beating and that, somehow, his own sense of honour had been attacked.

At seven-thirty Annie climbed into the car for the journey to the hospital. As they turned out of the gates Mahmoud looked at her in the mirror.

'I have found out about the girl. Her name is Joanna and she goes to the Raffles Girls School on Queen Street.'

Annie met his eyes.

'That was quick.'

'I merely asked the guard. He is a Sikh. We go to the same temple.'

'That was very clever. Can we drive by the school on the way, please?'

They rode in silence for a while.

'Mrs Annie.'

'Yes.'

'Do you believe this girl is your child?'

It was so unusual for Mahmoud to ask a personal question that, at first, Annie was taken aback. But he had the right to. She had involved him.

'I don't know. I think I have the right to try to find out. That's all. I mean her no harm, nor her family.'

'How will you know if she is your child?'

'She had brown eyes, something like mine, and black hair.

Her skin was not as light as mine. I have to see her. I can't leave without seeing her.'

Mahmoud drove to the gates of the school, now silent and dark, and pulled to a halt. Annie stared at it for a moment then signalled Mahmoud to go on.

'Mahmoud, during the war, this Mr Shinozaki you mentioned. Tell me about him.'

'I drove him only for about nine months or so. He was a pleasant Japanese gentleman, always polite and kind. Of course he did not speak to me of anything other than where to go and so on. He had a great deal to do with the Overseas Chinese Association on Hill Street and Dr Lim and also the Eurasian community and Dr Paglar who was head of the Eurasian Association. Also the sports club. He was generous with rations, which was very important in those days.'

'I see. Why did you stop driving for him?'

'I joined the Indian National Army. I was a Sergeant in the Azad Brigade.'

Annie's eyes darted to Mahmoud's face.

The Indian National Army had been formed out of the tens of thousands of Indian army soldiers captured at the fall of Malaya and Singapore. Their aim was to overthrow the British Raj but many were seen as brutal guards and collaborators with the Japanese. She was not sure how far she wanted to pursue this unexpected part of Mahmoud's life. But curiosity got the better of her.

'You fought?' she said.

'Yes. In Burma. After the war many of the officers were

arrested but most of us, like me, were repatriated back here.'

'Why did you join, Mahmoud?'

She saw a tiny shrug of his shoulders.

'For excitement perhaps. We believed in freeing India. And you see that came true. India is free.'

Annie nodded. 'Yes, it is. Do you wish for Malaya to be free too?'

'Yes, Mrs Annie. I think you do too.'

Annie met his eyes and, for the first time, Mahmoud allowed her inside.

'Yes, I do. But are the Maoists the right government?' she said.

'I don't know. Are the Sultans?' he said.

Annie was taken aback. She had not thought of Mahmoud as a radical but then she had not thought he would have joined the Indian National Army either, or go off and risk his life in the jungles of Burma. To understand that Mahmoud harboured sympathies for the Communists only made her realise how little one knows of our fellow man. That he had told her spoke of his trust and she was flattered.

At the hospital Mahmoud came to Charlie's bedside but Charlie was barely awake. Annie sat by Charlie's bed. Mahmoud left to wait for her. Several of his journalist colleagues came by but he was so groggy that, eventually, Annie decided there was no point in staying. The nurses assured her everything was mending. In a day or two the swelling would go down and he would be able to talk.

Sleep was difficult for her that night. The insects seemed

louder than usual. Sleeping in the day meant that, at midnight, she was still wide awake. Though she did not believe them, the warnings Charlie had given her nevertheless preyed on her mind in the dark. Madame Wing had gone home until the next afternoon as her aged mother was ill. The gardens were overflowing with people and she had asked Kumar to be vigilant. She turned over, determined to sleep, when she heard the clang of metal on stone. It was not outside. She knew the outside noises. This was in the house. She couldn't believe it. Surely a cat. But she hardly believed that. The cats were silent as ninjas unless they were screaming and meowing in the garden, fighting over a rodent or threatened territory. She did not turn on the light. She was now thoroughly awake, all her senses tuned, blood whooshing in her ears.

Metal on stone could only mean the pantry or the storerooms. Before her courage deserted her she got out of bed and slipped into her underwear and dress and moved quickly towards the verandah window and peered along the corridor. There was nothing. She took up the flashlight, the only heavy implement to hand and decided to stop being such a coward. She unlocked her door and stepped out onto the verandah, ran quickly along it to the living room over the porte-cochere. The moonlight was streaming in. She hugged the wall, seeing shadows everywhere. She thought she heard whispers downstairs and froze.

She felt for the light switch, wondering why on earth she hadn't put it on before. The light flooded the room and she went to the head of the stairs and flicked on the light there also. She stood a moment then went down the stairs. She saw a torchlight shining into the windows by the front door and pulled back with a gasp.

Then several things happened at the same time. She heard Kumar calling from outside and a certain rationality re-entered her brain. And she saw the tail of a pangolin disappear into the storeroom and burst into nervous laughter.

She threw open the front door and Kumar came rushing in. She pointed to the storeroom. It took four men two hours to remove the pangolin from the house. It is a creature that can imitate the pine cone, rolling itself entirely into a hard muscled ball and throwing up its scales, sharp as scythes. Two blankets were required to drag the pangolin from the house and deposit him in the garden. They were nocturnal creatures. He must have wandered in during the day and gone to sleep. Despite his eviction, however, they were not rid of him. He had left behind his calling card. Pangolins excrete a foul stomach-turning fluid, so acrid and powerful that Annie knew the stink would be in the hall for weeks.

17

'Maria Hertogh and her Malay husband yesterday turned down an offer of $15,000 from a foreign film production company for their life story and photographs with world copyright.'

The Straits Times, 9 August 1950

She watched nervously as Mahmoud pulled the car up on the opposite side of the street to the school gates. She got out and walked over to the railings. The girls inside were playing and running, standing in excited groups chattering. She remembered her own days at the convent, when, grown older and tougher, she had planned pranks with the others like her. Anything to discomfit the nuns whom Annie had grown to despise. Now, looking back, she saw that most of the nuns had tried to do their best, and only a few were utterly cruel. But it hadn't felt that way then, so it didn't matter. She still hated them.

She gazed over the schoolyard, walking slowly along the railings and to her dismay she realised how very much alike all these girls looked. All the little blonde ones looked like all the other little blonde ones, the brunettes likewise. And the majority with jet-black tresses were indistinguishable as to height, weight and even hairstyle. In their school uniforms, with their hair all cut to the same length, it was as if they had all been cast out of an identical mould. Occasionally, here or there, one would be taller or fatter, or have red hair or freckles, which helped distinguish them a little, but for the rest it was as if she was looking at a vast ice-field of penguins.

She realised she was hard-pushed even to tell how old most of them were. It was hopeless. She turned away and got back into the car. Mahmoud looked at her quizzically and she shrugged.

'I can't tell them apart.'

A knock came on the roof of the car and Annie saw a policeman's uniform at Mahmoud's window.

'What's going on here?' a deep English voice said.

Mahmoud got out of the car and Annie went to her window. Before Mahmoud could speak, Annie waved at the police officer.

'Sorry, Officer, I'm a bit lost. I'm looking for the Tiger Balm Gardens.'

The officer turned to her and touched his hand to his cap. She fluttered her eyelashes at him.

'The Tiger Balm Gardens? Well your man here is an idiot, Madam. The gardens are in the west.'

He threw a contemptuous glance at Mahmoud and Annie saw Mahmoud stiffen.

'Right, sorry. We'll be off. Thank you.'

Mahmoud regained his seat.

'Pasir Panjang Road,' the officer said slowly as if talking to a child. 'Back that way.'

Mahmoud looked straight ahead.

'Thank you,' Annie said gaily to the officer.

'Sorry, Mahmoud,' she said as they turned the corner. 'Just a little ruse.'

Mahmoud sat stiff and silent.

'Look, I'm sorry, for heaven's sake. I didn't want him asking me for identity papers and so on. They can do that if you act suspicious. Now he just thinks we're both a couple of idiots.'

When no reaction was forthcoming, Annie sat back, annoyed.

'Well just go home then. And I'll keep the car for today.'

They drove back to Peirce Road in frosty silence. Once he had parked the car, Mahmoud took his bicycle and walked, with all the dignity he could muster, down the driveway. Annie sighed.

She went to her room, took a sheet of paper and began writing a letter to Eileen Tan. No more of this hole-in-the-wall nonsense. Perhaps one woman to another, they might achieve something. She started several times but the words didn't seem to come out right. Whatever she wrote, it all looked as if she was threatening their happy home, without possessing the slightest evidence.

'Mrs Collins?' Madame Wing was at her door.

'Come in.'

Madame Wing opened the door and stood just inside.

'It's Joseph,' she said. 'He has a fever. I thought you would want to know. Saahan has been diagnosed with pulmonary tuberculosis.'

Annie forgot the letter and rose in horror.

'Where is Joseph?'

'He's in Saahan's hut. Saahan has gone to the hospital.'

'Bring him into the house, please. We will put him in the spare bedroom.'

Madame Wing hesitated.

'Is that wise, Mrs Collins?'

'He must be isolated from the other children. I will care for him. Send for Dr Chen, please.'

Joseph was tucked into the bed and Annie took his temperature. He was hot and feverish. She took some ice water and put a cloth to his brow, wiping away the sweat. He looked up at her, his eyes steady. Annie had never seen fear in this little boy's eyes.

'Now, Joseph. You will stay with me now in this nice room and I will help you get better. What do you say?'

Joseph nodded and she took his hand and put it to her lips.

Pulmonary tuberculosis, Dr Chen told her after examining Joseph, is highly contagious, spread by droplet infection. Doubtless he had picked it up from Saahan who, somehow, had escaped detection in the general health-checks.

'Saahan is not expected to recover, Mrs Collins, at his age. Joseph must go to the Middleton Quarantine Hospital at Moulmein road. The Government medical officer will not let him stay here. All the other children will have to be rescreened, as will you. This is very serious.'

'But is he not better off here with me? He will be so terrified to go there.' As she said this she knew it wasn't true. He wasn't terrified of anything; she was.

'Mrs Collins, be reasonable. There are nurses and doctors there, sterile environments. I cannot allow it. Actually it is illegal.

I will get an ambulance and he must go today.'

'Can I not drive him?'

Dr Chen ran a hand over his brow.

'You misunderstand the gravity of the situation. Hundreds of children in Singapore die every year from this disease. He must be isolated and treated. We have excellent drug therapies now. It's not the death sentence it once was. Please allow me to go about my business.'

Annie relented. She had little choice. Joseph lay quietly indifferent as the ambulance doors closed. Annie went to her room and moped until Madame Wing brought her a cup of tea.

'He will surely be all right,' she said. 'My friend's child had tuberculosis and he recovered very well.'

'Did they isolate him?'

'Yes, of course. But she was allowed to visit him when he stopped being infectious, after about a week or so.'

'A week. Oh goodness, Madame Wing. The poor child.' Madame Wing's words were a comfort however.

Now though she had to think about poor Saahan who was dying. What was to be done with him? He was a Hindu. Perhaps she should ask at the temple. Or would the hospital do that? Annie felt enervated and overcome. She felt a responsibility for the people around her, which was wearing her out.

She looked at the letter on her desk and shook her head. Tomorrow, she thought. Charlie's so poorly, and Joseph too, and now Mahmoud hates me.

She put her head on the pillow and fell asleep.

She stands with him, next to him, in the rain. He is taller than her, slim, broad shouldered. He takes her hand in his and they gaze down on ... On ... They are together, naked. He caresses her skin, touches his lips to her stomach and she laughs. I love you, she says. I ... He is speaking, his lips moving but no words sound. Everything is slow, slow motion, just out of focus as if the images are covered in a veil. His lips meet hers in a long slow kiss. I love you, she says.

Annie opened her eyes. The dream was so vivid she turned her head to look for him on the pillow next to her and put out her hand to the place where he ought to be.

She knew she had been the woman in this dream but who was he? She could never quite see his face or hear him speak. If she had been so in love with a man, how could she have forgotten him so completely? She closed her eyes, willing the dream to come again, but it had evaporated like dew at sunrise.

18

'I denounce the Muslim organisations who are against the
Laycock Bill. I appeal to all Malay parents to give consideration
to the fact that young Malay women have to lead difficult, sometimes
tragic, lives, due to the easy and light-hearted way in which Muslim
husbands divorce their child-wives.'
Che Zaharah, President of the Singapore Malay Women's Welfare
Association (September 1950)

Charlie smiled at her gingerly. He had been brought home by
Mahmoud and now lay on the living-room couch.

'No beds, please. Had enough of the things.'

So they had made cushions for him on the upper verandah,
under the fan. A week had improved his looks. The swellings
had receded, replaced now with a purple bruising over half of his
face. His eye was not damaged and his hands had healed. What
a miracle is the human body, Annie thought, and the moments
of her own resurrection came back to her more vividly than they
had ever done before. It was as if the veils that had clouded her
mind from that time were, one by one, lifting. It was being back

here with the heat and the scents and the tropical reverberations. The French called it 'retour sur les lieux du crime'. They believed it provoked memory and stirred spirits.

Madame Wing brought a pot of tea and adjusted Charlie's cushions. He smiled.

'Thanks,' he said, and she nodded.

'You look shocking. How are the ribs?' Annie said, pouring two cups. Nothing quite like a cup of tea, it was true. It kept you going. She had always felt awash with tea in Perth where her neighbours seemed to drink it every hour but here, even in the heat, she found it refreshing.

'Better. I can walk and take a shower, which is fortunate for you.'

Annie smiled and settled the tea cup on a low Indian teak side-table inlaid with tiny pieces of coloured glass, a relic of some former occupants of the villa. When the glass caught the light it sent a thousand reflections dancing on the ceiling like butterflies.

'Do you want to tell me?' she said. 'Do you still think it was Tan's thugs?'

'I can't think what on earth else it can be. I was minding my own business ...'

Charlie caught the movement across Annie's face.

'I wasn't doing anything shocking if that's what you think. Just hanging around down there. Fell in with a load of Aussie sailors and we had a few drinks. Went to the toilet, came out, two guys fell on me and thumped me good and hard for about two minutes and left me there. That's it.'

Charlie sipped the tea.

'Good to be home.'

Annie smiled.

'Made a statement to the police. Even Beaver turned up, for God's sake, as if I was meeting with Chin Peng. No witness, or none that wants to come forward. Mystery continues.'

He shrugged.

'A couple of days here then back to work. It's so damn boring lying in bed. And the Hertogh case has gotten very lively. Have you seen?'

Annie nodded. The debate on the legality of the marriage had gone back and forth. A letter to the press from Mansoor claimed that the marriage was based on affection and mutual agreement. No one had coerced Maria. Several prominent Muslims in the colony weighed in, saying the marriage was unwise but, in their view, legal. Given the fait accompli they questioned the wisdom of threatening friendly relations between Christians and Muslims in Malaya by continuing this barrage of criticism. Letters to the editors from all members of the community argued vociferously for and against. The Dutch newspapers claimed she had been drugged and it was an affront to European justice. The world had suddenly become hungry for news about Maria.

'Maria has come to represent what the Dutch have lost,' Charlie said unexpectedly. 'Their colonies, their pride. They couldn't win that fight but they sure as dammit intend to win this one.'

Annie nodded. It was quite perspicacious of him.

'She's not even white, is she? She's Eurasian. Something they might well, under ordinary circumstances, look down on. Yet they never stop calling her white in the newspapers.'

Finally the transcript of a tape that Maria had made to her parents surfaced. She made a plea to be left alone, reminding her parents of how Aminah had taken care of her during the Japanese Occupation and regretting the slander of her foster-mother's good name. She claimed she was happy in her marriage to an educated man and in living with the Muslim family that she loved.

Annie had read this with mixed feelings. Had it been dictated to her? Annie found herself indulging in the same wild imaginings of the Dutch newspapers. The level of emotion on the issue was running so high that no sense could be made of the whole thing. Annie stopped reading the letters to the editor. They just went over and over the same ground. But it was clear that pride was at stake on both sides. Finally the announcement was made that the Dutch Consul had full powers to act for the parents to get Maria back home and issued a summons under the Guardianship of Infants Ordinance. The affair was going back to court and a new bill had been laid before the government, the Laycock Age of Marriage Bill, restricting all marriage in the colony, regardless of faith, until after the age of sixteen.

'*The Mercury* wants a full piece bringing the story up to date, especially with this Laycock Bill. Nobby says there's a Nadra Fund being set up. The radical Muslims are getting worked up and I think sparks will fly.'

He looked at Annie who remained silent.

'You all right?'

'Saahan died.'

Charlie frowned.

'The mechanic who took care of Joseph. And Joseph is in the hospital with TB.'

Charlie put his hand out to hers and she took it gently.

'My word, Annie, I am sorry.'

She patted his hand. He was livelier but there was still a misery inside him somewhere she hadn't seen before. She was certain it was a woman and wondered if she should talk to him about it, but that agreement she had with him, not to interfere in his private life, stood in the way.

'I'm going to the hospital this afternoon. They say I can see him.'

'What you gonna do about that kid?'

'I don't know, Charlie. Really I don't. He's all alone, isn't he?'

'Yes. Look, I can't tell you what to do, but seems to me that little Jo needs a mum, maybe more than …'

Charlie stopped and picked up his tea cup.

'Say it. More than the Tan child who already has a mother and father. That's it, eh? But I can't let it go, Charlie. I feel I have the right at least to see her.'

Charlie lay back on the cushions and closed his eyes. Annie got up. The telephone was ringing in any case.

It was Maria Shepherd.

'Annie, I have some more news. I wrote to Jean about you and she's going to write everything she knows in a letter. Said she had to sit down and remember it in detail. She knows much more than me. She nursed you. She says she'll try to get in touch with Dr Worth.'

Annie thanked Maria. They talked a little longer and Maria

asked her to come to tea at her house the following week.

She got together some clean clothes, some food and some picture books for Joseph. Mahmoud drove her to the Middleton Quarantine Hospital. All the way there she was silent, trying to think.

The hospital was an old colonial building set in grounds filled with the lush beauty of hibiscus. Inside she was given a mask and allowed to hold his hand.

'The doctors tell me everything is going very well. Soon you will be so well you can come home.'

Joseph nodded and smiled. Her heart went out to him.

'I'm sorry about this mask. I look like a bandit.'

He looked puzzled and she laughed.

'Never mind. When you come home would you like to live with me in the big house? Poor Saahan, you know. He has gone to heaven.'

Joseph nodded gravely. She wanted to cuddle him, but the nurse forbade it. She showed him the picture books and they sat quietly looking at them. Then the nurse touched her arm.

'He must rest now and it will soon be mealtime.'

She saw Dr Chen as she went out into the corridor. She greeted him.

'Thank you, Doctor, for taking good care of him. Are you seeing him now?'

Dr Chen smiled. He was a warm man, she thought, nothing inscrutable, as they said, or oriental about him. That's how they talked in Perth. She was always amazed how very little Australians knew about any other race at all. She had known many Chinese in Ipoh and found them no more inscrutable than the Malays. He was a new kind of young Chinese man, filled with science and hope and vision. If these were the men who would lead Singapore into the future, it was in good hands.

'Hello, Mrs Collins. No, not Joseph. I saw him yesterday. He's doing very well. In ten days at the most I think he can go home. The children do very well on these new drugs, but actually I'm here for a grown-up patient who I have good hopes for too.'

She smiled. They walked down the corridor to the waiting room. Eileen Tan was in a wheelchair, waiting at the reception desk. She was wearing a mask. She looked up as Dr Chen approached and then saw Annie. Her eyes widened in surprise.

Annie was momentarily at a loss what to do. She desperately wanted to speak to Eileen but she dared not risk a scene, especially if Eileen was ill. Then she saw Eileen's husband approach the front doors. Two lanky English doctors, obviously senior, went to greet him. Annie walked quickly back the way she had come and turned towards the side entrance and out into the gardens.

19

'A suggestion that the United Malay National Organisation should intervene in the case of Maria Hertogh, the little Dutch girl, has been made by a columnist of the Kuala Lumpur Malay daily, *Majilis*.'

The Singapore Free Press, 14 August 1950

The letter on the hall table was from England. Annie picked it up and looked at the return address. Doctor Marjorie Worth. She had been one of the doctors at the internment camp. Maria had told her that Dr Worth was writing a memoir of the time in Changi, lest the world, in this brave new world, might forget.

Annie took the letter to the living room and slit its top with the paper knife and unfolded the thick wad of pages. She settled in the wicker chair.

My Dear Annie,

I hope that this letter finds you well. Jean has told me you are living in Australia, in Perth, in a climate that is most conducive to health. I remember that, when the liberation came, uncertainty hung over your future and you were so very alone. I hope you have found friends and loving companions in your new home.

I must tell you I miss the tropical nights on occasion when we are pinched and cold before the fire and the rain is teeming outside. Sometimes, even, you will be surprised to hear, I miss the companionship, amongst the hardship, of those prison walls. Now, when my belly is full and I can walk along a country lane with my dog in perfect freedom, I allow myself to dwell on the good memories of that time and the remarkable courage and often incredible good humour of the women with whom I shared those days. Women, more than men, take root in the present, whatever that may be, and the disturbance of the root is painful. In our case the roots were three and a half years old and they had flowered into loyal friendships, in much that was arresting, new and strange, and in a life permeated with an extraordinary sense of community and closely-knit fellowship.

Nobody, however sympathetic, can ever quite be able to grasp the stories we tell them or see the funny side of what we laugh at, or realise any of the intangible things that must be left unsaid. Eventually you cease to tell them. There is an air of almost obscene urgency to forget the past, which I still have to come to terms with. Even now, after five years, it is still strange to be free, to have the liberty of choice and not to bear the daily responsibility of playing one's part, however insignificant it might be, in a communal life against heavy odds. It has been difficult to become an individual again.

I am writing a memoir for I fear that this kind of history, the women's history, will be entirely forgotten, amongst the dramatic remembrances of men.

Jean has asked me in particular to write to you about your own situation and I am happy, if it can help you, to share with you what I know of that time.

You came into internment, as I recollect, around mid-June 1945, not April, as I understand Maria has indicated. You were brought to the camp hospital and it was I who took charge of you for the first days, though Dr Williams and Dr Small also had your care. We often rotated for the serious patients as three heads were better than one in those dreadful conditions. Everyone, you must remember, by that stage was absolutely exhausted and Dr Williams, indeed, was almost at the end of her tether, having been taken by the Kempeitai for many weeks.

You had a head wound, serious scalp lacerations to the right side of the skull. At first Dr Williams and I thought it was the result of a fall or a beating, but I recall that Dr Small said she thought the stitching presented more as a bullet wound. We could not be sure of the exact cause. I would guess that, by the swelling and contusions, this wounding had taken place some two or three days before you arrived. What was somewhat strange is that your wound had been cleaned, stitched and dressed very well, certainly by a qualified person. You were unconscious and our most pressing worry was a haematoma that could affect the intra-cranial pressure. Of course, we had no x-ray equipment or anything else to give us an indication of what was happening inside your skull but your blood pressure was steady and your pupillary response good, both of which were encouraging signs.

I suppose I did not give it any thought at all at the time but, now, looking back, it does seem that you were, shall I say, stabilised, in some way before you were brought in. Does this make any sense?

Annie shook her head.

With you, on the stretcher, came a small suitcase and inside this, along with some basic clothing was a quantity of penicillin, which was most useful in your recovery, for though we had no direct evidence of infection, it was certainly a possibility in such conditions, although we attempted to keep everything as clean as possible of course.

Annie read between these sensible and moderate lines the impossible medical conditions under which these women had worked. There were few women who worked in Malaya in the 1930s and even fewer were doctors. She and the others had been fortunate to have been interned with these women. But it must have been depressing for the doctors, with the lack of medicines and food, the appalling sanitation and, doubtless, watching the death of women they knew they could, ordinarily, have saved.

In fact, your arrival was something of a godsend, for the penicillin, I believe, saved the lives of several other women and at least two children.

Your recovery was very slow. You remained unconscious for two more days and we began to worry, very seriously, about dehydration. I want here to commend Jean and Maria and other women who, during that time, bathed you and in every way within their limited powers, kept you comfortable. Fortunately, you regained consciousness and took fluids, though you seemed dazed and confused and were unable to talk about what had occurred. From then on your improvement was good. It always amazed me, really, the resilience of the body, what it could survive. I think you must be of a good constitution. Your body does not give up easily. It fights on despite you.

Annie was struck by those words. Your body fights on despite you. She remembered the previous occasion, the time when Ronald had given her sleeping pills. She could not recall how close she had come to death then, but, in the end, he had not succeeded. Her body had fought for her then too. They were humbling, those two rebirths. One more chance at life, they seemed to say. How many more could she get?

You were able to drink normally and take food. What little there was of it. The women always kept aside some of their own rations for the sick in the noblest way. Your memory seemed impaired but this was, I have to say, the least of our problems at that time. Your physical symptoms got better, your head wound healed and you were finally able to walk around.

From that time you went into the general camp and shared a hut with Jean. You must rely on Maria and Jean for their account of your last months at the camp. I only saw you from time to time. Naturally I was glad to see you up and about but it was worrisome that your memory, certainly your memory of this incident in any case, did not return. I had thought that this was a short-term effect. There is something called repressed memory that the doctors are working on now. It is the theory that in the case of great trauma the brain protects itself from emotional breakdown simply by choosing not to remember. This science is in its infancy but this might explain, in some way, your continued memory loss.

Dearest Annie, I hope this has been of some use to you in some way. I wish you the best of health and happiness in your future. If you require anything else of me, do not hesitate to write and, should you ever find yourself in England, I hope you will call on your friends.

My warmest regards,

Marjorie

Annie went to the mirror and searched in her hair for any signs of this wound but there was little to see. A map of white lines between the hairs perhaps. This letter only deepened the mystery. She had come into the camp with a wound, a possible bullet wound or a beating, which had been cared for. So she had been to a hospital on the outside or at least been seen by a doctor. She had been moved only when it was safe to do so and with a supply of medicine. The only way this made any sense was if this had been, at the most, approved or, at the least, simply allowed to happen by the Japanese. Who else had access to such medicines? The only other group she could think of was the Indians. They had relatively good access to medicine and were trusted by the Japanese. That's what she'd heard after the war when accusations of collaboration and blame had been on everyone's lips. Was it an Indian doctor? The other possibility was the man who had been put in prison, the Eurasian doctor; what was his name? Mahmoud had talked about him. The British had locked him up after the war for collaborating but she thought they had let him go? The Japanese man, Shinozaki. His name kept coming up. He seemed to be involved in everything. Could it have been him? And where was he now?

She went back to the chair by the window and looked out onto the garden, watching the dogs playing and the children weeding the vegetable garden. It was maddening. Her mind went round and round in circles. It was impossible to have lived outside of the system in Syonan-To. She was a Eurasian with a British husband. She should have been interned within weeks of the Japanese arriving. But she wasn't. So where had she been? No, not where but, more importantly, with whom. Only a person of some importance could have protected her. Inescapably, that meant, first and foremost, a Japanese, but it could also have been a powerful Chinese collaborator or even an Indian. Whoever it was, Annie now knew, she had loved this man and that, in some way, this man had taken care of her after her injury, even to the point of having her moved into internment where, she guessed, he thought she would be safe. Safe? Safe from whom? Who would have harmed her, did harm her?

She got up, tired of thinking, and went into the garden. Madame Wing joined her for tea. The two women sat under the trees and spoke of domestic things and watched the children and the dogs.

20

'More letters promising financial aid and support
have been received by Maria Hertogh and her Malay husband
from Indonesia, Pakistan and Saudi Arabia.'
The Straits Times, 21 August 1950

'A raging volcano is in the vicinity.'
Utusan Melayu, September 1950

Annie picked up the newspaper. The battle for Maria Hertogh was back on in the courts and the mother, Adeline, had flown in. Despite herself, Annie found the story as compelling as everyone else seemed to. Today the mother had met her daughter for the first time in eight years.

THE STRAITS TIMES (16 NOVEMBER 1950)
After eight years of separation, Mrs Adeline Hertogh and her 13-year-old daughter, Bertha Maria, met in Mr M.A. Majid's house in Rangoon Road, Singapore, yesterday morning – and disagreed.

Shaking with emotion, Mrs Hertogh shook hands with Che Aminah, when she arrived at the house and was taken into the sitting room. 'Why do you keep on fighting?' asked Che Aminah. 'You gave your child to me to adopt as my own daughter.'

Mrs Hertogh replied that she had only asked Aminah to look after her during the war. Her eyes searched the room. She kept on saying, 'Where is my daughter?'

Che Aminah went into her bedroom and called Maria, saying that 'Adeline' was here to see her. After a few minutes Maria came out hesitantly, dressed in a pink baju and a blue sarong and sat down with the others at the table. 'Why did you say you didn't want to see me?' scolded Mrs Hertogh, mother-like. Maria replied: 'I am not going away from here where my husband is. Why have you come? I have had enough trouble.'

They argued together in Malay. Che Aminah sat between them. 'Whatever may be the difficulties, I will stay here and overcome them until I can take you back to your father and brothers and sisters in Holland.'

Annie found the account of this meeting distressing not only for the gulf between mother and child but for the obvious presence of the press around them. They were like dogs with a bone, and this included Charlie.

He had received a phone call from his editor, pleased with his story. It was making big headlines in Australia as it was all over the world.

He came to breakfast and read the *Straits Times* article

quickly, stuffing toast into his mouth.

'Slow down, Charlie,' Annie said.

Charlie made a face.

'The case is gonna begin any day now. It's gonna be sensational. I have to go.' He threw back his coffee and rose.

'Be careful, eh,' she said.

'I'm fine. Don't fuss.' He turned away.

Annie said nothing. She rose and began to walk towards the house. He turned back to her almost instantly.

'Sorry. I'll be careful.'

She looked up at him and smiled and he bent and kissed her cheek. He had almost entirely recovered from his injuries. Only the faded yellow bruising on his face remained and she touched it gently. In a few days that, too, would disappear. It was nice to have Charlie at home again and spend their evenings playing cards and listening to music. All too soon he would chafe and go back to his old ways. He was, like most journalists, she supposed, only truly happy in the company of his peers.

She'd asked Nobby about this one evening.

'Newsmen are like the noble elephants,' he'd said. 'We travel in herds and think alike. We don't trust the jackals and hyenas who try to trick us in our never-ending pursuit of the green grass of truth. We have big ears and we never forget.'

She smiled now, remembering it, as Charlie took her hand and kissed the palm. It was an entirely natural gesture, made in the affection of the moment, but she felt a jolt of electricity fizz through her hand. Charlie didn't notice; his mind was already downtown, on his story. He turned and strode across the grass.

The kiss, the touch of lips on her palm, the jolt, had nothing to do with Charlie. In a sudden rush another face had come to her. Lips touched her palm, full lips, sensuous lips and above them a straight, almost aquiline nose and then she saw his eyes. They were dark and liquid like shady mountain streams, and narrow and hooded as the hard edges of a wind-worn ravine.

She closed her eyes and felt his lips and saw the fall of his heavy black hair onto his forehead. She knew now she had been in love with an oriental man but she could not tell, from the intense detail of those eyes, anything more. She saw those things and felt those things yet she did not feel the rush of emotion, of love, she supposed, that such remembrances should bring. She laid it aside, this knowledge, for the moment, because it frightened her. If she had spent years being the lover of such a man in Syonan-to, she was what everyone had so despised, a collaborator. She still recalled the stories she'd heard as she waited and waited to be sent to Australia. Stories of the aftermath of the surrender, the lawless void the Japanese had left as the troops withdrew to barracks and hid themselves away, during the weeks before the British returned authority to the streets and Mountbatten took the formal surrender.

Retribution and revenge. The settling of deep bitter scores. Against the Japanese in the first days, but the oppressors had been smart enough to secrete themselves away. Thereafter, revenge had been sought amongst each other. The Chinese sought Malay blood as collaborators. And the Malays saw that some of the Chinese had made money, had built fortunes on the back of the Japanese authority, as blood-suckers, though Annie was certain the really vicious ones had melted away like the Japanese. The murders and reprisals went on until there was no longer any sense or reason to them and it was all done out of pure hatred and pure revenge for the years of fear and misery. She had also heard about the shaven-headed women, mistresses of the Japanese or Chinese men, beaten and bloody, who were paraded through the streets, their faces covered in spit, their bodies bruised. Many ended up in an alley, smashed to pulp or with a bullet in the back of their heads. She might have been one of them.

She turned her face away from these thoughts. The taxi arrived. She checked the bag of food and fresh clothes she had prepared for Joseph, picked up the bouquet of flowers and her handbag and left. Joseph was on the mend. He could come home in two weeks. His treatment would continue for six more months. It was long and complicated. Tuberculosis required a cocktail of drugs and the regimen had to be adhered to absolutely, Dr Chen had told her. Absolutely. If she could not be responsible for him and the proper management of his treatment, then he must stay in the hospital. The moment she had agreed she knew she had set her foot on an irrevocable path. She would adopt Joseph.

She meant to speak to Desmond about the procedures involved in letting a half-white single woman adopt a full-blood Malay child into pure white Australia. She smiled as she thought of the complications it would cause but she had no doubt, now, of her resolve to see it through. It made little difference to her search for Suzy, but rather strengthened it, and she put the terrible meeting between Mrs Hertogh and her daughter out of her mind.

At the hospital she asked that the nurse deliver her flowers to Lady Tan along with her note.

21

'The disclosure that threatening letters had been written to Mrs Adeline Hertogh, Maria's mother, and her supporters came as a climax to yesterday's hearing in the Singapore High Court.'

The Straits Times, 24 November 1950

Joseph was no longer infectious. He was able to mingle with other children, and Annie found him in the hospital garden, playing football with the boys. He had gained weight. The food at the hospital had done him good. His slim brown figure was lithe and soon it would be strong again.

'Joseph,' she called to him and he turned and raced towards her.

She picked him up in her arms and held him as tight as she dared. He wrapped his legs around her waist and clung to her like a tender little monkey. She felt the most overwhelming love for this little boy and the pressure of his cheek against her shoulder told his love for her. She set him down.

'Joseph. Soon you can come home with me.'

Joseph's face burst into a smile of warm radiance.

'Would you mind if I became your Mummy, Joseph? Would that be all right?'

Joseph frowned. She knew him a little by now. He was trying to think about this seriously before he spoke.

'I have no Mummy,' he said.

'No,' she said. 'I didn't have a Mummy or Daddy either. That means we are quite the same, you and I. Maybe we can be happy together?'

Joseph looked at her with his serious brown eyes. 'Yes,' he said and put his arms around her neck again. She kissed him and kissed him and, finally, she let him go.

'You never leave me?' he said.

'No, Joseph. Never. But you understand what it means? If I am your Mummy?'

'I have to go to school,' he said and looked downcast.

'Yes, indeed,' she said, smiling. 'And try very hard so that one day you will be a fine clever man.'

He considered this a moment. 'OK,' he said.

She kissed him once more and waved as he ran away to play with the other children.

She sat for a while watching them, listening to the cries and happy laughter. She knew he would come back in for the afternoon tea. She wandered along to his bed and put the clean clothes in his drawer. The Chinese nurse chatted to her for a while, telling her what supplies Joseph might need in the coming week, and Annie enquired, casually, if the nurse knew whether Lady Tan was still in the hospital.

'Oh no,' she said. 'She was discharged yesterday.'

Annie felt the buoyancy go out of her.

'But, if you go to the reception, I think I heard there was a note for you.'

Annie raced away, leaving the nurse looking alarmed. Yes, indeed, said the receptionist. A note, where was it? Annie kept her temper. When the note was finally handed to her she ripped it open.

Thank you for the flowers. I saw you when I came into the hospital. I would also like to talk. Please allow me some time to recover. I will telephone you. Eileen Tan.

Annie danced a little jig down the corridor under the reproachful gaze of the English doctor in charge and went to meet Joseph for tea.

When she left the hospital she took a taxi and directed the driver to the Indian shops on High Street. She wanted to look at material. A bolt for Madame Wing and the other families, a new dress for herself, clothes for Joseph and for the other children as Christmas presents. The day was cool and cloudy. She walked a while before the shops, the Indian owners coming to greet her and press their wares.

In the distance where High Street meets the Padang, she saw crowds, thick crowds of men. She suddenly remembered that this was the day of the verdict on the Hertogh case. What did the mother look like? And the little girl? She felt a curiosity to see them all, the same curiosity, she recognised, that fed the news frenzy. She wandered towards the High Court Building. A cordon of Gurkhas, in their impeccable brown uniforms and wide-brimmed hats, kept the crowds from entirely filling the road, whilst the police directed traffic as best they could. The Gurkhas had formed a line to permit passage into the court and remained still and stony-faced, their weapons held to the ready.

She stood under the big trees that shaded the walls of the Cricket Club. This building was as familiar to her as the convent at Ipoh. Ronald had been a member and played games on the grassy Padang that stretched behind it. She had sat, bored stiff, pregnant, watching the men running to and fro, the click of the ball on the bat sounding from time to time, while the mems drank gin-and-tonics and either patronised her or ignored her. A couple of them had been quite nice, the younger ones, not quite so stiffened by custom and time out East.

An English woman emerged from the club and stood, waving her fan, waiting for her car. She darted nervous looks at the crowd across the way and had clearly decided to go home as quickly as possible. Something about her, the way she wore her hat and carried her fan was familiar to Annie. The memory came back so suddenly, it was as if she had been struck.

Annie had stood here, under the porte-cochere, exactly as this woman was, waving her fan. Not the same fan of course, but a fan like it, made of delicate bamboo and silk. It was not when she had been waiting for Ronald to finish his interminable cricket games or drunken evenings with his friends. She had not been surrounded by the white-flannelled Hooray Henrys with their pip vowel sounds and their red swarthy complexions, but by Japanese men, in uniforms, and by women like her, Eurasian or else Chinese, dressed in long silk perfumed gowns. She knew exactly, at that very moment, that she had been the mistress of a

Japanese man. She could not quite recall his face but she almost heard his voice, somewhere on the edge of recollection. He spoke English, or was she just imagining that. Who are you?

A loud horn sounded and a taxi turned onto the main road and drew to a halt. The crowd surged forward, locking the car in a mass of waving, screaming bodies. Only when the crowd parted at the urging of the Gurkha rifles could she see the woman and the child. It was Aminah and Maria, heads down, with the Muslim man, Majid, who was their guardian. He turned to address the crowd and the Malay woman stopped, clutching Maria. She looked exhausted and cast down. The child at her side stared at the crowd, blank-eyed. Solicitors in black, holding boxes and files, rushed past them. Majid gave a final wave of defiance to the roaring, banner-waving masses and they disappeared inside the court.

'Well, how surprising, Mrs Collins, to see you here.'

Annie looked up into the sneering face of Beaver, his eyes shaded by dark glasses despite the lack of sun. He was with a middle-aged, shaven-headed Chinese man, also wearing a pair of round dark glasses. They looked like a pair of hoodlums out of *The Maltese Falcon*.

'Sightseeing?' he said and lit a cigarette.

Annie felt herself flush. That's exactly what she was doing and it was mortifying to be caught at it by the likes of Beaver. He knew very well she had not been at the Cricket Club of which, doubtless, he was a member.

'I was in the vicinity.' She heard the defensiveness in her voice and slapped herself mentally. 'Are you looking for Communists,

Captain?' she said more assertively.

Beaver blew smoke from his nostrils. The Chinese man stood impassively by his side, his head turned towards the crowd.

'I'm always looking for Communists, Mrs Collins,' he said menacingly and curled his lip.

Annie's assertiveness melted away. She felt intimidated by this man and saw how it might be in an interrogation room with him. Alone and isolated, in the wavering half-light, she felt sure he could convince her that she corresponded daily with the Malayan Communist Party. She trembled. He continued to watch her and she had no idea how to go on with this unpleasant exchange or how to move away.

'Hello, Annie.'

The familiar voice of Nobby Styles sounded at her shoulder and she turned to him, a feeling of utter relief and gratitude washing over her.

'Oh, Nobby. How lovely to see you,' she said, much too effusively. Beaver's lips twitched.

'Morning, Beaver. Checking the crowd for subversives? Think I saw a couple of your men.'

Nobby gave him a broad grin.

Beaver crushed his cigarette underfoot. Small pink spots appeared on his cheeks. He ignored Nobby and turned to Annie.

'I shouldn't stay here, Mrs Collins. This crowd could get ugly and turn on women they see as being like Mrs Hertogh. Refuge for you in the Cricket Club will be impossible, obviously.'

The implication was plain. She felt another flush rise in her cheeks. The man had a way of making her feel like she was nothing.

'Funny,' said Nobby, taking Annie's arm in his. 'I heard that the kid's pure white, as Dutch as tulips. Heard, too, there was a touch of dusk in your family, Beaver. Burmese, isn't it? I was there before the war.'

Beaver's face clenched. He stared at Nobby so hard and unmoving that he might have been turned to stone. The Chinese man remained utterly immobile. Then Beaver turned on his heel and walked towards the crowd and his companion followed. The dark car of the Netherlands Consul-General, its flag fluttering, arrived. The crowd surged and chanted 'Allahu Akbar' over and over, their voices rising to a frenzy as Mrs Hertogh left the car.

Annie squeezed Nobby's hand and he smiled. She caught a glimpse of Adeline Hertogh in her simple white blouse and grey skirt. Adeline glanced once at the crowd. She looked hollow eyed, nervous and harassed, looking neither left nor right, shepherded by her guardians quickly into the court house.

The crowd settled down and the chanting ceased.

'Come on,' said Nobby, heading towards the Cricket Club. 'Charlie will join us. The decision will take a while and one of my reporters has a man on the inside.'

Annie looked up at the building. She was not sure if she wanted to go inside.

'Are you a member?' she said.

Nobby laughed. 'Why would anyone want a dreadful hack in their exclusive club, that what you're saying?'

Annie frowned. 'Well …'

'You're right. They gave it to me before I became one. My

grandfather was a very fine cricketer and the personal private secretary to the much-moustachioed Sir Federick Weld, sixth Premier of New Zealand, eighth Governor of Western Australia and fourteenth Governor of the Straits Settlements.'

They headed towards the steps.

'My father was in the Burmese colonial service and then here. I was at school here in Singapore, played cricket for the club and made a member long before they suspected I would turn into a hack. They have, very kindly, not kicked me out. I come here from time to time to chat with the high and mighty and enjoy a cricket match.'

'Does Beaver really have Burmese blood in him?'

Nobby laughed. 'I don't know. But I found out his great grandfather had fought in one of those Anglo-Burmese wars and served in the Burmese government in Rangoon at a time when they all had native wives and concubines of one sort or another. I know that he can't be absolutely certain.'

They went inside and the ancient Indian doorman bowed slightly to Nobby whom he clearly recognised. Nobby signed her name and Charlie's into the visitors book, and they made their way upstairs to the long elegant upper verandah that curved to give a view of the vast open space of the Padang, fringed by the rain trees and the civic buildings on either side of its length, the cathedral to one side and, facing it, in the distance, The Recreation Club.

She went to the wrought-iron railing and gazed down over the green expanse and the now-muted, milling crowds.

He held my hand here, she thought. We looked down together

like this but the Padang wasn't a smooth grassy open space then; it had been a field, covered in the riffling leaves of plants. Her mind shuffled pages in the dim photograph album, moments glimpsed in frozen celluloid. He had a cigarette case. It bore a crest but she could not make it out clearly.

'Annie.'

She turned. Charlie came out onto the verandah.

'You all right? Not very safe down here.'

'Really,' she said sarcastically.

'Now, now, children,' Nobby said and ordered drinks.

The men discussed the case and Annie left them to it, content to sit here on this breezy verandah and stare out over the Padang to the glimpses of the sea between the trees. She tried to recall that crest but all she could see were his fingers, his perfectly manicured, elegant fingers, and that was when she felt the most visceral kick inside her, the galvanising jolt of those fingers touching her skin.

She drank the iced lime juice and took out her handkerchief, glad the men were busy, and touched it to her temple, waiting for her pulse to return to normal. What power had this man had over her that the mere thought of his fingers could bring such an eruption? But how is it that I cannot recall all of this? How can I not see his face?

She searched again but the page would not turn. Charlie came to her side. They watched the crowds turning, moving like the restless waves on the sea.

'Come on, let's go see what's happening. Annie, will Mahmoud take you home? He's around.'

Annie nodded. She felt the thud of a rock fall on her arm and cried out. A hail of stones landed around her, hitting Charlie on the chest. They both moved back instinctively to the safety of the inner verandah. Annie held her arm.

'Are you all right?'

Nobby came to her, worried. More stones flew over the parapet, thudding into the wood floor. The waiters rushed around ushering their charges, like children, inside the building.

Charlie rubbed his chest and smiled ruefully at Annie.

'You OK?'

'Yes, it's nothing. I want to go home.'

Charlie nodded and they left the building. A police cordon prevented the crowd from approaching the Cricket Club. Tom Masterson came up to the two men, smiled at Annie winningly and lit a cigarette.

'Hearing's going on and on. They usually break at five but arguments are still being heard. Could be a few more hours.'

Charlie nodded at Tom.

'Been a bit of stone throwing on the other side. Annie got hit. This could get nasty.'

Tom frowned. 'Sorry,' he said.

Annie smiled.

'Charlie got hit too, but we're all right.'

She turned and kissed Nobby on the cheek.

'Thank you,' she said and they shared a smile.

Charlie walked her to the car, past the now ever-growing crowd jostling at them angrily. Suddenly there was a flurry of movement and the crowd pulled away, as if the tide of humanity had ebbed away from them, and flooded towards the court. They both looked back. Maria and Aminah had emerged and they were engulfed by the frenzied mass who must have believed victory was theirs. The police waved batons over the crowd and, before Annie turned away, she just caught a glimpse of the two of them, the old woman and the little girl, encircled by police.

Mahmoud came forward, clearly surprised to see her.

'Take her home, Mahmoud,' Charlie shouted as he raced away.

She settled back into the car, closing her eyes and leaving their little world to its anger and misery.

22

'Nadra Adabi (Maria Hertogh), after five gruelling days in the High Court in the claim brought by Mrs A.P. Hertogh for her return, was "not available" this morning to reporters who called to see her. Mrs Hertogh too was "resting" and would not consent to an interview.'

The Singapore Free Press, 25 November 1950

Annie smoothed the clean white sheet in Joseph's bedroom. He was coming back the next day. She wondered how it would be for him, sleeping here in this big room in this big house, a child used to so much less. A chik chak tutted at her from the ceiling, then raced away, its body zigzagging across the wall. She wanted to spoil him, lavish him with gifts but had had to restrain herself. He would have to play with the other children here. It would not do to increase even more the distance between them.

She had told Madame Wing about her plans. She was not certain that her housekeeper approved but she did not openly criticise it. She had made it known that Joseph would stay in the big house whilst he was being treated for his tuberculosis. She intended for him to continue with his classes with the other boys for the moment, retain a semblance of normality, even as she wished she could begin a new kind of life for him. She felt vaguely uncomfortable. Of course the life she wished for him was a white life but she dismissed that thought instantly. He would have a better life but they would come back here often. A better life, she said to herself and shook her head.

'Everything as normal as possible,' she said to the fluffed pillow.

Charlie was in the garden eating an early lunch. He'd had a very busy day and had risen late after a night out into the small hours. He was entirely back to his usual self. The police had been unable to find the men who had beaten him and both of them were sure nobody would be charged with his assault.

The busy day was because the judgement on Maria had come down. The court had found for the mother, Adeline, the marriage had been declared invalid and Maria had been taken to the Girls' Home of the Convent of the Good Shepherd in Thomson Road. The crowd had been angry and verging on the riotous. The Gurkhas and police had had a hard time dispersing it. Charlie had spent hours at the convent with a photographer, getting interviews whenever possible. The press had been allowed access and it was clear, as Charlie told her, that the Dutch government considered this as something of a coup.

'A convent,' she'd questioned when she joined him, tapping the picture of Maria sitting, looking sullen, next to Mother St. Colomba.

'Odd choice, eh? Guaranteed to stir the Muslims into a frenzy, I'd have thought. I asked the police superintendent but he didn't seem bothered. Said it was the mother's choice.'

He drained his teacup.

'My word, I'm done in. But gotta go. There's yet another appeal by Aminah's lawyers. It never ends. I'm not complaining though. *Mercury*'s delighted. Got a byline.'

Charlie grinned. He was high on the drug of the story.

'Tom and I are off to Sultan Gate. The mosque there is a bit of a hot bed and we want to get some comments.'

Annie wandered back to the house. Madame Wing often played the radio and she heard it now, low, in her room.

'Meigui, meigui, wo ai ni.'

Annie spoke no Mandarin but she knew what those words meant. Rose petal, rose petal, I love you. She had heard this song many times.

The song came to an end and there, on the pane of the small window in the corridor, as if projected by her memory, she saw some signs, Chinese signs, standing out clearly, red against white. She had no idea how to read them but dared not pull her eyes away, trying to imprint them on her mind. Then she blinked and they disappeared.

She ran to the verandah and took a pencil, drawing quickly what she could remember. A box on two legs with a tilting lid. A flat roof with a vertical line crossed by three horizontals under it, then some boxes and four legs. She drew them out quickly.

She went to the head of the stairs.

'Madame Wing, can you come, please?'

She heard the radio go off and Madame Wing appeared in the hall.

'Finally that pangolin smell has faded. I've had the floor swabbed twice a day and it's taken this long.'

Annie went down the stairs, the paper in hand.

'Can you help me, please?'

Madame Wing looked at the paper and frowned.

'What is it?'

'Chinese, I think.'

Madame Wing glanced at Annie.

'Chinese? Are you learning Chinese, Mrs Collins?'

Annie smiled a little testily.

'No, no. I don't know what I've written. Or if it makes sense. I just saw these, what do you say, signs just now and wrote them down. Can you make sense of them?'

Madame Wing stared at them. She put her finger to the second figure. She took a pencil from her pocket and traced the figure. Annie watched her.

'I think this is backwards,' Madame Wing said and quickly wrote it the other way.

'Yes. You've somehow got it backwards. It is "Soldier".'

She looked at the other sign and her face froze and she looked up into Annie's eyes.

'You say you saw these, just like that, out of thin air.'

'Yes, I suppose so. They just came into my mind somehow. What do they mean?'

'In English you might say "Law Soldier", in Chinese we say – well that doesn't matter. In Japanese it is "Kem Pei".'

Annie frowned.

'In Japanese? I thought it was Chinese.'

'It stands for "Kempei", the military police. You understand, the Kempeitai were the military police here during the war and tortured and murdered thousands of people. How can you see this in your imagination?'

Annie snatched the paper and stared at it, then up into Madame Wing's dark, enquiring eyes.

'I don't know. I'm sorry. Forgive me.'

She ran up the stairs and into her room. She stared at the signs again and then ripped the paper to shreds, threw the pieces into the bin.

No, no, no: the words rattled in her brain. She had been madly in love with a man who was a murderer, a torturer, a member of that feared and dreadful army. How was that possible? Was that the reason her brain chose not to remember?

She ran a cold bath. She flung off her clothes and sank into it, submerging her head under the water. When she emerged she had made a decision. She wanted nothing more to do with these memories. She had started to half indulge herself in them, will them back into her mind with some idea of a romantic and heady love affair. But she knew that could not be so. Not in Syonan-to.

She got out of the bath and towelled off. That was over. She would not think about this anymore. What hideous things would she discover if she did? About him, but more importantly, about herself?

Forward, not back. That was the direction.

She dressed. Desmond was coming to dinner and she was going to ask him to facilitate the adoption of Joseph. This would serve two purposes. She would set in train this momentous step and it would, doubtless, scare Desmond half to death. A Eurasian wife might be all right, but a Malay child would surely give him pause.

Annie spent time gardening for a while, keeping busy. The sweet potatoes were growing like a weed and the cassava towered. The children came to help and she chatted with them. She fed Yellow and the other dogs then rested a while, taking tea. She avoided Madame Wing's eyes.

She bathed again and washed her hair and put on the radio, humming along to the songs. 'Mona Lisa' by Nat King Cole and 'Some Enchanted Evening' by Perry Como.

She put on her makeup and switched the radio to the classical channel. Mozart was playing. From below came the sounds of the kitchen. Ah Moy was making dinner. Annie had asked for all Chinese food, anything he wanted to make, but it seemed that he couldn't stop himself from preparing a western dish, as the evening's surprise. Ordinarily she liked to see what he had got up to but just today she wished there would be no surprises.

She put up her hair and selected the earrings Desmond had given her, small drop-pearls on a silver mount. She put them in her ears and shook them and there he was, in the mirror, looking at her with the dark liquid eyes of his handsome face, his hair falling on his forehead.

The earrings are pale-green jade butterflies. He touches them with his fingers and she puts her cheek to his hand. His cheek touches hers, and he whispers in her ear. 'Don't blame me. I will never forget you.'

Annie gasped and turned. She looked for him but there was

nothing, just the last of the sun slanting in onto the wooden floor. She turned back and stared into the mirror but he wasn't there either.

Don't blame me. What did that mean?

She heard Desmond's car coming up the drive and went to the verandah. Somehow this man had taken her and made her love him and then he had … What? Tried to kill her? Just like Ronald. The thought filled her with fury.

33

COURT SITS UNTIL SEVEN AT NIGHT

1,000 people waited three hours to see Maria leave court
for home. As Maria Hertogh Adabi left the Singapore High Court
last night after Mr Justice Browne had reserved his decisions on
her future, a waiting crowd of 1000 people broke through
a police cordon and surged around her.

The Straits Times, 25 November 1950

Joseph smiled and raced around the room. He didn't look in the least intimidated. Perhaps the long weeks in the hospital had accustomed him to a big bed. He bounced on it and ran backwards and forwards, checking every nook and cranny. She had put books in the bookshelf and they sat looking at them in the wicker chair, Joseph on her lap, until Madame Wing came in with a tray and said it was time for Joseph to take his medicine and have some milk and rest.

The telephone rang. Madame Wing looked up.

'I'll go,' Annie said.

She picked the phone from its cradle.

'Hello.'

'Mrs Collins?'

'Yes.'

'It's Eileen Tan.'

Annie dropped onto the marble-bottomed Chinese chair by the telephone table.

'Oh, thank you so much for calling me. Are you better?'

'A little. Drugs make you weak, but I expect you know that from the little boy. Of course the young do so much better than us.'

'Yes, he is home now and doing well.'

'I'm very glad. It is a kindness you are doing for him.'

'Oh, I like him a lot, so not really.'

Annie was anxious to move the conversation away from politesse and any further discussion of her happiness with another child.

'Mrs Tan, may we meet, do you think?'

'Yes. That is why I am calling you. I am able to leave the house now and it is very unwise for you to come here again. I am sorry for what happened the last time.'

'It's all right.'

'I can't promise anything, Mrs Collins.'

'No, I know. Please call me Annie. I just want to talk to you.'

'Yes. Well, would you meet me at a friend's house in North Bridge Road next week?'

'Yes, of course. I am most grateful.'

Eileen gave Annie the address and the two women arranged a time and date. Annie hung up, euphoric. She raced back up to

Joseph's room and read *Mother Goose* with him until he dozed off. This afternoon, after lunch, she would allow him to play with the other children for a few hours under Fatimah's watchful eye.

In the meantime, she had her own plans. She had arranged to meet the Eurasian doctor that Mahmoud had mentioned. His name was Dr Charles Paglar, and Maria had told her he was the current president of the Recreation Club.

The phone rang again.

'Desmond,' she said, recognising his voice.

'How's the boy?' he said and she smiled.

To her surprise, Desmond hadn't been in the least bit shocked at her notion of adopting Joseph. They had talked at length and he had been supportive. Perhaps he hoped she had given up her idea of finding Suzy. Perhaps. In any case, he said he would go ahead and find out the procedures for legal adoption. Once Joseph was legally her son, getting him back to Australia would be no problem at all, despite the white Australia policy.

'He's fine.'

'Can you come along at some stage to talk to the fellow here who understands this kind of thing?'

'Yes, of course. When?'

'Oh, next week sometime. In the meantime there's a do, a sort of Christmas bash at the governor's residence. Loads of people. Will you come with me?'

'Oh yes, lovely. Thanks.'

She hung up. She had been on cloud nine and now she felt plummeted back to earth. This could be a long procedure. Her single status was an issue, she could see that. But she had a house in Perth and money, and that must make a difference surely? She knew, too, that Desmond was avoiding the obvious question of the prejudice that a boy like Joseph would encounter in Australia. She had thought about this a great deal. Did his advantages in upbringing outweigh such dangers?

Perhaps Desmond believed she would be refused and therefore had decided it was just as well not to raise the question.

'One step at a time, Annie,' she said to herself.

Dr Paglar was a tall large man with a solid square face and dark sharp eyes behind round glasses. He received her at the verandah.

'Welcome,' he said, rising.

'Thank you for seeing me, Doctor,' Annie said.

'Not at all. Maria said you had some questions for me.'

He put out his hand to her and they shook. He signalled to the waiter to bring refreshments. They sat under the fan. The day was still and grey. The monsoon was upon them.

'This might be a strange request but may I ask you whether you have ever seen me before? During the war I mean.'

The doctor contemplated Annie's face for a moment or two.

'No, I don't think I recall. Can you tell me where you think we might have met?'

'Well, I'm not sure we have ever met. But, you see, I received the attentions of a doctor sometime in June 1945 just before I was interned, and I wondered if it was you.'

'Just before the end of the war. How strange.'

'Yes. It is precisely because it is so strange that I am here today. You see, I can't recollect at all what I did for almost the entire Occupation.'

Annie took off her gloves and put them to one side.

'Except I think I might not be very proud of it.'

Dr Paglar's eyes softened.

'I think you should not blame yourself for anything that happened during the Occupation, my dear. The entire island of Singapore was a prison, in one way or another, for everyone. Some had more obvious walls but everyone was forced into fear and hunger. People can't be blamed for what they do to survive inside a prison, one not of their own making.'

'Well, I believe I might have been ... the mistress of a Japanese man.'

Dr Paglar nodded.

'I see. Women were in an even more invidious position than men. What could they do if a Japanese officer happened to see them? What choice would you have had? Were you married?'

'Yes, to a British man. He was made a POW.'

'Unprotected and suspect. Did you attend the registration? You know there was ...?'

'Yes, yes. Maria told me. I don't think so. I don't recall.'

Dr Paglar wiped his brow.

'I don't want to dwell on horror but many women were simply raped, you know, and murdered, or thrown into brothels. I'm sorry to be so blunt, but I want you to understand how limited were your choices. No choices really. Don't blame yourself.'

'I'm not sure if I blame myself. I just want to try to understand. I had a head wound, you see, and I can't remember.'

'You think this head wound was cared for by a doctor.'

'Definitely, yes. I've heard from the English doctor who had attended to me at camp. She recalls very well. It was stitched, a possible bullet wound. And dressed, and everything. And I came in with penicillin.'

Dr Paglar fell silent, looking out over the lawn. Annie waited for him. She knew he was a clever, astute man and he had lived through every minute of the Occupation.

'Then the man must have cared for you. Doubtless, he thought you would be safer, at the end, interned. We know now that the war ended abruptly, with the atom bomb, but that was not at all the case in June of 1945. We thought the Japanese would fight to the bitter end, street by street, tree by tree, turn Singapore into rubble and kill everyone. I'm not sure he would have been right. I'm certain that the Japanese would simply have murdered every single POW, but in the end it turned out well, I suppose.'

'If I had been the mistress of an officer of some kind, would you ever have met me?'

The refreshments arrived and Dr Paglar waited until the boy had moved away.

'Not necessarily. I was head of the Eurasian Association, which was run by Mr Shinozaki. This meant, in effect, I was called on to make speeches of support for the Japanese as required, attend various functions, round up the Eurasian community to wave flags, sing songs, that sort of thing, when some dignitary turned up or some festival came round. Really it was a sop to the Japanese but it kept things sane. Keeping things sane around the volatile nature of the Japanese Occupation was no small thing, I can assure you. The military administration had someone to go to and Shinozaki acted as a buffer. I was able to practise medicine and do what I could.'

Annie nodded.

'Unless you and this officer, or whatever he was, turned up at such events, there is a good chance we would never have met. Are you sure he was an officer? There were many civilian Japanese in Singapore after the first months. Teachers, doctors and so on.'

'No, I have no idea what he was. I can hardly recall him at all.'

'May I ask why you want to?'

Annie frowned.

'I need to know I suppose. That gap in my life has become important. I had laboured under the idea that I had been a prisoner of war for the entire time. This was a shock.'

Dr Paglar nodded and drank his tea.

'Yes, I see that.'

'This Japanese man, Mr Shinozaki, is he still alive?'

'I believe so. At least I haven't heard any different. He was a prime witness and interpreter at the war-crimes tribunals. He spoke for me, actually, which got me released when the Brits locked me up for treason. I presume he is back in Japan.'

Annie thought. What else could she ask this man?

'I'm Eurasian,' she said at length.

Dr Paglar smiled. 'As am I.'

'Do you know of any other Eurasian women who, let us say, did what I did? Became the companions of Japanese men during the Occupation.'

Dr Paglar frowned.

'I mean,' Annie went on quickly, 'it is only because, you know, they might have known me. We might have moved in the same circles. Do you think?'

Dr Paglar shrugged.

'It's possible. Whether they wish to talk about it now, after so long, is another matter.'

'Yes, of course.'

Annie struggled with what else she could ask him. He had not known her. She had not been part of the purely Eurasian community. She had lived with a Japanese man, had moved in more Japanese circles. It was as simple as that. But other women, perhaps other women like her, were out there, silent.

'Dr Paglar, may I ask one last favour? Can I give you a photograph of myself and can I ask you to somehow circulate it to the membership of the club, simply asking anyone who knows me to get in touch? Would that be all right?'

'Well, I suppose …'

'If I said I had lost my memory and was seeking help, perhaps someone would come forward. It would be private.'

Dr Paglar looked at his watch.

'Yes, that would be all right.'

He fell silent a moment and looked out over the trees to the seashore and the boats moving quietly on the swell.

'History remembers war, you know, but not its aftermath. That can be as traumatic and tragic as the war itself. Picking up the pieces of your shattered life.'

Annie sensed that Dr Paglar's aftermath had been anguished. To be locked up and accused of treachery by men who were not there, when you had tried so hard to hold together the tenuous strings of sanity in the face of such madness.

He roused himself and rose.

'If you prepare a circular I will see it is distributed and ask anyone who has information to contact you directly. Will that do?'

Annie stood and put out her hand. Dr Paglar took it into both of his huge ones.

'Good luck,' he said warmly.

'Thank you.'

Annie walked along the road in front of Raffles Institution, the trishaws pinging their bells wildly, begging to take her wherever she wished to go. She ignored them. If she looked at them or waved them away they just got more insistent. She walked into the Raffles Hotel. She wanted to see if any memories came to her here and if not, relax a while in its lovely arms.

24

'The chief grievance appears to be that Maria has already
been put under Christian influence. Criticism would subside
temporarily if Maria were to be placed in neutral religious custody,
for example, the Social Welfare Department.'
Recommendation to the Colonial Secretary by A. Blades, Assistant
Commissioner of Special Branch, CID (7 December 1950)

She spent half an hour with Joseph in the bathroom. She found the most intense pleasure in soaping his little body and getting him into his pyjamas. She had bought him a wooden boat and he played with it whilst she watched him. He was a boy used to sleeping practically naked so she had made sure the pyjamas were very light. The room had a fan and she wanted him to be covered a little. As she dressed him she saw the little white flecks on his smooth, soft dark skin. They were like tiny pin pricks here and there, perhaps a dozen, hardly noticeable except this close and there was one quite long white thin scar on his shoulder. She felt upset for him. Had someone abused him, beaten him? It was so horrible she had to stop herself thinking of it.

She read him a story and tucked him in. His eyes drooped almost instantly and she leant and kissed his cheek. She pulled the net around his bed and watched him for a moment, sleeping, his brown skin and tousled black hair against the white pillow. He was beautiful and she felt as possessive of him as if she had given him birth.

Over the next days they got to know each other a little better. Joseph went off to his little lean-to school with Mr Pillai. He had gotten behind, and the other boys were now better than him and he had a temper spat, but she helped him in the evening and they went over all the letters and numbers until he remembered them.

The drugs made him tired and she put him to bed early the evening of Desmond's do. Wei Wei had strict instructions to stay nearby but Annie trusted her so little that she asked Madame Wing to look in on the child from time to time. Madame Wing had suggested an amah and Annie had thought about it. Did he need an amah, like he was some silly white child? He, who had lived such a life, a beggar child of the streets who had then lived alone with an old man for so many years? But here he was, in this big house and not in the grounds, surrounded by the other children.

She put it out of her mind for now and dressed. She had had the tailor make a dusky rose silk dress, which set off her skin, and had even paid a visit to the hairdresser. When Desmond called for her he whistled. Desmond looked elegant in his white suit. Charlie was going too with Nobby and many of the press corp. He had already left.

'We are quite handsome, I must say,' she said as she took his arm. She felt a certain excitement at this unusual outing.

As the car turned into the gates of Government House, however, she felt that sensation of deja vu wash over her. She had been here before. Who had been the Japanese occupant, she wondered.

The long drive was full of flame and the grand elegance of the house was enhanced by its position on the small knoll. A driver relieved Desmond of the car and they entered the hall. It was dominated by a gigantic Christmas tree made cleverly, as far as Annie could see, from bamboo. Portraits of the King and Queen stood on either side of it. An English soldier in a red coat and white gloves came forward to greet them and ushered them through to the garden where several hundred people were already gathered. The band on the verandah was quietly playing Christmas carols in the tropical night.

To the strains of 'God Rest Ye Merry Gentlemen', Desmond pointed out the important dignitaries, and the waiter offered them Champagne and orange soda. Annie saw the journalists huddled together like suspicious herds of wildebeest at the water hole. Desmond left her with them to speak to a group gathered around Sir Henry Gurney, the High Commissioner in Kuala Lumpur.

With Charlie and Nobby were Roy, Tom and four other correspondents from the English-language press. Charlie had brought along a beautiful young Chinese woman with a severe, straight-fringed haircut that made her look like a Twenties film star; she was clad in an alluring soft velvet and silk cheongsam of deep blue. She introduced herself as Yu Li, a freelance journalist who wrote for Japanese and Chinese magazines. Annie was almost sure Yu Li was the woman she had seen at the house.

They chatted for a time and then Desmond came over and whispered something to Charlie, who glanced at Yu Li and smiled. The two men wandered away. Annie and Yu Li sat at one of the tables scattered about the lawn. The natural sunlight had died away and the sparkle of electricity and flaming torches gave the garden a festive air.

'This is a lovely house. Have you been here before?'

'Actually I lived in this house during the war.'

Annie's mouth dropped open. Yu Li smiled.

'Everybody does that.'

'I'm sure. Tell me about it.'

Yu Li crossed her knees, showing her slim ankles and her fashionable high heels.

'Terauchi lived here,' Yu Li said and reached for another glass of Champagne from a passing waiter's tray. 'Count Hisaichi Terauchi, Supreme Commander, Southern Expeditionary Army. He's buried here in Singapore, did you know?'

Annie shook her head.

'Good heavens.'

'I'll tell you something stranger than that. The Japanese prisoners of war who remained here as labour for the years after the war, you know, they quietly collected the ashes of the 10,000 war dead, which were at the Chureito Memorial at Bukit Batok. It was blown up but those Japanese labourers got the ashes anyway. They brought them to the Japanese Cemetery in Hougang. Also brought the ashes of the Japanese executed in Changi and Malaysia for war crimes. The British have no idea because they don't read Japanese. The pillar says "A memorial to the ashes of 135 martyrs.""

Yu Li laughed.

'Japanese martyrs, those war criminals. How stupid the British are. They live amongst the honoured ashes of the Japanese who destroyed their empire and murdered their people and they don't even know.'

Annie found this statement outrageous and frankly almost unbelievable.

Yu Li waved her hand as if to dismiss it.

'Terauchi had a stroke when Japan lost Burma,' Yu Li said and laughed. 'Poor man. Then he surrendered to Mountbatten and died of a second stroke at a camp in Malaya.'

Annie sipped her Champagne, somewhat flabbergasted. Should she mention this to Desmond?

'How do you know so much about that time? How old were you?'

'Seventeen.'

Annie gazed at Yu Li. She hardly looked even twenty now.

'My father was Japanese. My mother is Chinese. She married him in Shanghai. When he died, she remarried, an English man who worked for Jardines. I went to an English school in Shanghai. When the Japanese took China, we came to Singapore.'

Her father was Japanese: this went someway to explaining this rather strange set of information she had.

'Do you remember him, your father?'

'Not at all. There is a picture of me with him. That's all.'

'What about during the Occupation?'

'My stepfather was sent to Japan as a prisoner of war. He did not survive.'

Yu Li's voice did not change as she said this. What did this woman feel about the death of her stepfather at the hands of the people of her real father? It was impossible to say. Yu Li didn't seem to feel anything but amusement.

'My mother became the mistress of General Seishiro, who was hanged in 1948. That's when we lived here. He lived here.'

'Good heavens.'

Annie didn't know what to say. There was a moment of silence then Yu Li burst out laughing. She had beautiful even white teeth and full red lips. Perhaps everything was so awful she could only cope with it by dismissing it.

Hardly daring to continue, Annie looked up towards Desmond and Charlie but the men were in intense conversation.

Annie sighed. In for a penny.

'Is your mother still living in Singapore?'

'No, we were taken to Tokyo after the war. She was a sort of witness at the Tokyo war-trials. She married an old American general and lives in San Francisco. My mother likes men and money.'

All the facts of Yu Li's life were extraordinary but she related them with a deadpan delivery as if discussing someone else.

Annie put her glass down and suddenly saw Beaver. He was standing to one side, staring intently at them both. She gazed back at him. He turned and walked away.

Charlie and Desmond wandered back to them and Yu Li swayed into Charlie. Annie saw how Charlie ran his arm possessively around Yu Li's waist and gripped her to him.

He's in love with her, Annie thought. Madly in love.

Desmond slipped his hand into hers.

'The governor's about to do his loyal toast and little speech before dinner. Shall we go inside?'

They joined the crowd heading slowly into the house.

'I saw you talking to Yu Li Cavanagh?' he said.

'Cavanagh, is that her last name? How British. With such oriental looks. It suits her extraordinary life.'

Annie looked up at Desmond. 'She told me something very strange.'

'She's a strange woman, and an untrustworthy and dangerous one.'

'Oh?' said Annie, her brow furrowing slightly.

'Yes. You can't believe anything she says. She's full of lies and has fingers in lots of different pies. Some say she's red, as Maoist as the Chairman. Special Branch keeps an eye on her.'

Annie looked at the swaying figure of red Yu Li in her blue velvet dress. Was everything Yu Li had just told her a pack of lies? It hardly seemed possible.

'Does Charlie know she's so untrustworthy?'

'Of course he does. He just chooses to ignore it.'

Desmond drew her to one side and the guests moved passed them.

'I didn't tell you before but the beating Charlie took, Beaver thinks it was a triad thing. Nothing to do with Tan. Yu Li mixes it up with everyone and I think she's borderline delusional. Thinks she's Mata Hari. She's supposed to be the occasional mistress of

Yang Chu Wei, a triad boss here.'

'Does Charlie know that?'

'He does now. He should drop her but perhaps he thinks he'll get an interview with Chin Peng or something, through her. I don't know.'

'Maybe he's just fascinated with her.'

Desmond smiled grimly. 'Yes, I'm afraid so. Men are. Let's hope it won't be for too long.'

Annie frowned. It sounded like Charlie really was in some danger.

They joined the stragglers.

'Sorry to be so serious,' Desmond said quietly.

'It's all right. Better to know these things. I was going to try to see something more of her myself. She's so interesting.'

Desmond stopped walking and gripped her hand.

'It's all right,' she assured him.

'I'm serious, Annie.'

'I know. It's all right.'

'You understand that seeing her means Special Branch will be all over you.'

Annie grew momentarily tetchy but it melted away in the face of Desmond's concern. She changed the subject.

'When shall I come over to talk about Joseph?'

Desmond was visibly relieved.

'Next week. We shall need, if humanly possible, a copy of his birth certificate. But that's probably impossible. Still any paperwork is good. You said he was in the care of the sisters at the Convent of the Holy Infant. Do you think he was baptised?

Could you find out?'

Annie nodded. A first step in making Joseph hers.

The band starting playing 'God Save the King' as they passed into the house.

25

'Hearing of the appeal against Mr Justice Brown's refusal to grant a stay of his order returning Maria Hertogh to the custody of her parents will come up before the full Court of Appeal on Monday.'

The Straits Times, 9 December 1950

Annie had no chance to speak to Charlie over the next few days. He did not return home that night or the one after. She called his office.

'Bit busy at the mo. See you when I see you,' he said and rang off.

That he was totally involved in the Hertogh story she did not doubt. The reporters were invited every day to camp out at the convent in Thomson Road and take pictures of Maria with the Mother Superior, of Maria playing the piano, of Maria with Adeline. There was a report of Maria kneeling to the Virgin Mary that threw the Muslim community into paroxysms but no pictures were taken and it seemed it was false after all. In addition she knew that dozens of reporters from Holland and all over the region had arrived for the verdict of the appeal.

At night she did not know where Charlie was but she could guess. She put that matter to one side.

Tomorrow she was to meet with Eileen Tan and today she had an appointment with the Mother Superior of the Convent of the Holy Infant Jesus.

She did not immediately ring at the convent's main gate. She went first to the Gate of Hope, the door where unwanted babies were left. This was where Joseph had been placed by a despairing mother. What had been her thoughts as she had left the child, swaddled in a sarong, on the forbidding doorstep of an alien religion? Only absolute despair could have driven her to it.

Annie walked back along the wall and rang at the gate. She was admitted and asked to wait. It was a hot day and she sought the shade of the gothic chapel. As she stepped out of the daylight she was, for a moment, stunned by the hushed air and muted light that greeted her inside. It was as if she had stepped into an undersea cloister. The narrow stained-glass windows were dark from dirt and age, many of them cracked. The war had left its marks here too as everywhere. This patina of age and battle, to her mind, simply enhanced their beauty and cast a peaceful light on the pews below. She sat in the mute glow and gazed at the beatific faces of Mary and Joseph contemplating their child in the crib, and she thought of all the shattered hearts and scattered dreams that the war had made.

She had never believed in this God. The sisters had crushed that belief out of her. But now the thought came that, even with the horror of the war, she had been unable, honestly, to give up the idea of the god that could be found in the innate goodness of most human beings. The human divine, she supposed, which she found more fully expressed in Buddhism, though she found that philosophy both uplifting and gloomy in equal measure. Only sitting here in the chapel could have inspired such an unlikely train of thought. She was not often given to existential musings.

'Madame Collins.'

She rose and greeted the Mother Superior, a Frenchwoman who possessed the weathered face of a Christian soldier and had spent years in the harshness of country missionary work. They walked without a word to the lounge in Caldwell House, the sisters' quarters. Annie had explained her situation in the letter she had written to the Mother Superior. Annie's eyes were drawn to the words on the circular wall, 'Marches en ma presence et sois parfait'. Be perfect? Was it possible, even if you were convinced you were in His presence?

They sat in the lounging chairs and the Mother Superior took up from the low table what Annie recognised as her letter. She seemed a woman of few words and great efficiency as befitted her role in a life spent amongst the destitute and poor. And perhaps amongst quarrelling women, Annie thought. The sisters at the Ipoh convent had not been all sisterly love; their arguments and bad tempers were well known and the cause of much secret girlie gossip.

'According to the information you gave us, the baby who became Joseph was possibly left at the Gate of Hope some time in 1941, certainly not later than the surrender in February 1942. Is that correct?'

'I surmise. Is it possible he could have been left later than

February 1942, after the Occupation?'

'Perfectly possible. I have made enquiries of the Chinese and Malay sisters who were here during that time. Hundreds of babies were taken in during the Occupation. It was fortunate that the Japanese, believe it or not, were quite generous in their rations to the convent. What strange people they are.'

'Yes. As you say. Is it impossible then to find him?'

'No, indeed not. Very few boy babies are left at the convent. The majority are girls. This year we have had a vast number of Chinese girls. It is the year of the Tiger, as the Chinese term it, and girls born in that year are considered bold and difficult, or so I understand. To give up a child on such a pretext. Such superstition.'

The Mother Superior's face expressed her disapproval. Annie looked at the pictures of the saints and at the religious relics on the wall around her and refrained from expressing her thoughts on superstitions to the good Mother.

'The boy is less quickly given up in Asian societies, as you may know, and usually only when they are extremely sick or crippled in some way.'

She took up the paper on her desk.

'However, I want to be quite sure of what we are talking about. According to our records in 1941 no boy was left at the gate. However in January 1942, a boy aged one month was taken in. No child was taken in for several months after that. The war would have unsettled everything. The European sisters were interned. Another boy was left here in August of 1942 and then another boy in November. That is all for that year. Three baby boys in 1942.'

The Mother Superior looked up at Annie.

'Older boys came in, you understand, young children, toddlers. But no babies corresponding in age to the child you mention, a child born in 1942.'

She put the paper back on the table.

'Madame, the child you are caring for, is he a sound child? I mean sound of limb and healthy in every way, his eyes, his hearing?'

'Yes. Of course he has tuberculosis now. He caught it from his guardian. But otherwise he is healthy. Quite normal.'

The Mother Superior sighed and rose.

'Will you have some refreshment, Madame Collins?'

'Thank you, no.'

'I shall order tea nevertheless.'

Annie sat turning back the fingers of her gloves. She could not imagine what could possibly be the problem, but she got the distinct impression that there was a problem. When the Mother Superior returned with a young nun bearing a tray, she spoke up quickly.

'Is there some kind of problem?'

'There is possibly a ... complication.'

The Mother Superior put up her finger to hush Annie and waited until the door had been closed.

'I want to explain to you everything very clearly so you may be sure of what I say.'

Annie nodded. The woman seemed serious minded and careful, Annie thought. She kept her tongue and accepted a cup of tea.

'Only one of the babies in 1942 was baptised Joseph. His age was established by the physician who examined him. Our records are clear. He was a healthy baby boy, a little thin but otherwise normal. He had some superficial shrapnel wounds and was covered in blood, which had looked alarming but was not fatal. After that there are two other boys baptised Joseph, a boy of a year or so who came to us in 1943, very sick. He, God bless his soul, he died. The other boy baptised Joseph was two when he had been left here in 1944 and he was deaf.'

Annie finished her tea and put down the cup. She knew instantly. The marks she had seen on Joseph's skin were shrapnel marks.

'So, this baby in 1942, this boy must be Joseph. Is that what you're saying?'

'Yes.'

'Well that's wonderful. I can get a copy of his baptismal certificate.'

Why on earth was this woman being so long-winded, Annie thought.

'Yes, you can, but there is something else before you can take ... before we can take that step.'

'Well?'

'The boy came with a letter.'

'A letter?'

'Yes. Amongst his clothes there was a note. In Malay.'

Annie felt dryness in her throat and swallowed hard.

'From the mother?'

'From the father.'

'I see.'

'Yes. I have had it translated into English.'

The Mother Superior took an envelope from her desk and held it in her hand.

'Madame Collins, do not read this letter here. Go home and read it quietly and think about what it says. If, after you have read it, you wish to come back and talk to me, my door is always open.'

The Mother Superior rose.

'God Bless you, my dear.'

Annie stood outside the gates and stared at the envelope. She could not go home. She could not wait that long. She walked quickly along Victoria Street and into Bras Basah, heading for the Raffles Hotel. Once inside she selected a big wicker chair in the shady inner courtyard. It was only two o'clock but she ordered a gin and tonic.

When it came, the ice cubes clinking against the glass, she gulped down half of it. Then she opened the envelope.

26

'If saner counsels do not prevail, we are ready for stronger doses of Cold War mixture. You know how the German Nazis were defeated by the Russian winter. Our pen can become sharper than the sword. Enough organisation exists in the framework of the Islamic Brotherhood to deal with any situation that may arise.'

Open letter to the police by Karim Ghani, Muslim leader, Editor of *Dawn, Sinaran, Melayu Raya*, 11 December 1950

Annie was glad to get back to the house on Peirce Road. It had begun to feel like home now that Joseph was back and healthy. She wished that Charlie was there too but the Hertogh hearing was due to start any time soon and she knew he would not return until it was over, if then.

The contents of the note required action on her part but she had no wish to speak of it to anyone as yet. Madame Wing came out to greet her and pointed out a letter on the hall table. Annie smiled and thanked her, hardly hearing the words she spoke, and went in search of Joseph.

He was helping in the vegetable garden with the other

children. She heard his voice raised in laughter and Malay chatter and merely stood, watching him from the upper verandah. She did not want him to see her and run to her. His health had improved and his skin flashed golden brown as he and the others wandered along the rows of beans and tomatoes. She saw Yellow lying under a flowering cassod tree, his head on his paws, fast asleep. She stood painting the peaceful happiness of this scene onto her mind until Madame Wing came and asked about some domestic issue and broke her reverie.

She wandered down the staircase to the hall and took up the letter. The name on its back said 'Jean Morrison' and Annie could not place it. She sat on the verandah and threw off her shoes, curling into the chair. The fan turned noiselessly overhead and the crickets buzzed to a crescendo in the shrubberies. The clink of ice and glass sounded and Annie saw Ting place a tray with a jug of iced lime juice beside her. She smiled at him. The thought of him and all these people and what would become of them after she left had begun to enter her thoughts. Ting was a hard-working young man who had the care of his mother and his wayward sister. She wanted to do something for him but she had no idea what. She sipped the cold lime juice and put her head against the back of the chair.

She opened the letter and began to read, realising quickly it was from Jean Barker.

Dear Annie,

Maria has spoken to me of your search for your past. I consider this journey of yours a serious undertaking and I have taken some time to write to you as I wished to gather my recollections carefully.

It has, of course, been some time since I thought of my life in Singapore at all, either before the war or during the Occupation. When the British troops returned I met my husband, Doctor Keith Morrison, a captain in the army. We married in 1946. We came to England in 1948, a foreign country for me, full of coldness and austerity, and it has taken me a certain time to settle in to the life of a country doctor's wife. There is still rationing and the food is bland and joyless. I admit to longing many times silently for Malaya, the home of my birth and a happy childhood, the place of my marriages and the grave of my first, still remembered, husband. Despite the darkness that fell on us all, Malaya remains like sunlight in my heart.

We have two children. I am grateful, every day, that we all survived that time but when I watch my children I am sometimes reminded of those youngsters who grew up in internment. Perhaps it is a lack of patience on my part. Almost certainly a fault in my motherly instincts. I know it is not charitable, but my most vivid memory of those prison children is resentment. Their incessant shrill screaming and noise, their constant to-ings and fro-ings, their feet clattering on the iron steps or the concrete floors. They made the women's prison something of a nightmare, like living in a very dirty and woeful kindergarten day in and day out, with no escape.

I'm know you cannot know all this but we talked a great deal of it at that time and my words might help jog your memory to speak a little of that life.

Annie, it is a strange thing to say perhaps, but it is only now, with the knowledge of the absolute horror of those camps at Belsen and Buchenwald, that I can look upon Changi as something of a heaven in comparison.

We, the women and children, confined in such conditions for so long, were petty and fractious and argumentative, the severe lack of food and space made clashes over an inch of ground and a piece of pineapple almost inevitable. The noise, the heat, the dust, the runny dampness of the concrete, the rain, sickness, the gaps of all types that lay between us, the feelings of hopelessness. All these contributed to varying degrees. The Japanese on their side, with their drunkenness, their aggression and petty tempers, made life annoying and difficult, but they largely left us to get on with everything ourselves, some of them occasionally even displaying behaviour that was decent and humane in a way that no woman or child in Belsen could ever have experienced. I don't thank them for any of it, but it still makes me shiver, even now, to think of what we might have had to endure instead.

Everything became much worse after what we now know as the Double Tenth, when the Kempeitai took over the running of the goal. This was when we had the pleasure of meeting Tominaga, a man of great coldness and cruelty. Women and men were arrested and taken away. Many did not return and we saw some women, including Dr Williams, only after months, when they returned in appalling condition. Increasing numbers were coming into Changi at that time. The population of children doubled yet all privileges were refused. Food became very bad. School was not permitted for the children, nor was exercise in the yards. I think we should all have utterly perished but for the decision to move all civilians to Sime Road Camp in May 1944.

As you now know, you came into Sime Road Camp in June 1945, almost a year after we had been moved there. The camp had been a British military camp but was used by the Japanese as a transit camp for POWs returned from Siam. It was our first news of what happened to those men. There were hundreds of messages scrawled on the walls. You may remember them. 'B force went up 2000 strong, returned 600,' 'Death caused by beri beri, typhus, dysentery, malaria, starvation.' Messages about the living and the dead that had filled us with horror. We had no idea of the death toll. We made a list of the names, you may remember, and circulated it around the camp, which was terribly dangerous of course for us and for those POWs who were still alive but a record had to be made.

Annie looked up from the letter and drank the rest of the lime juice. Now that Jean spoke of it, she did remember those messages and names and something of the Sime Road camp. This had been Ronald's fate. Those scrawled messages on the walls recorded the horrors he had endured until he too had perished, breathing his last in the heat and mud of that filthy place. She had never understood how he had died and her heart, so filled with loathing for him for so long, flooded now with waves of pity. His body had never been found. His bones had sunk, like thousands around him, into the dank earth. She thought of Mabel and her grief at his death. A grief she had not felt and thought she never could. She waited, watching the butterflies beneath the window, until she could return to the letter.

It was on the outskirts of the city near the MacRitchie Reservoir and a golf course. Fresh air, open space, so much green after the grey walls and the screaming confines of prison. There were those kajang huts and, here and there, the graves of the poor POWs who had died and been buried. One woman found her husband's name on a cross, the first and only indication of his fate. It was a terrible thing.

The hospital hut is where you came. It stood on a hillside. It was always cramped but under those conditions and when the men had built us some decent toilets, it was, I suppose sufficient. You already know from Maria about how you came into the camp and about your treatment there.

What you don't know about is the attitude to Eurasian women, which more or less began when we moved to Sime Road. Can you remember that the Japanese guards, who had been kept under control in Changi, simply started wandering around the women's quarters as and when they liked? They consorted freely with the young Eurasian girls. It was said that they didn't find European women attractive but I believe that there were European girls who were 'visited' as well, though the British women would not have it. These girls shared the huts with the other internees and the Japanese men came to them there, day and night, without any regard for the other inhabitants. Can you remember any of this?

Eventually they built the 'White House,' where they kept these girls. There were drunken fights over these women too and many of the English women considered all us Eurasians as potential spies and harlots, despite the fact that most of us took no part in such goings on. For many, you know, it was simply better food and accommodations that drove them. But of course it created resentments.

So Eurasian women who came in late in the Occupation were thought to have done the most dreadful things outside, whether they had done so or not. The truth never mattered much once gossip got going. The already scarce food and space would go a little thinner – that was the bottom of it. Maria and I, actually Eurasian women in general (considered 'easy' and lacking in the true morals of the white woman) had to face this when we came in. We were fallen women, in and out of the beds of the Japanese or Chinese men, living high on the hog. It didn't matter that sweet, blameless Maria had lost her brother and spent months of horror in the hands of the Kempeitai, or that I had endured much the same.

Fortunately, you were not in the least aware of all this at the time, but you may recall it having happened later, when you were up and about. Dr Worth and Dr Williams took very good care of you and the nurses did a wonderful job. On the whole, the fresh air and greenery did all of us a power of good and our life in Sime Road was marginally better than Changi.

Which brings me to one evening, not long after you came in. The Japanese from time to time both in Changi and Sime Road invited visiting dignitaries to 'view' us women, in what we called Zoo Visits. Really it was a pointless parade to show us all off, especially the Englishwomen of course. The almighty British, how they are fallen, that sort of thing. Also there were constant impromptu visits at any time by the guards with their flashlights looking at us, usually drunk. It all added to the feelings of stress and insecurity.

At Sime Road the same sort of thing went on, especially with the guards wandering in and out of the huts at night on any whim. I happened to be on duty at the hospital just after rounds and before sundown about a week after you arrived and saw one of the guards, whom we nicknamed Acid Drop, a pernickety man but not totally vicious, and another man come into the hut. I jumped to my feet, of course, to bow. Not bowing, you will remember, always occasioned a slap or worse. The women really never did bow satisfactorily as I remember, which put the head of the internees, the sour and hateful Tominaga, into a temper. He was hanged after the war, for which hurrah!

Acid Drop ignored me and looked along the row of patients and pointed to you. You were in the middle of the row. The dusk was practically over and the night was coming in. The man knelt by your side and put his hand on your arm. I became alarmed and even dared to speak to Acid Drop, who simply turned and told me to shut up.

I thought he was going to slap me but I didn't care. I had decided to start to scream blue murder when suddenly they both left abruptly. I ran to you and you were perfectly all right, sleeping quietly. The man had placed a flower on your pillow. It was most extraordinary. It was a white orchid, like the ones that grow so tremendously all over Malaya.

I don't want to shock you but I have to tell you that the man was dressed in the uniform of the Kempeitai, with the white arm band. I threw the flower away. That a Kempeitai officer should come and give you a flower seemed beyond belief. I never told the commandant.

The odd thing was that for a week after that we received our full Red Cross parcels, all of us. Usually they never got through, their contents diverted to the Japs, and so this was a very big thing. Just to have tins of food with English names was such a boost to morale. No one could account for it at the time, but it occasionally happened, on the Emperor's birthday or celebrations of the Fall of Singapore, that sort of thing. I wonder now if it was because of that man who came to see you, but I can't be sure of it.

That is all I can tell you. I did not speak of this to you at that time because you were generally not in a state for such information and also because a visit by a Kempeitai officer would have been confirmation of what many of the women in prison had already assumed. That you had been a collaborator and a whore. I can offer no consolation except to say that I believe that the man who came to see you cared for you and wanted to see if you were well. I can't otherwise understand why he would have done what he did.

I cannot add anything useful to this account except to say, as Judy Garland used to tell us, Chin Up! Cheerio! Carry on! Easy for her to say, wasn't it.

Good luck with your search and your future life. Please write to me if you care to. I would love to hear from you.

Yours most warmly,

Jean

Annie reread the last paragraphs. An orchid. He had come to see if she was all right and had placed an orchid on her pillow. A man who was a Kempeitai officer. That was the man whom she had adored, who had then tried to kill her. The man she had loved. She could not believe it. She rejected it utterly. She could almost entirely see his face now. He was handsome with his dark hair falling on his forehead like a boy. A Kempeitai officer. This fact stuck in her throat and she felt sick.

She rose and walked to the edge of the verandah and sought Joseph but the boys had disappeared somewhere. She folded the letter and put it back inside the envelope. She did not want to think about this anymore. She went downstairs to call Joseph inside.

27

'If the police want, I can arrange, Inshallah, to give you thirty-three Natras to control any Muslim crowd, provided each Natra is armed with a Quran. Natras are enough to tackle a Muslim mob. The police pistols are for the Gog and Magog.'

Open letter to the police by Karim Ghani, Muslim leader,
Editor of *Dawn, Sinaran, Melayu Raya*, 11 December 1950

Mahmoud smiled as she came out of the doors. He had finally forgiven her for her transgressions with the policeman.

'Good day, Mahmoud,' she said, smiling back.

'Mrs Annie,' he said, and bowed slightly.

She told him the address, located on the North Bridge Road near Arab Street, and sat back.

Yet again Charlie had not come home and Desmond, too, was away from Singapore. His office had politely declined to say where he was or when he would be back.

She looked at the back of Mahmoud's head and noticed how the folds of his turban were so perfectly aligned. She briefly wondered how long his hair was. She knew the Sikhs didn't cut their hair but wasn't quite sure why. How beautiful it must be for his wife to admire it, knowing it was for her eyes alone.

She took the sheet of typewritten paper from her handbag and read it for the fortieth time.

This child is Hari, one belonging to God. He is my son. His mother is dead. Because I am Indian and she is Malay our families cursed us and here is the end of this curse. She is dead and this boy is hurt by the bombs and soon I will die on the battlefield. So be it. God forgive me. I will not leave him with anyone who will despise him. I have no choice but to leave him here. Please care for him and raise him to be a good child, loving god. I have to go. I have to fight. If I live I will come back. Harnam Singh.

Harnam Singh. A Sikh. Joseph was like her more than she knew. A little half-blood child, loved by his father and his dead mother but despised by their families. What foolishness it all was. Had it been the same with her? Her own mother and father dead, and the grandparents, ashamed, had dropped her at the Gate of Hope.

She gazed out of the window.

If this note had been all there was in the envelope she might, possibly, have been able to ignore it. The mother was dead and possibly the father too. But there had been an additional sheet and on it, also typed, was an addendum.

2 January 1947: A Sikh man named Harnam Singh came today enquiring after Joseph, the son he calls Hari, left at the Gate

of Hope in January of 1942. After enquiries were made we could
not find this boy and the father departed in great distress. Mother
Superior and the sisters can only imagine that either the child died
unrecorded, ran away or was taken away during the turmoil of
the post-war period. There is no one here who can remember. It
troubles my soul that we have failed in our duty of care to this
child. God forgive us.

5 January 1947: Harnam Singh returned and left his address
in case of any news of the boy. God bless him and care for him
and his son.

Sister Immaculata

Annie looked at the address, located in Serangoon Road.
She didn't know if Harnam Singh was still at this address but
she knew she had to find out. The car came to a halt. Mahmoud
opened her door.

Eileen Tan's car pulled to a halt behind them and Annie
waited for Eileen to get out of the car. Annie watched as Eileen's
driver ran quickly round to her door and opened it. She got out
slowly, adjusted her walking stick and looked at Annie.

Annie went to her side.

'Can I help you?'

'No, thank you. My friend's apartment is just down there.
Not far.'

She dismissed her driver who pulled away smartly and the
two women began to walk towards the building where her friend
lived.

A roar went up in the distance and Annie glanced towards

it and saw a crowd of men surge round the corner. Mahmoud looked up. He had not moved and Annie looked at him as they passed.

'It's all right, Mahmoud. I'll get a taxi home. Thank you.'

At that instant the roar of the crowd rose and a hail of bottles crashed onto the ground and splintered a few yards away. Both Annie and Eileen turned in alarm. Flames flew up from a parked car. The crowd suddenly and alarmingly swelled like a dark balloon filled with air and began moving down the street as if carried on a wave of water. Banners and flags waved wildly and the burning car exploded in a great boom and shot sparks into the air and began raging. The crowd pounded every car they passed with their sticks and hacked at them with long parangs.

'What is it, Mahmoud?' Annie said, not understanding.

Another crowd of men came from the other side, appearing suddenly in a riot of screaming and boiling anger. A rain of stones came down onto them, one striking Eileen on the shoulder. She cried out and staggered. Mahmoud caught her.

'Get in the car, Mrs Annie. Quick.'

The crowd was surging from both sides. A European man stopped his car and got out, remonstrating with the crowd, bellowing foolishly. Men wielding parangs and long sticks fell on him. The sound of bursting glass came like shots and was followed by the screams of a woman. She was dragged from the car and surrounded. Annie cried out and helped Mahmoud with Eileen. She shut the door and screamed at Mahmoud.

'Get in, get in. Hurry.'

Mahmoud slammed his door shut and started the car but

before he could move the car was engulfed, locked between walls of white shirts, bare chests and wildly gesticulating brown arms. With the windows rolled up it was steamily suffocating, and sweat rolled off them. Annie's heart pounded. Faces peered inside, comically insane, shouting and screaming, their voices rising to a fever pitch. Spittle oozed down the glass. Clubs began beating on the roof of the car like jungle drums. Hands grappled with the handles of the door, desperate to get to the inhabitants. Then a long stick crashed through the windscreen. Distorted faces of fury peered in, their mouths working in anger. Perhaps they saw Mahmoud and his turban. Perhaps they did not see the two women crouched on the back seat. The mob rolled away and Annie caught a glimpse of men hacking at another European man who had been foolish enough to get out of his car. He fell, clubbed into the swirling mass of brown bodies and faces as if swept down into a whirlpool.

A new mob then descended on them, and bricks landed on the car and cracked the windows. Mahmoud engaged gears and began to move forward. Thumping on the roof began again, and legs began to swarm all over the car. A foot shoved into the broken windscreen and a high scream was heard as the glass caught it. It disappeared, pulled away in a stream of blood. Then the rocking began. The car was shoved from side to side but it was heavy and the rocking suddenly stopped. Despite the heat, Annie felt a shot of intense cold pass through her body. She knew absolutely that if they didn't get away immediately they would all be killed. Eileen lay huddled in the corner, her face white. Annie screamed, terrified.

Her scream seemed to galvanise Mahmoud. He revved the engine loudly and jerked forward. The bodies slipped off the car and the shouting was mingled with screams. Mahmoud put the car in reverse. He jerked backwards quickly and men scrambled to get out of the way. Perhaps some of them had lost their courage at the thought of being mown down or had decided to search for other prey, but the mob relented. As the crowd thinned, Annie saw, to her shock, two Malay policemen watching it all, unmoving, the whites of their eyes unwavering.

A car, trapped like theirs had been a moment before, burst into flames and she heard the screams of the occupants.

Mahmoud screeched the car into gear and roared away. Annie fell sideways on the seat, sobbing with relief. Mahmoud punched out the broken glass of the windscreen with his arm.

'It's all right, Mrs Annie. It's all right.' Mahmoud's voice was soothing, rocking. She closed her eyes and felt the rush of air through the broken windscreen.

The car suddenly careered sideways as a stick flew in through the side window like a spear and almost caught Mahmoud on the head. Annie screamed again. Mahmoud fought to bring the car under control and the brakes screeched but he could not prevent the car from careering into another. A shower of stones clattered down on the roof and Annie smelt petrol. There was a burst of orange and flames began to lick the front of the car.

'Oh my God,' Annie screamed.

A rock came through the window, catching her temple and she collapsed and fell to one side. Everything went black.

28

'The violent incidents that have taken place in the Colony
today have no support from devout Muslims. I appeal to all
Muslims to refrain from violence and to assist the authorities
in restoring and maintaining the peace that we all as merchants
and workers depend on for our livelihood.'

Radio broadcast by the Chief Kadi of the Colony,
Haji Ali bin Haji Saleh, on Radio Malaya, 11 December 1950

Waves and wind. And sudden cries of seagulls. She heard
them from a great distance, reverberating inside her head
as if she were lying on the sand at the beach.

'Annie.'

Her name came up from the bottom of a deep well.

'Can you hear me?'

The voice grew louder, the mist rolled away and she opened
her eyes. She looked up into the face of Eileen Tan.

'Thank God, Annie.'

Eileen was pale as tissue paper. Annie tried to move her head
but it felt as heavy as a boulder.

'Don't move. We're all right. Inside a house.'

'How ...'

The act of speaking was painful. She stopped.

'Ssh, don't speak. We are inside a house. Mahmoud brought us here. He is safe too but has some burns.'

Eileen moved away for a moment and Mahmoud's face appeared in front of Annie's eyes.

'I'm all right, Mrs Annie.'

Annie tried to smile but it was too hard. Eileen returned.

'Rest now. We're safe here inside. You've got a cut on your forehead but we've bandaged it. The town's gone mad. I've telephoned my husband. He'll come and get us when he can.'

Annie closed her eyes.

When she opened them again her head was splitting with pain. She moved her neck which, this time, responded, and saw Eileen sitting at a table. She was coughing. A Chinese woman by her side was eyeing her anxiously.

'Eileen,' she said and the woman next to Eileen got up and came to her and said something soothing in Chinese.

Eileen broke out in a paroxysm of coughing. The telephone rang and the Chinese woman got up quickly. Mahmoud appeared out of nowhere.

'Oh, Mahmoud. Help me sit up please.'

Mahmoud looked doubtful but nevertheless placed an arm under her and lifted her to a sitting position. She touched the bandage on her head.

'Do you think there's an aspirin in the house?' she said and he disappeared in the direction the Chinese woman had gone.

She realised she was in the upper storey of a shophouse. Somewhere outside she could still hear shouting and the waves of crowds passing by. An ambulance sounded in the distance. Mahmoud returned with a glass of water and a powder of some sort, which she took. It tasted bitter and she looked at him.

'Chinese medicine. This is a traditional medicine shop.'

As he said this a tall middle-aged Chinese man appeared.

'I am Wee. You take this,' he said, pointing to the powder. 'Feel better. Your head is OK.'

His wife came to his side, carrying a tray with Chinese cups and a tea pot. She put it down and poured some tea into a cup. Hot, green Chinese tea.

Annie drank it gratefully. It was fragrant and the hotness felt good on her throat.

'What's happening?'

Doctor Wee sat opposite her.

'Rioting at Sultan Mosque. Police are out but too many people, too much trouble.'

'Why?'

'The court case,' Mahmoud said and she looked at him. His hands were bandaged. She frowned.

'What happened, Mahmoud?'

It was Doctor Wee who answered.

'Burns. But not serious. I have put ointment. He bring you here to this house, from the burning car. Look.'

He rose and helped Annie to her feet. He pushed back the shutter and she saw the old Ford lying twisted into another car, smouldering, about a hundred yards away. The police were nowhere to be seen. The crowd completely controlled the street. If anything there were more people than before. The doctor quickly closed the shutters.

'You stay here tonight. Cannot go home.'

She nodded. 'Thank you,' she said, and he smiled.

She went to Eileen and saw blood on the cloth Eileen was holding to her mouth. She stared, dismayed, but Eileen just waved her hand a little.

'I'm all right. We can't leave anyway. Christopher says he can't get down here just yet. The police have barricades up. He's sending an ambulance but it looks a bit hopeless right now.'

For the next hours the rioting raged in the streets around them. The radio reported that the violence had become widespread. From Tanglin to Geylang. Nobody should leave their homes. The police were trying to bring things under control. Rioters had set up their own barricades at North Bridge Road, Victoria Street, Beach Road, Jalan Besar and Sultan Mosque. At least two journalists and several civilians had been either killed or injured. Details were yet to come in. Military vehicles had been attacked and set alight.

Annie's heart twisted and she looked at Mahmoud. Charlie, Nobby, the others, they had been in the thick of the rioters outside the court.

'Do you think Charlie's all right?' she said to Mahmoud. 'And the others?'

'I think so. I hope so.'

'Should we call his office?'

'I will try.'

Mahmoud came back a moment later.

'No answer. The Reuters office says the reporters are still out.'

The Chinese doctor treated Eileen with some traditional medicine and, to Annie's relief, the coughing and blood stopped. He led Eileen to his son's bedroom and Annie went along and waited until Eileen fell asleep. His son, the doctor told her, was at school. He had received a telephone call and warned the boy not to come home. He would spend the night with a friend.

It was now clear that they would all be staying here. The Chinese doctor and his wife prepared a simple meal then laid out some bedding. Mahmoud called his wife and made sure they were safe. Annie spoke to Madame Wing and told her to make sure the gates were shut and locked and everyone stayed inside. It was calm, Madame Wing told her, around their streets but that was no surprise. It was clear that the frenzy was in the town and more and more Muslims were joining the rioters.

They all settled down for the night and Annie had never been more grateful to be safely inside a building. The sounds from outside were ferocious, of crashing glass, of intermittent gunfire and of screams of 'Allahu Akbar.' The doctor had locked down the shutters of his shop but, he told her, the rioters were largely, he felt, interested in attacking Europeans and Eurasians. He had seen the mob stopping buses and taxis and searching for Europeans to attack. She and Mrs Tan must not go outside at all until they could safely go home. The night was punctuated with the sound of breaking glass and hysterical yells. Only when the sun appeared did the sounds die away.

At seven o'clock, Eileen's husband turned up with an ambulance and his eyes showed his surprise and displeasure at seeing Annie. However, he said not a word. He helped his wife downstairs and thanked the doctor. When Eileen was in the ambulance he turned to his driver.

'Take them home and come back for me.'

The driver nodded. Tan, without a further look in her direction, got into the ambulance with his wife. Eileen turned her eyes to Annie's but the doors shut and the ambulance drove away, threading its way through a street littered with rocks and broken, burned-out cars.

Annie and Mahmoud thanked the doctor and his wife and got into Tan's car. As they rode down Orchard Road they saw that Cold Storage, the bastion of European shopping, had been transformed into a burnt-out smoking shell. A police patrol stopped them and ordered them home. A curfew was being imposed. No one was to be on the streets.

Tan's driver dropped them and sped away. Mahmoud refused any food. Annie begged him to stay but he refused and rode away on his bicycle. She watched him go. He was worried for his family.

'Shut the gates,' she ordered, 'and don't let anyone in or out.'

She turned to Madame Wing who was standing calmly to one side.

'Is Mr Ransome home?'

'No. No one came home last night. Are you all right, Mrs Collins?'

'Yes, thank you. A rock. It's nothing. Could I have a cup of tea, do you think?'

She went to the phone and called *Reuters* but the man in the office had no idea. All the reporters were still out.

She went to her room and took off the bandage. The wound was deep. Dr Wee had put in three stitches. She cleaned it gingerly with some Dettol and put a fresh bandage around it then went to the verandah for the tea.

'Where's Joseph?' she asked Madame Wing.

'With Fatimah. He wanted to stay with her boys and I thought it would be all right.'

Annie waved a hand. 'Yes, yes, it's best. Has he had his medicine?'

'He's had breakfast and his medicine. He's all right. Shall I fetch him?'

'No,' Annie said wearily. 'I need to rest a little. Later.'

She looked at the stoical face of the woman opposite her.

'Is your family all right?'

'Yes, there were no disturbances where we live. It's localised, I believe. The army has taken over. It was on the news. I believe there is a curfew. You were fortunate to get home.'

Annie put her head back on to the cushions. She was fortunate to get home but what had happened to Charlie?

29

One cup of tea. His name. It means one cup of tea.

Annie tossed from side to side. Her head hurt and she woke twice and took an aspirin, then returned to troubled sleep. The voice came from inside her dreams.

One cup of tea.

What did it mean? She searched until her mind ceased its turmoil and she drifted away.

She woke to a knock at her door. She raised her head gingerly from the pillow.

'Yes?'

'Mr Ransome on the phone, Mrs Collins.'

She got up, a wave of relief washing over her

'Tell him I'm coming.'

She picked her way downstairs, holding her head erect. The bruising extended all down one side of her face.

'Charlie?'

'Annie, it's me.'

'Oh, thank God.'

She burst into tears and obviously filled Charlie with alarm. He made soothing noises.

'My word, Annie. It's all right. Don't cry. I'm all right.'

She wasn't crying only for Charlie, she knew, but for herself and the night she had endured. She stopped crying and wiped her nose.

'Where are you?'

'At the hospital. The AP man, Tom, has been badly injured.'

'Nobby, the others?'

'All right. Everyone else is OK. We got into the Cricket Club but Tom got the first fury of it at the court. He was mobbed and by the time the tear gas and the Gurkhas had split up them up he was on the ground. It was crazy. Majid came out and tried to speak to the crowd, to tell them that the decision had actually been postponed but the crowd wouldn't hear it. They presumed they'd lost and Karim Ghani was pumping up the rhetoric.'

Annie suddenly felt angry at Charlie.

'Where've you been? I haven't seen you for days.'

There was a silence at the other end of the phone. She had sounded like a shrewish wife. She didn't care. She'd had enough of it all.

'Mahmoud and I got caught up in the rioting at North Bridge Road. Mahmoud was burned saving me and Eileen Tan, and I got a rock in the head. Your car's burnt to a crisp.'

'My God, Annie. I'm sorry. Are you OK now?'

'Yes. Are you coming back?'

She was suddenly impatient with him and his news nose and boyish desires for glory.

'No. Can't. Story's on and so is the curfew. You're safe now. I'll catch some shut eye here at the hospital then I'll call Mahmoud.'

'All right.'

She put down the phone abruptly.

She turned on the radio. The Chief Kadi of the Colony had called for calm and condemned the rioting. What good it would do Annie was not sure. The mob seemed out of hand.

She went to lie down. She was not annoyed at Charlie. Worried perhaps. The source of her anger was within herself.

The insistent and senseless mantra of 'one cup of tea' returned to her nightly. She had begun to half fall in love again with this unknown man, at least in her dreams. In the night she loved him and in the day she was horrified at herself.

She closed her eyes and waited. She heard bird calls and the familiar sounds of the house but nothing else. No voices in her head. She felt the tension go out of her body and drifted into dreamless sleep.

30

'Mr Tom Masterson, Chief of the Singapore bureau of the *Associated Press*, had his leg broken and his head injured when attacked by rioters. His colleague, Mr Larry Allen, was reported missing last night. Mr Allen was last seen being chased along a street near Jalan Besar. His car was overturned and burned.'

The Straits Times, 12 December 1950

'Singapore Police last night arrested 187 people throughout Singapore for violating the curfew and detained an additional 76 under the Emergency Regulations. This brings the total number arrested since the rioting on Monday to 1,107.'

The Singapore Free Press, 16 December 1950

After three days the twenty-four hour curfew was lifted. The night curfew remained but life began to return to normal.

Annie's head felt better. She went to see Dr Chen and he pronounced her well and told her to come back in four days to remove the stitches.

She had brought Joseph back into the house. He was bursting

with energy and, since none of the children could go to school, and Mr Pillai couldn't come, he spent most of his days pottering about in the vegetable garden or playing with the other children and Yellow.

The post-mortem began: the police were blamed for not opening fire; an inquiry was called for and so on. Annie read and discarded the newspapers.

She had been too idle over the time of the curfew, cooped up here. She'd talked to Maria on the phone and chatted for a while about Jean and the contents of her letter. But other than that she had been bored. Everyone was glad to go out, do some shopping, go back to school, to welcome their return to normality.

Charlie came back home last night, late. He hadn't come to see her and had gone straight to his room, with Ting following in his wake. She waited now for him to get up. She looked at her watch. Eleven o'clock. She didn't dare wake him. She was aware that he had worked non-stop for four days.

Annie picked up her bag and took out the address of Harnam Singh. She called a taxi and gazed at the scores of men cleaning up the rock-strewn and chaotic streets.

The address was on Serangoon Road, near Race Course Lane. The police had cordoned off the area from Jalan Besar south towards the mosque and the streets were crowded with people making their way around the cordon. The Traction Company headquarters nearby had been burned and workmen were clambering all around it. Annie stopped the taxi at Buffalo Road and walked the rest of the way.

She looked at the numbers, finally locating the address and

stood on the opposite side of the street staring at the shophouse. On the ground floor was a store with colourful saris on plastic mannequins, carpets and displays of cheap gold jewellery. Above, the green and white shutters were closed. She waited. The sign on the clothing store said Veeraswamy in English, with curly Indian writing above it. Next door was a pawn shop and on the other a sign for Batu Pahat Goldsmiths. It had been over three years since Joseph's father had come to the convent. She hardly knew what she was hoping for.

She crossed the road and entered the shop. She touched the material of the sari on one of the mannequins. It was that new material, Terylene, a man-made cloth she had read about. It was not a natural fibre but it felt silky nevertheless and beautiful with its vivid oranges and golds. The owner came forward smiling, his teeth gleaming white in his dark face.

'Welcome,' he said, obviously surprised to see her. 'You are my first customer. Very lucky. The riots have been very bad.' His gaze went to her forehead and its sticking plaster.

She showed him the name on the paper. Harnam Singh. He shook his head. He would ask, however, at the local shops. He called a young boy, his son perhaps, and gave him the paper, rattling off instructions in his native tongue.

She thanked him and purchased two saris and a good deal of cotton cloth for his trouble. Mr Veeraswamy offered her tea and a seat and they discussed the rioting and the Hertogh case for a while, neither venturing into any difficult or contentious opinions on the matter. The boy came back in twenty minutes without success. No one knew of Harnam Singh.

Mr Veeraswamy suggested she try the Sikh Gurdwara Temple on Queen Street. Annie gathered up her parcels, and Mr Veeraswamy hailed her a taxi. She had done her best to find him. She went home.

Charlie had still not left his room. Ting had taken him fruit and tea, Madame Wing said, and Mr Ransome had taken a bath, she believed. Annie gave Madame Wing a parcel of cotton cloth and asked her to distribute the rest as she thought fit, the saris to go to Mrs Kumar. Madame Wing thanked her. Annie sensed she did not entirely approve of this generosity, but Annie didn't care.

Maria called and invited her to tea, now that things had settled down. Annie knew Maria would want to gossip endlessly about the violence and the newspaper reports but didn't know how to refuse so she agreed but put it off until the following week.

She wanted to telephone Eileen Tan but lacked the courage in the face of her husband's implacable aggression and Eileen's fragile state. She missed Mahmoud too and wondered about his hands. She wanted to see Charlie and decided to invite him to the garden for lunch. She relayed the instructions to Madame Wing and walked to the door of Charlie's private sitting-room and knocked.

He came to the door and smiled at her. She was so glad to see him she threw herself into his arms and he hugged her. He felt so good, so warm and she hardly wanted to let him go.

'My word,' he said, releasing her. 'I wasn't in a war, you know.'

She smiled and kissed his stubbly cheek.

'I missed you. Will you come and have lunch with me on

the lawn?'

He looked tired still, or was it sad, she wondered, despite the long sleep. And thin. He'd lost weight.

'Come on,' she said, taking his hand. 'Please.'

He nodded his head.

'Give me a minute.'

She left him. Something had happened. She was almost sure he had filed loads of stories over the last three days, so it wasn't disappointment over the news. Yu Li. She was sure it was her he was moping over.

When he sat under the trees he looked fresher. He had shaved and after a long iced lime juice he perked up slightly. They discussed the rioting. He'd got what the journalists call a 'herogramme' from his editor, full of praise for his coverage.

'Owe most of it to Nobby. Those Reuter guys are stars. Share the reports with me, you know. Greater love hath no journalist than that he should lay down a bit of his story for his friend.'

Ting brought lunch. Madame Wing soon glided across the grass. There was a phone call from Mahmoud. Charlie rose. Joseph ran across the grass and jumped on her knees and she hugged him and kissed his cheeks. Mr Pillai had returned and set up his classroom. The boys had extra lessons and, after a drink of juice, she let Joseph go, waving. Whatever the concoction of drugs Dr Chen was using on Joseph was, it was working. The thought of drugs and tuberculosis made her think of Eileen again. She decided she would call her this afternoon.

Charlie joined her.

'Mahmoud's fine. Hands OK. Bit of a hero, eh? My word.

He's arranged to rent a car for a few weeks from someone he knows until we see what the office says about a new one. Not likely I should say, even second hand, but you never know. I need to interview you. OK? Get your story of the attack. I've got paperwork to do and police reports and so on and a story to file. Mahmoud's picking me up in an hour.'

Annie wanted to ask him about Yu Li but didn't quite dare. She knew it would change his sunny mood to gloom. She didn't want to see Mahmoud and when the car drew up, an ancient Austin, she did not go down to greet him. It was churlish but she knew, in her heart, if she saw him she would have to ask him to do something about Harnam Singh, and she wasn't ready for it.

She had done enough about it, she told herself. She had sought him out, but he was not there. He might have moved anywhere, to Malaysia, to India, anywhere. That argument became less convincing though as time went by and when she had seen Joseph in the classroom, his little face full of light, glad to be back at his lessons this time, she knew she had to make a further effort. Despite her growing love for Joseph she could not truly, and in all decency, not make an attempt to understand what had happened to his father. She would feel guilty then, during all their days together. But not yet. For a few more days she would have him totally to herself.

After Charlie left, she screwed her courage to the sticking place and picked up the phone. It rang in Eileen Tan's house and the voice of the butler came on the line.

'Lady Tan, please.'

'Who is calling?'

'I ... a friend, Mrs Collins.'

The butler hardly hesitated a second. He was very good.

'Milady is indisposed,' he said.

'Oh,' Annie said, nonplussed. This could very well be true.

'Can you leave a message?'

The butler cleared his throat slightly.

'If you wish.'

Yes, I do wish, you pompous fool, she thought, then sighed.

'Just tell her I called, please, and wish her good health.'

There was a crackling on the line and suddenly another voice spoke.

'Mrs Collins. This is Christopher Tan.'

'Oh, I see.'

Annie had removed the phone from her ear slightly. His voice was strong and aggressive.

'My wife is unwell. I would like to thank you and your driver for helping her when she needed it. However, let me say, she would not have been in that part of the town at all if it had not been for you.'

'Mr Tan, I only wish to speak to her. That's all.'

'That is not all you wish to do. Please leave us alone or I shall have you removed from the Colony.'

The phone clicked and the line went dead. Annie replaced the receiver. She felt hot with anger, her first reaction to such a threat. Could he have her removed? Was it possible? Somehow she thought it might be. The anger faded and she felt consumed by hopelessness.

She slowly climbed the stairs to her room and lay down. Tears sprang to her eyes and she turned on her side and watched the leaves of the cassod tree moving in the breeze.

31

CURFEW BRINGS A QUIET NIGHT.

DEAD CITY WITH EMPTY STREETS – EXCEPT FOR TROOPS.

DEATH TOLL NOW 16, OVER 180 INJURED.

'Singapore's dawn to dusk curfew which ended at six o'clock this morning brought rioting incidents down considerably and a quiet that was a marked contrast to the savagery that prevailed on Monday night.'

The Straits Times, 16 December 1950

Desmond roared up the drive and flung on the brakes.

He rang the doorbell insistently, impatient. Annie opened the door and without a word, Desmond lifted her into his arms.

Annie laughed, embarrassed, and pushed herself away.

'Desmond, really. I'm all right.'

He looked at her face and touched his finger to the plaster on her forehead. He took her hand and led her up the stairs to the verandah. Annie frowned. What was all this manly behaviour about?

The rioting had been over for a week but he had been in

Malaya throughout and, clearly, had just heard about the attack on their car.

He pulled her to the sofa and sat.

'Desmond. What on earth?'

'Are you all right?'

'Yes, of course I am. It was ages ago.'

Desmond looked stricken.

'I just heard. I couldn't call you. I was in the jungle up country, you know. Didn't even hear about it until it was over. I came back as soon as I found out about you.'

Annie patted his hand and he withdrew it instantly and took her by the shoulders.

'Don't do that. Don't you know how I feel about you? Don't act like I'm your brother for God's sake.'

Annie pulled herself away from him and rose. She felt oppressed by his intensity. He stood up and took her hand. She frowned. Really, what was he doing? She pulled her hand from his and opened her mouth to speak, to tell him to calm down, when suddenly he produced a box from his pocket and sank down on one knee. She didn't know whether to laugh or scream. She simply stood, dumb-faced, looking down at him.

'Annie, I want to marry you,' he said and opened the box. Inside lay a ring with a quite large square diamond, sparkling against the blue velvet.

She felt as if her heart were literally in her throat and swallowed hard. She stared at the ring, blinking, as if she could blink it away. Desmond rose.

'I bought it in Kuala Lumpur. I meant to wait, you know,

for a more romantic setting but when I heard I just had to come straight away. If anything had happened to you … you know.'

She pulled her eyes away from the ring. He waited and she knew, with each passing second, his heart was growing more and more hurt.

'Desmond. It's a cliché, I know, but this is so sudden. You've taken my breath away.'

Desmond smiled, glad of some response and buoyed by the fact it wasn't a refusal. Annie saw her mistake. She was going to refuse him and she should have done it immediately. She felt, as she supposed most decent women would in this situation, utterly embarrassed for him and for herself, and could not face the hurt and silent recriminations that would follow. She had never led him to believe she cared for him that way. She had allowed him to kiss her of course, and perhaps that had been enough. But Lord in Heaven, how could he have made such a leap, from a kiss to commitment? It spoke of a kind of desperation and she suddenly, awfully, felt contempt for him, totally unjustified and then, instantly, felt ashamed.

'You haven't said no,' Desmond said and she felt nailed to the wall, the sharp points of darts and the hammer blows pinning her. He must have read something of this on her face and quickly put the box back in his pocket.

'I've given you a shock. Annie, I love you.'

She looked into his face then and saw that it was true. He did love her. But she didn't love him. Of that she was absolutely certain. She should have told him right there and then but she didn't. A riot of thoughts crowded her mind: he was a good man;

she could do worse; he would protect her and care for her; he would be a wonderful father to Joseph and any other children; he was reliable, sturdy, steadfast. These momentary flashes felt instantly mercenary. But she could not yet face his response. She took the coward's way out.

'Give me some time, will you, Desmond, please?'

His face was caught between relief and anguish. He had professed his love for her but she had not, like a woman in love would have done, thrown herself into his arms, covered his face with kisses, accepting him instantly.

Annie saw he was becoming filled with embarrassment. He grew stiff.

'Of course.'

He took her hand and kissed it. She looked at him tenderly. Perhaps that look gave him hope for he smiled.

'I'll go. You're all right, I can see.'

She walked with him to the front door.

'Don't make me wait too long. Will you, Annie? I can't bear it.'

He got into the car without a second glance and drove away before she could respond.

Annie went back to the verandah and sat for a moment. She looked around the room and it seemed to close in on her. In that moment it didn't feel like home. It felt like a cage. The same cage that Ronald had put her in. She could still feel the weight of Ronald's heavy-gutted frame crushing her on their wedding night, his drunken hands rubbing all over her, lascivious and sweating, his lips on her breasts, sucking at her, biting her, as if he was a cannibal devouring his prey. He had bought her, those lips and hands said. I've bought you, lie still. There had been nothing tender about that night. She hadn't known what to expect when she married him, just thrilled to leave that old life behind as quickly as possible, but she had found out.

She had lain still and paid her dues for this escape. This was the price, she'd said to herself and had bitten back her cries and the bile rising in her throat and kept her eyes on the unblinking orbs of the gecko on the ceiling, staring down at her. She didn't feel free except in his absence. His presence was oppressive, bullying, critical. After a month, he did not come to her every night. Usually he'd grab at her when he was half drunk, and then it had been violent, an assault, bordering on rape, though she had never fought him. Though she'd been only seventeen, she'd realised that he had woken from some strange dream and he looked at his urgent sexual need for her youthful, half-blood body with disgust.

She had endured this and said nothing, and when she'd found she was pregnant she'd been relieved that he would rarely come to her bed. After the birth of Suzy and his complete disgust at what he saw as the depths to which he had sunk, he'd almost never even talked to her and had lost interest in her as a wife. He'd turned his rabid attentions elsewhere, to the pleasures of the club and the women of Chinatown. By then the whole of Singapore was in conflagration and the days of the Japanese Occupation were almost upon them.

Desmond was not Ronald. He was only thirty-five, strong and fit. And he loved her. It couldn't be the same. It was unfair to compare them. She said this to herself over and over, but she knew she could never be married again to a man she did not feel passion for, did not love with all her soul, no matter how ephemeral those feelings might be.

To begin, again, that same life, was unimaginable. Desmond was, also, white. She had, for most of her life, been in a position of feeling constantly inferior: the nuns who thought their tiny charges were full of original sin, which had to be prayed and knocked out of them; the white ladies who came to eye them up and down as if they were a species of walking evil because they had been begot and abandoned, or smile at them condescendingly for the luck they'd had at not being left in a ditch but raised to a semblance of civilised life; the memsahibs of Ronald's acquaintance who had been envious of her exotic looks and disdainful of her foul associations, a woman that a pukka white man had clearly married because she was sexually promiscuous and lascivious, not proper like them. She recalled Jean's words about the view of Eurasian women in the camp. Even there, where they had all laboured under the most horrific hardships and starvations, even there, it had not gone away. Here and in Australia it would be exactly the same. She didn't belong; she wasn't white. They would never let her forget it.

Somewhere in the back of her mind came that niggling phrase again. One cup of tea. He had been the man she had given her soul too. Did it mean she could never love again?

She rose, confused. She went to the garden to find Joseph.

She had made up her mind. She was tired, tired, tired, of indecision. She would tell Desmond tomorrow and she would set Mahmoud to find Joseph's father. Then she would leave Singapore. She suddenly felt the heavy yoke of its oppressive heat, its endlessly clicking and whirring insects, the poverty and need reflected in those all around her. She was sick of the memories this place evoked, the discoveries she was making, which she wanted to reject and bury deep and cover with miles of earth.

She longed for Australia and its cool autumn nights. Perth's blue skies and blue seas, the sound of the crashing surf on the endless coastline and the feel of the sea breeze in her hair. She felt free in Australia, the land where she had been reborn into this Annie Collins. How many immigrants had done that? Run away to its vast shores, its distant vistas, and left old lives behind. She wanted to go home, to the only true home she had ever known. The house with the big ghost gum she had inherited from the woman she had grown to love and who had loved her. Mabel's house, filled with good memories of tolerance and kindness.

She would try to speak again to Eileen Tan for that was why she had come here. She would reject all the rest of these strange, syrupy, foggy remembrances and new affections, find Harnam Singh, or not, but one way or another it would be done.

32

Inept handling of situation – UK press

'Concern over the Maria Hertogh case and its bloody sequel, which found expression in the Commons yesterday and the leader columns of this morning's newspapers, is combined with criticism that the matter should have been allowed to develop to this grave state. The police are criticised for their handling of the riots. "The handling of the situation by the government has been inept" says The Manchester Guardian, which states that the Government's inability to prevent the riots "has been matched by its incompetence in policing them."

It is not yet clear how Maria Hertogh, the Muslim girl, came to be placed in the charge of a Christian convent. This was a challenge to Islam of a kind that a wise government avoids.'

The Straits Times, 14 December 1950

Charlie was not entirely drunk but he was half way there. Mahmoud had delivered him home in this half-folded inebriated state and helped him upstairs to his private sitting room.

He had, Mahmoud informed her, been drinking with

Mr Styles and the other reporters in Mr Toenails' Bar.

It hardly seemed possible but people were still dying and trying to recover from those terrible events. The girl, Maria, had disappeared, spirited away somewhere by the police.

She poured the coffee Ting had placed on the low Chinese table. She shook Charlie slightly and put the coffee in his hand. He drank it all down in one gulp and she poured more.

He revived and sat up.

'Annie,' he said and smiled lopsidedly. 'Sight for sore eyes.'

His speech was very slightly slurred and she put the coffee cup in his hands again. He cradled it a moment then drank from it and dropped the cup to the floor. Annie bent down to pick it up and suddenly felt herself lifted into Charlie's arms. He pulled her against him.

'I'm very unhappy, Annie,' he said.

She pulled away from him.

'Yes, I know.'

'I dunno what to do,' he said and put his hands to her cheeks and looked into her eyes.

'I know you don't. It's Yu Li, isn't it?'

His eyes closed and his whole face frowned at the utterance of the name. His head lolled and she wondered if he had fallen asleep. She got up.

'Don' go.'

He looked at her but she saw his eyes were unfocused. Suddenly he rose as if galvanised by a greater power than the alcohol and took her in his arms.

'Charlie, stop,' she said and tried to pull away.

He wrapped one arm around her waist and took her head in his hand and put his lips to hers. She tasted the fumes of the alcohol and the heat of the pressure and suddenly responded, wrapping her arms around his neck. He swayed and pulled back from the kiss, then, as if drawn back by an invisible magnetism, his lips came down on hers again, hard. She felt her response to him, hot and urgent, felt the length of his hard body against hers. She wanted him. She wanted to make hot, sweaty, passionate love to him, without a single thought in her head.

His hands came to her buttocks and he pulled her against him, grinding her into him. She groaned and gripped his hair. He bent and swung her into his arms and started to walk unsteadily towards his bedroom. She had a sudden vision of them making love, joined in mind-numbing physical passion. She kissed his neck, overcome, grasping him to her.

Then the nightjar whirred loudly and its spinning song blew away the force of this sudden whirlwind of desire and she was in another man's arms. Akira, she murmured and saw his face. She lifted her head to his, wanting her lips on his. Charlie kissed her and she suddenly pushed him away.

'Stop,' she said and Charlie came to a halt.

'Stop, please.'

Charlie, too, seemed to come to his senses at the sound of her voice, which was not the right voice. He put her gently to the ground, turned and walked towards his room.

'Ting,' he called loudly. 'Bring me a beer.'

As she heard Ting's feet scurrying towards them she turned and went to the verandah. She poured herself a gin and tonic over lots of ice.

Akira. His name had come from the depths of her. That was his name. Akira what? He must have another but that refused to appear.

The phone rang. Madame Wing had gone to bed and Annie picked up.

'Annie, it's Eileen.'

'Oh, Eileen. How are you?'

'Better. A little. Well enough to come and see you. I've told Christopher I want to see you. He's not happy but he won't refuse me whilst I'm sick.'

'Thank you, Eileen. When can you come?'

'Next week. On Monday. I have a doctor's appointment and will come after, at two o'clock.'

'Yes, yes. Please. I can't wait to talk to you.'

'Goodnight.'

'Goodnight, Eileen, and thank you again.'

She put down the phone. She went to the desk and took out a piece of paper and began to write a note to give to Mahmoud.

The next morning she and Charlie avoided each other. Whilst he was bathing she found Mahmoud who was waiting by the car.

'Nice car, Mahmoud. Even better than the Ford, I think. Less inflammable perhaps.'

He smiled. She looked at his bandaged hands.

'How are your hands?'

'They will be all right. How are you?'

'Yes. I will also be all right.'

Annie went forward and took his hands in hers. Their eyes

met.

'Thank you.'

Mahmoud nodded. She released his hands and took out the note she had written from her pocket.

'Mahmoud, I have to ask you a favour, which requires your discretion. I would like you to find someone. I have written everything in the note. If you find out anything about the man in the note, could you please tell me first?'

Mahmoud put the note in his pocket without a word. When Annie heard Charlie on the stairs she smiled at Mahmoud and darted away.

33

MARIA IN CALCUTTA

'Maria and her mother Adeline Hertogh, passed through Calcutta this afternoon, on the way to Holland from Singapore. They left Singapore secretly, says *Reuter*, on Tuesday afternoon, in a plane specially diverted from its normal route of Karachi.

They were sent on Monday to St. John's Island from the Girls' Home of The Convent of the Good Shepherd and travelled to Kallang airport by launch. They were taken from the flying boat jetty to the airport building under strong armed escort.'

The Straits Times, 14 December 1950

'I'm glad you've come to see me.'

Eileen leaned back on the long sofa in the verandah, a cushion behind her neck. She looked pale and ill but there was some colour in her cheeks, though her fine skin was mapped with veins.

'Are you very sick?'

'I have scars on my lungs. What the doctors call fibrotic nodules. I had tuberculosis and it leaves these nodules on the

276

lungs. They can contain active cells. I'm not currently infectious or I should not have suggested meeting you. But I have to go back into hospital again for a week or so. It's very tedious.'

Eileen turned her face against her cushion. She was like a painting so delicate it showed the etchings of her bones and skin.

'What a scourge. But the new drugs are marvellous. The treatment is very long though. They say more than six months. I plan to go to Switzerland in a few months, to a clinic. The air there is supposed to help.'

Eileen gazed at Annie.

'I will take Joanna with me. She can study French and carry on her violin studies. She's very talented.'

'Joanna?'

'Yes, the little girl, Joan. Our child's name was Joanna.'

'You are sure this is your natural-born child?'

Eileen said nothing for a moment.

'The one thing I am sure of is that she is *not* my natural-born child.'

Annie's heart nearly jumped out of her chest. She rose from the chair, agitated.

'How can you know that?'

'Because my baby had a mark, a birthmark on her upper arm. Joan, my Joanna, does not.'

'But you took her in anyway. You raised her.'

'Yes, of course. There were three. Do you know the story?'

'I know there were three Eurasian babies that Mrs Loke and Rose Lim took care of when the Japanese came.'

'Yes, three. All from different families, but like sisters. I think of them as sisters, your little girl …'

'Suzy.'

Eileen smiled.

'Yes, Suzy and my Joanna and another, an unknown little one who was either Mary or Theresa. I've been there, you know. To Bahau, where my daughter and the other little girl are buried.'

Annie sat down. 'Did you find them?'

'I found many graves. Perhaps they were marked once but wooden markers rot away.'

The loneliness of the Malayan forest covering those small graves caught at Annie's throat. She felt tears come to her eyes and took out her handkerchief. But she felt an inner elation, too, which she fought to disguise. This Joanna could be Suzy.

'I'm sorry. Your child is buried there. You know that at least.'

Eileen looked at her, an eyebrow raised, and spoke with heavy irony.

'It was hardly a comfort.'

'No, of course.'

'You are relieved. Of course you are. There is a chance, a slim hope in your mind.'

Eileen shrugged and her voice returned to its calm, unemotional tones.

'I left flowers for them, for Mary and Theresa, for everyone there. It is a small thing isn't it, pointless really, but I could not have left without doing it. Rose Lim, I found her grave. I didn't know Mrs Loke. Rose Lim was my housekeeper before the Occupation.'

'Do you think Joanna is Suzy?'

Eileen shrugged, the movement so slight it was almost imperceptible.

'Did Suzy have any distinguishing marks? Joanna has none. Her skin is unblemished.'

Eileen turned her birdlike eyes onto Annie.

'So is her mind. She must have had wonderful care from those two blessed women and then Rose's husband, who had his own child to care for when he lost his wife and his friends. When Christopher found her she was bonny and sweet-natured. He brought her to me and she saved my life ... and his.'

Annie shook her head. 'No distinguishing marks. She is darker skinned than me, her baby hair was black but ... No, no special marks.'

'You want to see her.'

'Yes.'

'Of course you do. But will you know? Will you?'

Eileen's voice had risen and Annie sensed the other woman's distress.

She put out her hand to Eileen's but it was ignored.

'I have no idea. I think it is fair to let me see her. Does she know? Joanna, does she know she is not your natural child?'

'No.'

Eileen looked sharply at Annie. 'Up to now there has been no reason for her to know any of this. Have you been following this case of the little Dutch girl?'

Annie knew this would come up.

'Yes. It was horrible.'

'A battle for that child who was perfectly happy, at perfect peace, living in a quiet community with her foster mother, loved and loving. She was special there, you know, probably a little spoiled. Her white skin would have made her so. Now what is to become of her? One amongst so many, her mind always dwelling in Malaya.'

'Do you think the mother gave her daughter away?'

'Yes.' The answer was emphatic and Annie stared at Eileen.

'How can you know?'

'I know it. The woman was desperate. Five mouths to feed and a newborn. And no idea of the next day, never mind the next month, with the Japs crawling over everything and the husband dead perhaps. She would have given up a daughter, not the sons. The youngest daughter was Maria. She was the obvious choice. It is terribly common, you know, in Asia. Girls are sold or given up for prostitution, cheap labour, because of poverty, for many other reasons. It still goes on today.'

Annie was struck. Of course they were given up. Girl children were the last thing anyone wanted, a commodity to be traded. Perhaps she really had been lucky, as the nuns had ceaselessly told her, to have found refuge in the convent.

'I am quite certain she meant it to be forever, thinking her husband dead. When the husband came back perhaps she was ashamed or scared and told him something different. And now the poor Malay woman has to be pulled on the rack for it.'

Annie didn't know what to reply. The same thoughts had been in her own mind. Eileen's voice took on an edge of strain and shrillness.

'Anyway, I understand that. It is the rest that is so hard to bear.'

Eileen closed her eyes. Annie sat down and poured some tea and allowed the silence to wash over them. She knew Eileen would not have come unless she had something to say. She put the cup in front of her guest.

'I've told you my story. Will you tell me yours?'

Eileen opened her eyes.

'Yes. I want to tell you. You are the only person I would ever tell this story to, and I will tell you because my child is the sister of yours, whether she is living or dead. Those three brown babies who shared their first smiles with each other, they are all *our* children.'

Annie did not speak once as Eileen told her story.

Christopher Tan had been partner in a law practice before the war. In 1940 he had joined the Chinese Brigade of the Straits Settlements Volunteer Force, an auxiliary army; then in December 1941 he had joined Dalforce. This was an irregular guerrilla brigade of Chinese volunteers formed by Lt. Colonel John Dalley. They were so ferocious they had earned the nickname of 'Dalley's Desperadoes.' When the surrender came Dalforce was disbanded but many of the soldiers, including Tan, joined the Malayan People's Anti-Japanese Army in the jungles of Malaya. He fought there for the entire duration of the war.

Annie remembered Desmond telling her that this anti-Japanese brigade formed the backbone of what was now the Communist insurgency in Malaya. When the surrender came Tan had lost half his bodyweight but had still marched with his fellow soldiers victorious into Singapore, then set out to find his family.

What he had discovered was devastation. His parents, his brother and his parents-in-law had been murdered, his child was lost and his wife was near death's door.

After her long, slow recovery, her husband, Eileen told Annie, could not again speak of her experiences for which he felt utter shame.

'If he had stayed it would have made no difference. I've told him. They would simply have killed him and probably still have done the same things to the rest of us. But he has difficulty with this.'

Three days after the Japanese took over, they'd come to her house. They had obtained a list of Dalforce fighters, who had killed many of their comrades, from a tortured prisoner and come for Tan. When she'd seen the Japanese soldiers roar up to her door and realised what was going to happen, she had entrusted her baby, Joanna, to Rose Lim, never believing she would not see this child ever again.

Not finding Tan, they'd taken the entire family to the YMCA building, the Kempeitai headquarters, and held her there for two months, alone, in conditions of the most unspeakable brutality. She had discovered only after the war what had become of her mother and father and Tan's family. In the YMCA they had tortured her for information about her husband and his fellow fighters. The Japanese tortures were not subtle. Water torture forcing water down her until she bloated then placing a board on her stomach and jumping on her. Her nails were ripped out. She was forced to remain crouched, unmoving until she fainted, then beaten. The lack of food and water and light, the incessant beatings and the filthy cells almost brought her to the point of death. Then, one day, for no discernible reason, they took her out of the cells to a doctor, cleaned her up, gave her food and put her into the army brothel.

Eileen turned her eyes to Annie who could hardly bear to look in them. She forced herself to, desperate to share in this woman's suffering.

'This place was a different kind of hell. We serviced up to fifty men a day. We became like raw meat inside and were covered in bruises and cuts from the rough hands and the slaps. A douse of disinfectant and on to the next one. It was excruciatingly painful but if you made the slightest sound or expressed disgust or pain you were beaten. There was no reprieve except to get so sick they let you take some rest. I didn't get pregnant, much too thin. But many did. That didn't stop those girls from being used until the last moment, then the babies were drowned. The mamasan was a woman, like us, you would think, but she barely saw us that way. We were vessels, like pots, to be used and cleaned and used again. You'd think I would have rather died, but I didn't. The will to live was strong; I wanted to see my baby again. My insides were wrecked. I got syphilis and tuberculosis so they took me out, expecting me to die, but I didn't. I have no idea how I survived.'

Eileen turned her face towards the trees dappled with sunlight just beyond the verandah. Her eyes were tearless, hard and bright. Annie waited, silent. No words she could find would carry any meaning.

'Actually, no idea. Strange thing, survival, isn't it? Even at its worst, life seems so much better than death. Well, I suppose for a while anyway. Until it truly becomes beyond bearing. So many young women died. You could die whilst they were on top of you and they just finished their business on your corpse. What kind of men are they?'

Eileen's voice took on a razor-sharp edge as she cut away at these recollections.

Annie took Eileen's hand.

'Enough now. Enough. I am so sorry, Eileen. So very, very sorry.'

The two women sat, their hands entwined and watched the motes of dust dance in the sunlight.

After she left, Annie simply sat for an hour reflecting on Eileen.

They had not done a noble thing, Eileen was at pains to say, but had done the only thing that could rebuild their own lives, could save their own lives and that of this child. The Tans had known that Joan was not their Joanna, but it had made no difference. She was Joanna reborn, given back in spirit to them. Whether she was Suzy was not the issue for the Tans. Those three babies had blended into one. That was for Annie to understand. Eileen had promised she would telephone Annie when she had finished her treatment. They would meet again, she said. Annie could meet Joanna.

34

KARIM GHANI AND FIVE OTHERS DETAINED

'Six Muslims, three of them well-known in Malaya, were arrested in different parts of Singapore at three o'clock yesterday morning and are now detained under the Emergency Regulations.'

The Straits Times, 19 December 1950

'Gurdwara means the gateway through which the Guru can be reached.'

Her guide was elderly, his beard and moustache of a marvellous length and coloured pure white, like an Old-Testament prophet. He was tall and still upright despite his age. He had deep brown eyes, soulful. His turban was black with a strip of white at the edge, which set off his dark skin and white beard in spectacular fashion.

'The gurdwara has a darbar or main hall, as you see,' he said. Annie looked around. She had removed her shoes and covered her hair with a scarf. The room was devoid of idols, paintings and any kind of religious statuary. It was a simple, cool, open space covered in carpets. Anyone, of any faith, may, with respect, enter here, the old man had told her.

'Only the book is here, you see. The holy book, Guru Granth Sahib, which guides all Sikhs.'

Annie saw an open book on a blue and white cloth-covered stand, raised slightly higher than the floor and sheltered under a white canopy. The old man went forward and stood praying silently for a moment, then bent and touched the floor. He rose, paused, and rejoined her.

'I'm getting old,' he smiled and Annie shared it for a moment. 'This way, Sahiba.'

'May I ask,' Annie said, 'why you call me "Sahiba"?'

'It is a form of address, like "Mister" and "Misses" in English. We call men "Sahib" and women "Sahiba".'

'Oh, I see. But you also call the holy book "Sahib".'

'Oh, yes. Well it denotes also someone or something that you trust, or in our religion, give honour to.'

'The Guru Granth is then something like the Honourable Guru Granth.'

'Yes, something like that.' The old man moved on.

He led her to the communal kitchens and rooms behind the darbar. The gurdwara was, he said, a community centre for all to meet and share meals. Anyone could come, whether Sikh or not, and share in these meals. Charity was a central part of Sikhism.

Faith and justice, he told her. 'We believe in one god and the teachings of our holy scriptures, and the learned Sikh gurus guide us. We believe in the equality of all humans and reject discrimination on the basis of caste, creed and gender. We believe in the universal brotherhood of man and that a good life is found in the happiness of the family.'

Annie nodded. She had to know about this religion. Mahmoud had explained that 'Sikh' is a Sanskrit term meaning 'a student or disciple of a guru, an enlightened one'. Most Sikhs are Punjabi, he had told her, and almost all men take the name 'Singh' as a surname and all women 'Kaur'.

He had found Harnam Singh.

She had sat with Mahmoud in the kopitiam and shared Tiger Lolly ice creams. Away from the house he was always more comfortable and easy-going. He had invited her and she had been glad to accept.

'You have ice cream on your beard,' she'd said.

He'd glanced at her, taken his handkerchief and wiped his mouth.

'It is not very polite to comment on the appearance of others.'

She'd smiled. 'Very well. Next time you can go around all day with things hanging off you.'

He'd shrugged but she knew he was teasing.

Harnam Singh had been found through the Sikh temple. He had been in the British army before and during the war. He was now a member of the Malayan Police Force. She had been disappointed at how quickly he'd been found but she was now glad to know he was a respectable man.

'Was he, like you, in the Indian National Army?'

Mahmoud had shaken his head. 'No. He somehow got to India before Singapore fell and fought there. Very pro-British.'

He'd looked at Annie.

'Is that good?'

She'd understood he was asking whether he, Mahmoud, had been disloyal, a bad man, even a traitor.

Annie had smiled. 'Not good, not bad. You know I hold no lamp of loyalty for the British. If he is to have Joseph back I want him to be a good father, that's all.'

'He is a Sikh. We are all good fathers. Great men.'

Annie had looked at him and smiled.

He had laughed. It was, she'd thought, the first time she had heard him laugh. And it was at himself.

'Don't joke about it. I want Joseph to have a good father.'

'Yes, I know. We are no better or worse than anyone else. We have strong bonds of family. He seems a good man. He is married and has one daughter. What more can I say?'

'You can tell me he will love Joseph and take care of him.'

'I think that is true. There are no guarantees. You would also make a good mother for him. But he wants his son back so I think it is true that he loves him.'

Annie had met his eyes. 'Joseph has had such a strange life. What will it be like? Will he bully him?' Do you think he's like that? I worry so much.'

He had sighed. 'A boy needs a father,' he said. 'But only a good one. If it makes you feel better I will speak to him.'

Annie had nodded. 'Yes, speak to him, please, Mahmoud. I would speak myself but I feel it would be better coming from you, a man and a Sikh. Will you tell him about Joseph's life? How wonderful and clever he is. That the child needs kindness and understanding. Will you?'

'Yes,' he'd said.

She had wanted to know more about his religion so he had brought her to the temple in Queen Street. She had waited until he brought this old man and had left her in his hands.

She found him outside now, leaning on the car, under the shade of a tree. He always emanated a sense of great peace and calm, which was immensely reassuring.

'Thank you.'

At the house she went into the garden and watched as Mr Pillai finished his lessons. She waved to him as he departed and Joseph ran up to her. She took him on her knee.

They talked a moment about lessons. Then she took his hand in hers.

'Joseph, I have to talk to you about a serious thing.'

He patted her hand. 'It's all right.'

She swallowed and fought back the feelings that were threatening to overwhelm her.

'It's about your father.'

She waited. Joseph said nothing.

'I have found your real father.'

'I have no father,' Joseph said.

'Yes, Joseph, you do. He has been looking for you for a long time.'

Joseph threw himself onto her chest and hugged her neck.

'It's all right. You are not going anywhere. You understand, Joseph. You are staying here for now. It's all right.'

He began to sob and she held him tight, tears springing to her eyes. Then she steeled herself. She pulled him away and looked into his eyes.

'Listen. You trust me?'

After a moment Joseph nodded. His eyes did not quit hers for an instant.

'I will not let you go until you are happy to go, you understand. We will meet your father together, here, in the garden. It's all right.'

'I don't want to go,' he wailed and threw his arms, once again, around her neck.

She held him until his tears subsided. He looked around and saw the other children watching him curiously and wiped his eyes.

'We will talk tonight at bedtime. Go and play now.'

Joseph hopped off her knee, clearly happy to end this talk, and ran quickly into the trees.

By bedtime he had become curious. He was a child filled with curiosity and a precocious practicality. He had clearly thought this through during the day. She held him in her arms on his bed and told him his father was a brave man, a soldier who had fought in India and was now a brave policeman. He had a wife and a little daughter, a half-sister for him. His mother had been a Malay lady who had died in the war. Nobody had wanted to lose him. It just happened that way. By the time he had fallen asleep she knew that he was more than curious, that he wanted to meet this man and see for himself. Annie kissed his cheek and smoothed his dark hair. She closed the netting around his bed and watched him until it was dark. He was not frightened of the dark. His life had made him tough and resilient, even on occasion cruel. He needed a father, if a father there was. There was no moral dilemma here for her, just the twist in her own heart. The man was a good man, a good citizen, a brave soldier. He had loved a woman, a young Malay girl, had defied his family and his religion for that love of his youth. If she had lived, Annie knew that Harnam Singh would have married her and they would have been happy. But she had died and he had had to give his son away. But he'd thought of this child for all the years of the war. If he had been anything less than the man she believed him to be, she would not have considered surrendering Joseph to him. But he was a man she believed to be like Mahmoud, strong and loyal. And there was, Annie knew, no man better than Mahmoud.

She parted the netting and kissed Joseph once more on his cheek, letting her lips linger on his smooth skin. Tomorrow she would ask Mahmoud to speak to Harnam Singh.

35

The lawyer's offices were on Beach Road and she decided to walk a little. The curfew of the area around Sultan Mosque had been lifted. The investigation had begun.

The roads had been cleared and the man, Karim Ghani, had

been condemned by most of the Muslim community as a rabble-rouser; but this was hindsight. As the story began to unfold, everyone had been shocked at the dereliction of duty of some of the Malay policeman, at the strange participation of the Chinese, of the ferocity of hatred that had burst out. Everyone was careful. The situation in Malaya was so precarious and volatile, the people of Singapore felt shifting currents and it made them wary.

She had discussed the idea of a trust for Joseph and set, as one of its clauses, that the lawyer should visit him and his family once a year and deliver a letter from her. It was, she knew, an interference in their family, but it was a small insurance policy and, this way, she would receive news of him and his welfare. The trust would be a way of staying in touch. However, the trust could be approached by his father to pay for all his medical expenses and education until he turned twenty-one. She intended to make this known as soon as Joseph was happy to leave her.

She turned her steps towards the Chinese Medicine Hall of Dr Wee. She had not been back to thank him since he and his wife had rescued them and she felt that her time here was drawing to a close.

This afternoon she would meet Eileen and Joanna at Peirce Road. She was certain, at least as certain as she could be right now, that she had not the heart to turn Joanna Tan into Maria Hertogh.

She opened the door of the shop and stepped inside. It had the strange distinctive smell of such establishments, a mixture of earthy herbs and roots and mushrooms with something sweet and ill-defined that mingled with it. She stood a moment, looking around at the myriad oddities in glass jars. Her glance fell on the long counter marked 'tea'. A young Chinese assistant with a long face and buck teeth came forward, bowing.

'Good morning. I should like to speak to Dr Wee, please.'

The assistant stood a moment, clearly nonplussed. Perhaps few, if any, non-Chinese came into this shop. In Ipoh that was not the case. Many Indians, Malays and Eurasians consulted the Chinese doctor and bought his powders and potions. Even the sisters at the convent did. Perhaps he thought her a white woman. That was much rarer, certainly.

'Dr Wee?' she said again.

He bowed and disappeared through the door to the upper rooms.

Mrs Wee emerged and smiled.

'Oh, it is …'

'Mrs Collins,' Annie said and put out her hand in greeting.

Mrs Wee bowed and Annie dropped her hand.

'I came to thank you and your husband for your kindness to me and my friends.'

'Thank? Oh is nothing. My husband soon come back.'

She turned to the buck-toothed assistant who was hovering by the door and rattled some Chinese off to him.

'Cup of tea?'

A cup of tea. One cup of tea. Annie looked at the array of coloured tins with black Chinese characters displayed along the shelf.

'Yes. Thank you. The tea you gave me on the evening of the disturbances. Would that be all right.'

Mrs Wee looked confused. Annie realised, as she had not before, that Dr Wee's wife was predominantly a Chinese speaker.

'The tea you gave when my head hurt.' She touched her brow and made a drinking motion and felt foolish.

Mrs Wee's face brightened.

'Ah,' she said and spoke again to the young man, who left them.

The two women stared at each other, the lack of a common language throwing them into silence. Fortunately, within a few moments, Dr Wee returned and greeted her effusively.

'Hello. Welcome,' he said and exchanged quick words with his wife, who bowed smartly to Annie and went through the door from which, a moment later, the assistant emerged with a tray.

'My wife brought tea. Good, good.' He smiled and indicated two hard chairs and a small black wood scroll table in the corner.

Dr Wee poured the tea.

'I wished to thank you for your kindness. I might be leaving Singapore soon and did not want to go without visiting you.'

'Yes. Yes. It is all right. Are you well now?'

'Yes, thank you.'

'It is good things have settled down.'

'Yes.'

She sipped the tea then looked into it. The Chinese tea cup and saucer were pure white with pale blue characters adorning their sides. Against the white porcelain, the tea leaves and the liquid were brilliantly green, beautiful, like green jade and white pearls. It reminded her again of those butterfly earrings.

'Dr Wee, may I ask a question about tea?'

He looked surprised but nodded.

'Does a cup of tea have some special significance in China or even perhaps Japan?'

She saw him stiffen very slightly and regretted mentioning the loathed nation.

'In China perhaps?' she went on hurriedly.

'Tea is drunk for health but also for ceremonial reasons, at weddings and so on. Or, like the British, to welcome friends. The preparation of tea is an art, both in China and … elsewhere.'

He took his cup and drank.

'The green tea, like this one, is most delicate. The darker teas are more robust.'

'What is the Chinese word for tea?'

He pointed to the character imprinted in gold above the shelves of tea.

'Cha,' he said.

Annie couldn't think of anything more to ask.

'May I purchase some of this tea?' she said.

'This is Mo Li Hua Cha. It has a jasmine flower scent. Delicious.'

She smiled at him and finished the cup and put it gently on the saucer. The taste of the tea reminded her of nothing.

Dr Wee also finished his cup. He put it down and looked at her.

'Japanese tea is bitter. Not good.'

He spat the words like nails. In them she heard three and a half years of accumulated hatred.

'Yes. I'm sorry,' she said and he seemed to shake himself out of the mood.

He prepared her package with care, tying it with string and wrote the tea characters on it in black ink. She paid him and put out her hand.

'Thank you again.'

He took her hand and bowed slightly.

'Goodbye.'

At home she put the tea in the drawer with some other items she had purchased for her friends and acquaintances in Perth. She could smell its fragrance through the paper. It was pleasant, the perfume of tea.

She took a quiet lunch with Joseph. They didn't speak of the visit of his father, which had taken place two days ago. It had, she thought, not gone very well. Joseph had been shy and unwilling to be touched by this big man. Annie had seen how much Harnam Singh was affected by the meeting with his child. He had also brought along his wife and one-year-old daughter, and the woman had sat silently, her child in her arms. Annie worried about this woman. Joseph was not her child; he was the love child of another woman. Would she resent him? It made her tremble inside. Joseph didn't want to speak of it so they talked about school instead.

Mr Pillai had told her that Joseph had not paid attention. Annie couldn't scold the boy though. He was in a state of turmoil. She had asked Mr Pillai to be patient. She had begun to hate this whole process and wished she had never agreed to it. But the father, he had been so grateful, so emotional.

'Thank you,' he had said to Annie, his eyes meeting hers. 'Mahmoud Sahib told me about your kindness to him. Thank you.'

The visit had been brief, constrained. Harnam Singh had arranged to come again in two days' time, alone. Annie knew she would have to let Joseph go. There was no choice. This was his father and he had every right to his son. But the trust for him, the money for all his expenses, that was to forestall, in some measure, any resentment on the part of his wife. She knew about women, especially simple, not very well-educated women. They had only the most basic instincts and the strongest was possessiveness for her husband and her own children. It was perfectly possible for this wife to hate the Malay woman he had loved. Men were blind to this sort of thing but Annie, a woman, could see it as clear as light in a crystal.

She turned away from these thoughts. Tomorrow, Eileen had told her, she would bring Joanna to meet her.

36

MUSLIM PLEAS TO UK GOVT. ON MARIA

'The British Government will be asked to secure the appointment of a nominee of the Muslim Advisory Board to find out whether Maria Hertogh wants to stay in Holland or return to Singapore in the event that the Court of Appeal varies the present order giving custody of the child to her parents.'

The Straits Times, 19 December 1950

The day was heavy and humid and rain was in the air. Monsoon storms started with a breeze, in the still day, then turn into a gale, which clacked the shutters and tossed the blinds. Then as the sky grew dark the rain would fall straight and hard, in torrents, gushing off the roof, banging against the blinds, racing into the drains, drilling holes into the dry earth.

She loved the rain in the tropics. It swept everything before it, drawing down a curtain so dense nothing was visible. It cleansed the ground and the air and took the heat away, and left you cool and all the jungle sparkling and fresh.

She finished putting up her hair and straightened her dress.

As the first breezes grew stronger she went to the verandah to watch the heads of the trees tossing about as if they, too, were thrilled at the relief from the endless heat. The black clouds gathered, scudding closer and closer, the day darkening.

She could hear Wei Wei and Ting running around the house, lowering the chicks and shutting the doors with a clack, clack. Madame Wing called Joseph in from the garden but he didn't answer. Annie thought he had probably taken refuge with Fatimah's children, all of them huddled, laughing, in her small hut or jumping in the first warm rain. Sometimes, she knew, he found this big house strange and disconcerting.

She went to the verandah. The electric lights were on all over the house.

The rain began with a whoosh of wind and pushed the brand new chicks into the room, as if a hand had slapped them. It was their baptism of rain. She went to the covered verandah downstairs and sat. A boom of thunder clapped overhead and, despite herself, she jumped. She heard screams of laughter from the back of the garden, which was now entirely hidden from view by sheets of water. The noise was tremendous, and speech and movement in such a deluge were impossible. It stopped humans and animals in their tracks. A tropical storm was primaeval, untameable, exhilarating.

She rose. She wanted to feel the rain on her head, coursing down her body. They had done this sometimes at the convent, the bunch of them, the orphan girls, with the nuns screaming at them from the edges of the quadrangle. It was a moment of sheer joy, all of them laughing, voices raised, jumping and squishing their bare feet into the muddy grass. For the duration of the storm they were free. There was hell to pay afterwards, of course, Hail-Marys and penances, but it was worth it.

She stepped into the rain now and gasped. The sheer weight of the water felt like bricks pounding down on her head and shoulders, and, instantly drenched, she stepped back under the verandah and laughed. She had forgotten that feeling, the elemental force of such a storm. She stepped in again, ready now, and let it rush over her, pounding all thought out of her mind.

When it began to lighten she went inside and dripped muddy puddles up the stairs. The Malay maids giggled and brought cloths, following her like bridesmaids to the bathroom door, mopping and laughing. She turned and smiled at them and they went off into gales of girlish laughter. They probably thought she was demented.

She washed quickly and towelled off. She felt ready to face what this day would bring.

At two o'clock, she watched Eileen's car come up the drive. She had chosen the gothic, winged, 1925 Rolls Royce Phantom, the car Christopher Tan had used to bring Joanna home, or perhaps it was not her choice to bring it but his. Considering its history with the Kempeitai, she was surprised he could bear to ride around in it. However, the significance was not lost on her. She went downstairs to greet them.

She had asked Madame Wing to set out tea on the lawn. The rain was gone, soaked up by the greedy earth, dried up by the sun, as if it had never happened, with only the cooler air left behind to mark its passage.

She saw that everyone on the compound had gathered, dotted here and there, to look at the car. The Tans' Chinese driver leapt out and took a quick look round, enjoying the admiring examinations. He adjusted his cap and opened the door.

Eileen came out first and Annie took her hand, then slid her eyes to the child standing behind her mother, looking around, her lips straight and unsmiling.

Her hair was shiny black, curled into ringlets, which gave her an old-fashioned look. She was slim and pretty, brown-skinned and almond eyed. She was wearing a pink-and-white-checked pinafore dress over a white blouse. Annie tried desperately to see something of herself in this girl.

'Joanna,' said Eileen, taking the girl's hand and drawing her to her side. 'This is Mrs Collins.'

'Annie,' she said and put out her hand smiling. Joanna shook it, expressionless, and gave a small curtsey.

'I'm very pleased to meet you.'

'And I, you, Joanna.'

Before she could say more Madame Wing emerged and Eileen greeted her in Chinese and, with her hand firmly in Joanna's, entered the house. Annie trailed after them.

Madame Wing knew the significance of this meeting in every respect. She had attired the staff in their newest uniforms as befitted the arrival of the wife of Sir Christopher Tan, Legislative Councillor. The table was impeccable. Ting served tea, while Eileen looked around and Annie tried not to stare at Joanna. Madame Wing withdrew.

'Are you enjoying school, Joanna?' Annie said, pouring tea.

'Oh, it's all right. Some of the teachers are quite horrid.'

The girl, Annie saw, was at a loss to discover why she was here. Annie offered cakes and the girl perked up slightly and began to nibble quietly.

'Are you all right, Eileen? Your health?'

'Good, better. We leave for Switzerland in two weeks. Don't we, Joanna?'

'Yes, Mummy.' The girl smiled broadly, obviously thrilled at the prospect.

'Oh, how nice,' said Annie. 'Will you like the snow?'

Joanna nodded. Eileen took up her tea cup.

'I shall learn to ski,' she said. 'Daddy said I could, didn't he, Mummy?'

'Yes, Dear, but school comes first.'

Joanna frowned and looked a little cross. Annie thought the girl might get up and stamp her feet. She was obviously a child who was used to getting her own way.

'Obviously, Mummy. I'm not stupid.'

'Oh, no,' Eileen said quickly putting down her cup. 'No, Darling, of course not.'

'And eat chocolate. We shall eat chocolate,' Joanna said matter-of-factly.

Eileen looked relieved.

Annie looked at Joanna again and again as they talked about Switzerland and schools and her violin studies. She was a precocious child and opinionated, talking at length about the famous professor of violin she would study under, her musical ambitions. Annie let this conversation wash over her. Joanna could have been her child, there was a small resemblance, she supposed, but no more than to Eileen. She looked simply Eurasian, a pretty mix of bloodlines. After half an hour, Madame Wing glided over to them and replaced the teapot.

She looked at Eileen. 'May I take Joanna to the house to have some ice cream with the other children? Would that be all right?'

Eileen glanced at Annie.

'I thought it might be nice rather than sitting here with us. Just for half an hour,' Annie said.

Annie gazed at Eileen, her face immobile. Eileen hesitated a moment.

Joanna was looking towards the house. She looked surprised.

'Would you like that, Darling?' Eileen's voice had taken on a querulous tone.

There was a small silence as Joanna considered her options. Could she refuse, wondered Annie. Could she be so rude?

'Yes. All right,' Joanna said gracelessly then got up.

'Lovely, Darling. Come back when you've finished.'

'Oh, I shall come back if I'm bored,' she said.

Eileen threw a glance at Annie who made no reaction. The two women watched Joanna stride across the grass. Annie wondered if she had ever sat down to ice cream with such a motley crew of children but thought it might be good for her. Joanna was clearly well on her way to becoming a little snob.

'Well,' Eileen said. 'You've seen her. What do you think?'

Annie shrugged. 'I don't know. How remarkable that I don't know. I should have thought to see something, if not of me, then at least of Ronald.'

'The Asian side is strong. Somehow mixed children always look more Asian than white. I don't know why.'

Eileen had visibly relaxed. Annie knew she no longer felt threatened. Annie recognised that there wasn't the slightest possibility of her taking away this child. She was the Tan child, through and through, right down to her perfect white cotton socks. Nurture had overcome everything. She didn't especially like her, with her clipped English tones and her boldness. The idea of uprooting her from the wealth and social position the Tans held, to deprive her of Switzerland and violin lessons, and to stick her, some rich colourful plant, in the dry earth of Perth was ludicrous. If only they had all done this months ago.

But then, Annie mused, months ago I would not have seen it so clearly.

Joanna came back after ten minutes, manifestly horrified at the company she had been asked to keep. When it came time to leave, Joanna was visibly relieved. Annie walked them to the car. Eileen touched Joanna's shoulder and the girl, reminded of her manners, curtsied to Annie. She rose and looked up into her eyes.

'Thank you, Mrs Collins,' she said and smiled.

Annie saw it then, right there. The tiny white scar in the corner of one eye. Suzy had been in the garden, in her wicker cot, under the trees covered in the net. A palm branch had cracked suddenly and dropped from the tree, right onto the baby. She had been covered in green fronds and brown bark. A part of the hard bark had caught the corner of her eye. It had left a gash and there had been a lot of screaming and wailing but the baby had not been badly hurt. It had cleared up within a few days but had left a white scar on her brown skin.

'Come on, Mummy,' Joanna said peremptorily and got into the car.

Her child was alive and well, Annie knew. The feeling was overwhelming and she felt a state of utter confusion. Eileen shook her hand briefly and got quickly into the car. Annie heard the whining tones of the girl as she stood watching the car disappear down the drive.

37

'LONDON: The King said in a world-wide broadcast last night that mankind must make the most momentous choice of its history and decide between the creeds of love and hatred. For, he said, if our world is to survive in any sense that makes survival worthwhile, it must learn to love, not to hate, to create, not to destroy.'

The Straits Times, 27 December 1950

The next days were conducted in a state of mind that she could only describe as chaotic.

The child, her child, had lived. Other women had kept her alive. She wanted to go to her and take her in her arms and explain this to this spoilt little girl. Other women, other babies had died but she had lived. Was it in order to be turned into a rotten little snob? She almost couldn't bear to think of it. She changed her mind twelve times a day. She would write to Eileen, she would decide, would explain her thoughts. But she knew it would just throw the cat among the pigeons, distress Eileen, who was a good woman, and she decided against it. Then she would change her mind in the morning only to revert back at night.

Eventually, when her mind had rolled around the subject enough, she suddenly thought how marvellously and strangely fitting it had all turned out to be. She did not much care for the girl Suzy had become but she realised that the child had turned into almost exactly the sort of daughter that Ronald would have adored. Perhaps all of that instinctive self-worth and pomposity was actually Ronald's blood and nothing to do with the Tans at all, or even herself. It made her feel really much better. Suzy, the daughter he had so rejected, had turned out to be Ronald. If there was a hereafter, they would surely find each other in it.

At that moment, she also suddenly realised that she had made her peace with Ronald. She had found his child but, now, she also understood something of the dreadful conditions under which Ronald had died. Like the thousands of other men, he had endured the unendurable, had been bloated with beriberi, ulcerated feet and legs, riddled with cholera and typhoid, driven and starved until his heart had simply given out where he had stood and was then thrown into the heaps of arms and legs that protruded from the mud of the Siamese forest. No one deserved such tortures, no one, and certainly not the man Ronald had never revealed to her. To survive Gallipoli and die so cruelly at the hands of such unspeakable barbarism. The weight of her hatred for him fell away. She forgave him utterly.

She turned her mind to Joseph. The meeting with the father had been neither good nor bad. The little boy had, for the first time, allowed himself to stand near Harnam Singh and they had all shared an hour in the garden. Harnam Singh had told Joseph something about his mother and how he had come to be at the convent. When Joseph ran off to play, she had been harsh with this father, more cutting and questioning than she had intended. She had not dared speak of her true worries about his wife, but she had told him of her own love for this child. She needed him to understand that Joseph would be all right with him, in his family. Harnam Singh was a proud man, and she could see her questions did not please him; but she didn't care. When Joseph was ready he could go, she said, but not until that day. Not until the day when Joseph said to her he was happy to go would she let him depart. Harnam Singh had acquiesced but she saw he was annoyed. Annoyed at having her interfere in his life, now that he had found his son. But he was not angry. She saw he was not a man of temper, just pride, which he was keeping under control for the sake of his boy.

Before he left, he said to her, 'I love my son. Please don't worry.'

It reassured her a little. But only a little. Joseph was not his son, just as Suzy was not any longer her daughter. He was a boy raised to a very different way of life. He would need time to adjust and he might never, as she almost knew Maria Hertogh would not, truly accept that life. But he was much younger than Maria. Youth was on his side.

She was sick of thinking and sick of the compound, and she went downtown and walked along the edge of the promenade by the sea, then bought a little suitcase for Joseph. When she got home she hid in her room and only came out for dinner and to put Joseph to bed.

That night she announced to Charlie that she was leaving. As soon as Joseph was ready to go she would go. The Tan child was not hers. She'd accepted that.

He wanted to take her out, go down to the river for a drink and a meal. Get away into the life of the city. But she shook her head and left him. She wanted to listen to the radio, to Kenneth Horne and Richard Murdoch in *Much Binding in the Marsh*, and laugh out loud. Something totally English and disconnected from all the lives that currently surrounded her. As Mabel had grown increasingly bed-ridden they'd listened together, to *The King's Christmas message*, *Letter from America* and the *Light Programme*. She'd read to Mabel the books taken from the shelves of her home: Walter Scott, Kipling, Jane Austen and Agatha Christie. It was here in the warmth of this home and listening to Mabel that she had begun to understand something of the young Ronald.

Sleep came easily and, for the first time in several days, she awoke refreshed. She joined Charlie in the drive downtown and then asked Mahmoud to take her to Chinatown, barely paying attention until she realised that they were not in the city but passing the docks at Tanjong Pagar.

'Mahmoud, where are you going?' she said, leaning forward.

'To the Tiger Balm Gardens,' he said. 'It's on Pasir Panjang Road, so I'm told.'

She smiled.

'Don't be ridiculous. I've apologised for that.'

'You are leaving soon, I think.'

She stopped smiling. 'Yes,' she said. 'When Joseph is settled.'

'Then, if you don't mind, I should like to visit with you the

Tiger Balm Gardens.'

She leaned back.

'Well, well. You are most peculiar but very well.'

She was glad of this little excursion with him. She had never been to this western part of the island. The road passed the docks and from there the vista over the water looked lovely. She leant her chin on her hand and contemplated the view and when Mahmoud left the main road and climbed the hill up to the Haw Par Villa Chinese gate with its multiple, upturned roofs, she felt a small sense of excitement and began to enjoy Singapore again.

It was quiet but she imagined it would be heaving with people on a Sunday. They climbed to the first exhibit. An Indian snake charmer appeared out of nowhere and she thought he must have been asleep behind a rock. She had seen the rather amazing show many times and she gave him some coins and he took his basket and returned to his nap.

They read about the Aw brothers, Boon Haw and Boon Par, who had built these strange gardens before the war from the riches they had made from Tiger Balm. They walked through the strange and gaudy figures from Chinese mythology, the Ten Courts of Hell, the Buddhas, up the various paths to the pagoda. Here they sat and contemplated the vista from the hill.

'You like Harnam Singh?' Mahmoud said suddenly.

'Yes. When Joseph is ready, he will go.'

She looked at Mahmoud. 'Can I tell you something?'

'Yes.'

'I don't want to insult Sikh women so you must forgive me, but I don't trust his wife.'

Mahmoud was silent a moment.

'It is not Sikh women but this particular woman, perhaps. You don't trust her because you suspect she might be jealous of the first woman and dislike Joseph for it.'

'Goodness, yes, Mahmoud. That's it exactly. What do you think?'

'I think you might be right. My wife has already pointed this out to me.'

Annie turned to Mahmoud. He had never spoken of his wife before and she was somewhat curious about her.

'Your wife is clever then. She sees what I see.'

'Yes, she is very clever. She is not Sikh, but she is very clever.' He smiled.

'I see,' said Annie slowly. 'She is not Sikh. Then what is she and how is that you married her?'

'You are extremely nosy.'

Annie laughed. 'Yes I am. But you brought her up. Tell me. I thought you had to marry a Sikh wife?'

'I married my wife for all the usual reasons one marries a woman. That she was not Sikh didn't matter to me. Our children are raised in the Sikh faith. We were married in the gurdwara.'

'Mmm. So she is Punjabi?'

'No. She is Eurasian. Anglo-Indian.'

'Ah. Goodness. Eurasian, you say. And so wise.'

'Wiser than me, luckily.'

They shared a grin.

'The child is not yours, the little girl?'

'No,' Annie said, 'she is.'

It was Mahmoud's turn to look at her.

'No good can come of it. I realised that she is more like my dead English husband than me. She would hate me for even suggesting I was her mother.'

Mahmoud turned his face back to the view.

'You can leave it like that? You won't regret?'

'No, I don't think so. There is no way of knowing, is there? But I think she's got a good life.'

'Our children are not our children,' Mahmoud said, 'they are the sons and daughters of Life's longing for itself.'

'Good heavens. That's pretty profound. Is it a Sikh saying?'

'No. My wife told me that when you first came here looking for your daughter.'

He put his hand in his pocket and took out a small book.

'This is for you.'

Annie took it.

'It is by a man called Kahlil Gibran. He was a Sufi poet. My wife's father was a Sufi, her mother an English teacher. Their marriage was a great scandal but she and her sister loved them for it. She is proud of both her English and her Sufi blood. She asked me to give it to you.'

She opened it and saw a chapter marked 'Children'. She turned to it and read it silently.

You may give them your love but not your thoughts,
For they have their own thoughts.
You may house their bodies but not their souls,
For their souls dwell in the house of tomorrow.

She began to read it aloud to Mahmoud.

You may strive to be like them,
But seek not to make them like you.
For life goes not backward nor tarries with yesterday.

She rested the book on her lap.

'Do you think it's true?'

'I don't know. I'm no philosopher.'

Annie nodded.

'Please thank her for her gift.'

They rose.

'You're a lucky man, Mahmoud Sahib,' she said.

'Ah, so now I am a Sahib. But you may not be a Sahiba.'

'Forgive me. I didn't understand. Ignorance is the root of all evil.'

He smiled. They set off down the hill. The gardens were so empty and quiet her eye was drawn to a man and a woman near one of the grottoes that bordered on a small open area of grass. To her amazement, Annie realised it was Yu Li Cavanagh and was momentarily nonplussed. Then Yu Li, perhaps like her, noticing the movement of other people, looked over. She hesitated for the space of a few seconds then waved and came towards them. She had abandoned her Chinese cheongsam for western clothes and was dressed in a sun dress of yellow with billowing petticoats.

The man she was with walked down the hill and disappeared behind a large statue of the God of War.

'I'll be down in a moment, Mahmoud.'

He hesitated and she smiled reassuringly.

'It's all right.'

She watched Mahmoud descend, his tall figure lithe and upright.

'Annie, isn't it?' Yu Li said, smiling.

Annie got the feeling Yu Li rarely forgot a name.

'How surprising to meet you here,' she said and stared at Mahmoud's back with an eyebrow poised in a position of smug enquiry.

'He's my driver,' Annie said and flushed slightly.

Yu Li shrugged. She took out a packet of cigarettes and offered one to Annie.

'What brings you here?' Annie said quickly

Yu Li blew a long trail of smoke and looked around.

'A friend is visiting. I always bring them here. It's so gaudy and unusual, don't you think?'

'Yes. I am leaving Singapore soon and I thought I might like to see it before I go.'

'Yes, you are right to do so.'

They began to walk down the steps.

'I am leaving too. I'm going to Tokyo.'

'Oh. Does Charlie know?'

'I will tell him.'

'He cares a lot for you.'

Yu Li smiled.

'I care a lot for him. But life is life. And Tokyo is just coming back to life. Will you ever come to Tokyo, Annie?'

She was surprised by the question.

'I can't think so.'

'Well. If you do, leave a message at the Imperial Hotel. The American army people live there, you know. It was built by Frank Lloyd Wright, one of them, so they feel comfortably at home I suppose. But I have friends amongst them. My mother is married to an American general. Did I tell you?'

Annie gazed at Yu Li. Perhaps she is mad, thought Annie. Talking about Tokyo to people who have no reasons to care a damn about what was happening there. Her stepfather had been murdered by them. It was unconscionable. Perhaps she was just completely unaware of anything but her own life. It was really difficult to say, but God help Charlie. She'd have forgotten him in half an hour.

When they got to the cars Yu Li threw her cigarette on the ground and crushed it with her yellow high heels. The man she had been speaking to was a young good-looking Chinese in a white suit and a black fedora. He was in the driver's seat of a sleek cream Cadillac. He looked like he'd seen too many Hollywood movies.

Yu Li turned to Annie and kissed her on both cheeks.

'Goodbye, Annie,' she said. 'Perhaps we'll meet again. I hope so.'

Annie watched as the car roared away.

'I think she's selfish and probably mad but I can't help liking her,' she said to Mahmoud as she got in the car.

'Neither can Mr Charlie,' he said. 'But she's dangerous.'

'Yes,' Annie said, 'mad, bad and dangerous to know.'

38

'Fear that "senseless riots" had retarded the attainment of
self-government for Singapore "for at least 10 years" was expressed
in the Legislative Council last night.'
The Straits Times, 20 December 1950

The red suitcase sat in the middle of the black-and-white
chequered hall like a stain. The faint odour of pangolin still
hovered, caught somewhere in the crevices of the tiling beyond
the reach of bleach.

Mahmoud would be coming in an hour or so. Time to
say goodbye to this crew of strange companions she had lived
amongst for a while.

She had arranged with Mr Pillai to organise teacher-training
classes for Fatimah. Wei Wei had joined a hairdressing salon as
a 'lady barber.' Annie had decided not to ask what these duties
entailed.

Desmond had called to wish her well, which, since she had
refused his proposal, was very good of him. Perhaps his heart was
a little broken but men like Desmond, with their busy lives, soon

got over it.

She had left money with Charlie to cover the next four months. He would be leaving then and had told her that he'd been promised a posting to Tokyo.

'I'll get my war yet,' he'd said and they'd shared a bottle of Champagne. Charlie didn't know about war so he loved it or at least his youthful romantic notions of it. It would, he believed, bring him glory. Perhaps it would, but Annie was sure it would bring him something else as well.

She never spoke to him about Yu Li. She wasn't sure he knew she was in Tokyo, half-suspected he did, but then it wasn't really any of her business.

Charlie wasn't here now. She had already said her goodbyes to him.

Harnam Singh was here though, and she watched him in the garden with Joseph as the little boy said farewell to his friends, most especially Fatimah's two boys. Joseph too was packed and Annie had taken pains over his little suitcase, adding his reading books and his new pencils. She had waited until he was ready and now he said he was and so was she. The money had been discussed with his father. It had made a difference. Harnam Singh's wife was here today with the little girl. Annie had kissed Joseph goodbye and couldn't bear to do it again. It was too hard, too hard. She so wanted them all to love him.

She moved away from the window as Harnam Singh took his son's hand in his, the lead around Yellow's neck in the other. He had agreed instantly to take along the dog his son loved. Annie could see this man would be a kind and caring father. The boy would keep the name, Joseph. It had been given by those who had loved and taken care of him, that's what he said. He was Joseph Singh. As they passed by the window Joseph looked up. She walked round the verandah to watch them leave in the taxi. She wanted desperately to call to him but her throat grew thick and she couldn't make a sound.

The taxi began to move away and she felt her heart jerk with it. Suddenly Joseph pushed his head out of the window, searching for her. She moved forward and raised her hand. He smiled a huge reassuring smile and waved. Then the taxi moved away and he was gone.

She went to her room and cried until she was wrung out and dry as old paper.

Now she wanted to leave as quickly as possible. Ah Moy, Ting and Wei Wei had lined up as requested and made their dutiful goodbyes. Their farewells were heartfelt but they had merely crossed each other's paths a moment.

'Good luck,' she said to them all.

Madame Wing stepped next to her as she waited for Mahmoud.

As the car came up the drive, Madame Wing turned to her.

'I am grateful to you, Mrs Collins. Your search has made me revisit people and events I had buried for many years. It is always painful but it is good, too, to dwell a little on those that have gone and remember them fondly. Otherwise their memory is always distorted and twisted by sorrow and it becomes hard to get it straight and clear. It is good to untangle them from anguish and set them and oneself free. The Chinese have a rather strange saying but I find it quite apropos in my case. You can't stop the birds of sorrow from flying, but you can stop them from building nests in your hair.'

Annie nodded.

'Yes, I see. Is it best to go back, then, do you think, Madame Wing? I have to decide whether to go back one more time.'

Madame Wing, if she was surprised, made no sign of it.

'Yes. The truth is best.'

'Even if you won't like what you learn?'

Madame Wing turned her dark eyes to Annie's.

'I think you know the answer to that question.'

Madame Wing put out her hand and Annie took it.

Mahmoud had loaded her suitcases and now waited by the car door. She got in and he drove slowly away from the house, down the avenue of palms and tembusu trees, down onto Peirce Road, then Holland, then sped on and on, leaving the bustling town behind.

At the Kallang River the skies grew grey and rain began to fall, hard and heavy. They turned into the gates of the airport.

Mahmoud pulled up under the verandah. He carried her bags into the terminal and waited as they were tagged and loaded onto the trolley. The plane sat on the tarmac, its propellers just beginning to slowly turn.

She put her passport into her bag and turned and faced him. She felt tears again. She had hoped to cry herself out so completely there would be nothing left. But the human body, it seems, is capable of an inexhaustible supply.

'Goodbye, Mahmoud Sahib,' she said and put out her hands

to his.

'Goodbye, Annie Sahiba,' he said.

He opened his arms and she fell into them. It seemed as natural as taking a breath.

When he released her they both stood a little awkwardly.

'May the road rise up to meet you, may the wind be at your back,' he said.

'Is that a Sikh saying?'

'No, Irish.'

They shared a smile then she walked quickly away. The rain had stopped but the dark clouds sat low. She walked to the plane, glancing back once. Mahmoud was standing at the window. She waved and he raised his hand.

The plane thrummed, its engines building to a crescendo, the noise blotting out thought. It rose and turned sharply to the south, over the leaning palm trees of Tanjong Rhu. She looked down and saw Mahmoud, a tiny figure, standing by the car, gazing up, even in the rain. She clutched his handkerchief and watched until he and Singapore were enveloped in a swirling cloud.

She had set out on a road that led into the tangled past. She had thought it straight and narrow but it had turned out to be full of bends and drifts and invisible chasms. A certain peace had come to her from this journey. But on this path she had also caught a glimpse of something else, in the fragile rice paper of a Japanese fan and in the deep green leaves of tea. A dim sighting of her own unsuspected nature and a former life, which unnerved her.

A wise woman had said we all travel unexpected paths and navigate the bitter sea. She wasn't sure she wanted to go down into the bitter sea, but she wondered, briefly, whether she could ever live a proper life without seeing what kind of creature lay in its depths.

But not now, not yet, perhaps not ever. The past would always be there like a torturer's tool and she had been stretched to the end of endurance for such recallings.

She took out Milton and read the last stanza. Lycidas was youth lost, a reflection on the precariousness of existence and the irony of fate but, at its conclusion, the poet spoke of the most clamorous of human needs. In the darkest hours of existence we grasp tight, no matter how illusory, to the glimmering beams and starry gleams of hope.

The plane burst out of greyness into the dazzling brilliance of the sun and a vast lake of blue, spilling the past away like the day star sunk beneath the ocean waves.

Epilogue

Maria Hertogh arrived home in Bergen op Zoom to an ecstatic welcome from the public and her sisters and brothers. At first, Maria could only talk to her mother, the only one in the family who understood Malay. She demanded rice with every meal, resenting the western diet. She continued to say her Muslim prayers five times a day. A policeman in plain clothes was assigned to escort her whenever she left the house, for fear of possible kidnappers who might take her back to Singapore, following reported sightings of 'oriental strangers' around town. The house was also placed under surveillance.

Slowly, Maria began to adjust to her new environment. A nun came to the house daily to teach her Dutch until she was proficient enough to attend a local convent school. She also began to attend Mass with her family. In Singapore, Aminah and Mansoor had apparently given up hope of retrieving Maria after leave to appeal to the Privy Council was not granted. The affair died away.

In 1956, Maria married twenty-one-year-old Johan Gerardus

Wolkefeld and eventually gave birth to ten children. Maria did not seem to be content. She told *De Telegraaf* that she often had rows with her mother, who lived nearby. She also said she still longed for her Malayan homeland. Johan and Mansoor began corresponding. In letters both expressed a wish for Maria to travel to Malaya to visit the aged Aminah, but the trip was never made due to financial difficulties. Aminah died in 1976.

In August 1976, Maria's life took another dramatic turn when she found herself on trial in a Dutch court charged with plotting to murder her husband. She admitted in court that she had been thinking about leaving her husband but was afraid to start divorce proceedings in case she lost custody of her children. She had come into contact with two regular customers at her husband's cafe bar. The trio had bought a revolver and had recruited a fourth accomplice to carry out the actual murder. However, the last member had gotten cold feet and gossiped about the murder plan. The police quickly learnt of it and arrested all four conspirators.

In her defence, Maria's lawyers brought up her background, which the court acknowledged. In consideration of her past, and because the plot had not been executed and there was no proof that she had offered any inducement to the other three, she was acquitted. Meanwhile, Maria had also filed for divorce on the grounds of the irreparable breakdown of her marriage.

Maria returned to Malaya in 1998 to an emotional reunion with her adoptive elder sister. On 8 July 2009, Maria Hertogh died from leukaemia at the age of seventy-two.

The Straits Quartet

by Dawn Farnham

Singapore's most passionate series of historical romance

Drawing on real-life historical personalities from 19th-century Singapore, author Dawn Farnham brings to life the heady atmosphere of Old Singapore where piracy, crime, triads and tigers are commonplace. This intense and passionate romance follows the struggle of two lovers: Charlotte Macleod, sister of Singapore's Head of Police, and Zhen, triad member and once the lowliest of coolies who beats the odds to become a wealthy Chinese merchant.

Opium, murder, incest, suicide, passion and love ... an intoxicating combination in the sin city of the south seas.

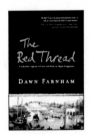

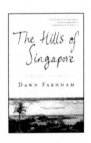

| THE RED THREAD | THE SHALLOW SEAS | THE HILLS OF SINGAPORE | THE ENGLISH CONCUBINE |